The Curse

CW01512478

Richa,

By the

The three novels in the Puglia series
Dancing to the Pizzica *(2012)*
The Demise of Judge Grassi *(2013)*
Leonardo's Trouble with Molecules *(2014)*

Long Shorts *(Revised Version 2015)*
(A collection of unusual and humorous short stories)

*(The three novels in the Commissario Beppe Stancato series
set in Abruzzo)*
The Case of the Sleeping Beauty *(2015)*
A Close Encounter with Mushrooms *(2016)*
The Vanishing Physicist *(2017)*

Puglia with the Gloves Off *(2019) – A travelogue*

Published by nonno-riccardo-publications
richard_s_walmsley@hotmail.com

Book cover design by Natalia Dalkiewicz
natalia.dalkiewicz@gmail.com

Front cover design: a photo of the town of Penne in Abruzzo taken by the author and adapted by Natalia Dalkiewicz.

Author's Preface

Welcome to my seventh novel. Unusually for me, it does not form part of a series of stories. Needless to say, it is firmly based in Italy - in an entirely fictitious town called Collemaga. However, three characters from the Abruzzo novels do make a cameo appearance towards the end of the story.

The town name Collemaga translates as 'The hill of the sorceress'. The setting for this story is a small mountain town in Abruzzo. It weaves a tale about a town which purports to be 'the most cursed town in Italy'. This much is factually based, although the actual town which inspired this story is further south than Abruzzo. The details of the plot are almost entirely fictitious, however.

I suppose the story can be described as a thriller - although I am always wary of attaching a specific genre to any of my novels. It will, I believe, keep you sitting somewhere near the edge of your seat for most of the time! The mystery element is uppermost in the plot as the principal character, Luca Fontana, begins his research into why Collemaga should merit its unusual epithet. He rapidly unearths sinister undercurrents within the structure of the town.

There is a strong element of the 'psychological thriller' in the narrative which emerges half way through the novel. But before Luca himself is literally dragged into danger, he meets a host of colourful and entertaining local characters – some delightful and others more sinister. I have, I believe, been very influenced in all my novels by a number of remarkable Italian television series. They do not shy away from involving children in the plots – and there is often a hint of the supernatural woven into the story. The current novel shows these influences very clearly.

I would like to acknowledge, with immense gratitude, the contribution of Rob and Karina Graham, who live with their son and daughter in the Lot-et-Garonne region of France. It was Rob who discovered the original article about 'the most cursed town in Italy' upon which the story is based. I am sure he would be amazed and amused to see how his original discovery has been transformed. Karina has read the novel piecemeal – pointing out my moments of inattention as regards spelling, punctuation and an annoying habit of accidentally changing the names of minor characters as the story unfurls. Karina has proofread all seven novels and has been kind enough to say how involved she became in the plots. I think she is astonished that her former French teacher has shown signs of possessing such a vivid imagination in his autumn years.

If, on completion of your reading this story, you are curious to know the name of the real town in Italy which earned the dubious privilege of being nicknamed 'the most cursed town in Italy', just write me an email (see title page) and I shall tell you. The details and history of the real-life town are all on the internet. The articles are intriguing enough to stretch one's credulity to the limits. Italy is an unfailing source of wonder and mystery.

For the fifth time running, I must praise my artwork designer for producing such an evocative book cover, which sets the atmosphere of the story so cleverly. Natalia Dalkiewicz was only sixteen when she designed the book cover for 'The Vanishing Physicist'. Now, two years on, she is studying – not surprisingly – Graphic Design, at the University of Norwich Arts School. Thank you Natalia! Your talents and your generosity in devoting your time to my book covers are much appreciated – off the usual scale of ordinary compliments!

Finally, I would just add one 'footnote'. You will find a glossary of Italian words and phrases used in the novel at the end of the book – both in the Kindle and the Paperback versions. If a word is marked in the text with an *, you will find its translation at the end of the book. The characters are, with one exception, all Italian, so it seems only proper that they should be allowed some words in their own language! This also adds a bit of local colour to the narrative. Just occasionally, I have added Italian expressions simply because I like the sound of them. For example, Acqua in bocca! *It means literally,* "Water in the mouth". *It's the Italian equivalent of* "My lips are sealed". *Presumably, if you have a mouth full of water and open your mouth, the 'secret' will be out. Surprisingly, the expression* "A little bird told me" *is an exact translation of* "Me l'ha detto l'uccellino". *Languages fascinate me. If you do not fall into this category of person, simply ignore the glossary at the end of the book. Most of the foreign words used are apparent from their context.*

Richard Walmsley. December 2019

Prologo

A conversation between the mayor of a hilltop town of barely two thousand inhabitants somewhere in Abruzzo - and his unofficial henchman - one Luigi Bonifaccio:

"Luigi, that man is not the simple tourist he is claiming to be," stated the *sindaco** of Collemaga. "I sense it *here,*" the mayor added, tapping the side of his nose with a knowing finger.

"What you want I do about him, *signore?*" asked Luigi, speaking in his local dialect – the only language he could speak fluently. He was hoping any action would involve employing what he liked to call his *talenti speciali.*

"For now, I just want you to keep an eye on what he does, where he goes and who he speaks to. Give him the usual treatment. Where's he staying by the way?"

"In that backstreet hotel, *signor sindaco* – the one called *L'ospite inatteso.*"*

"Ah, *that* hotel - the one where those two young Moroccan call girls work from, isn't it?"

Luigi Bonifaccio nodded, avoiding looking at his *capo* directly in the eyes.

"Exactly the place where I would have expected someone to stay who didn't want to attract attention to himself," continued the mayor, ignoring the fleeting look of guilt on Luigi's face. "Did he tell the proprietor how long he intended to remain in Collemaga?"

"He was vague about it, *capo* - or so the hotel owner, Dario Frassica, told me. He booked a room for seven nights but said he wasn't sure how long he would be staying in this area. He said a 'colleague' was due to join him in a few days' time," added Luigi whose narrow head had begun

1

nodding up and down mechanically as if to add a sense of intrigue to the banality of his words.

The mayor looked away, irritated by his junior collaborator's repetitive gesture. He might have looked less ridiculous, reckoned the mayor, if he had not had that thin line of black moustache beneath the beaky nose that went up and down in time with the nodding head.

The mayor dismissed Luigi with a peremptory wave of the hand.

"That will be all for now, Luigi. You know what to do," he said managing a fleeting smile which vanished the second his lackey was no longer facing him as he headed for the mayoral office door.

"And don't forget to go out through the rear entrance..." he added unnecessarily to Luigi's departing back.

"Sissignore," muttered Luigi wearily without bothering to turn round. He was familiar with the routine. He knew his place. His main objective was to get outside the building and light up one of his very own personalised roll-up cigarettes.

As soon as he was on his own, the mayor looked at the crucifix hanging on the wall opposite his desk, not far from the official photo of the incumbent President of the Republic. He let out a deep sigh which expressed the heavy burden of responsibility that lay upon his shoulders. He wondered what the President – or Jesus come to that - would have made of his peculiar situation.

Why couldn't he have been elected mayor of some ordinary *comune?** He would like to have believed that both Jesus and the President would have sympathised with his plight had they taken the trouble to sit down with him for a few minutes and listen to his problems.

He made the sign of the cross, touched the President's photo reverentially –and went home for lunch.

1: *Il forestiero...* *(The Outsider)*

Luca Fontana was a name that rolled easily off the tongue. He had always avoided telling anybody remotely associated with the media what his real name was. He had worked for Rai News and for *Il Corriere della Sera** as an investigative journalist using this pseudonym. He had, through a police protection scheme, even acquired an official identity card with this name on it. He was certainly not going to alter this arrangement now he had decided to get to the bottom of the mystery surrounding this seemingly insignificant hilltop town – if indeed there *was* a mystery to reveal.

He could just about afford to 'go it alone' as an independent journalist. If the venture succeeded, he should have no trouble interesting some TV channel or weekly news magazine in the story of Collemaga. If nothing came of it, he would simply return to Milan and pursue his life's mission of revealing the corruption and the involvement of the mafia in almost every walk of public life. He had already written and had published several books about the infiltration of the *'ndrangheta** in the cities of northern Italy. He was amazed that he had not been the target of threats or reprisals over the last decade. He had even considered the possibility that the absence of any form of underworld retribution was due to the fact that the Calabrian mafia clans welcomed the notoriety that his publications bestowed on them. Perhaps his writings succeeded in creating that aura of fear upon which their operations flourished.

But now he was forty and had a wife and two young children, he felt it was time to avoid the risks of antagonising the darker elements of Italian society. Investigating why Collemaga had acquired the unusual reputation of being 'the most cursed town in Italy' appeared to be a less hazardous undertaking. His 'alternative' ID card, however, gave him added reassurance when engaged in such exploits.

This was the reason why he now found himself in a tawdry bedroom of a two-star hotel which bore the somewhat sinister name of *The Unexpected Guest*. For the first hour or so, he had assumed that he was the only resident in the hotel. The owner had greeted him with a smile that had faded instantly, to be replaced by the listless countenance the journalist had registered as he had stepped through the main door. He had not even asked Luca for any identification document. Maybe the hotel owner would remember his legal obligations the following day. Luca assumed the man must be glad of *any* custom in this out-of-the-way hotel.

Luca had ironically nicknamed his accommodation 'The room with a view'. The single window overlooked the characterless backstreet which he had walked up after parking his car. There was a second murky window high up above the desk through which he could just make out a wrought iron staircase leading up to the floor above. An apology for a fire escape, he assumed, until he had seen two pairs of shapely stockinged legs topped by two miniskirts vanishing on their way to the upper reaches of the building. He looked at his watch. It was just past midnight.

"A side-line activity for the hotel owner," he had assumed. This impression was modified when he saw the unmistakable lower half of the shady individual who had initially directed him to this hotel making his way up the staircase in pursuit of the two girls.

"Punter or pimp?" Luca wondered. He opted for the latter choice. The man had struck him as being 'sleazy' - that was the word which had sprung to mind as he had stepped out of his car in the little *piazza* to ask where the nearest hotel was. He had detected the whiff of something other than tobacco on the man's breath. His first taste of life in Collemaga turned out to be depressingly banal.

But there had to be more to this town's soul than banality, surely? Its name for starters! You don't call a town 'The Hill of the Sorceress' for no reason. At least historically, there must be some mystery surrounding its reputation. But it was now, in the 21st century, that people called it the 'town whose name is left unspoken'.

He had read and re-read the claims about the town being cursed; babies born with strange deformities, plagues of vipers invading the gardens of any who defied the unspoken laws of those in charge of the town, even citizens who disappeared without a trace -the list was endless. And then, way back in the 1920s, a distinguished rogue lawyer of considerable weight within the community had declared to a crowded courtroom:

"If I am lying to you, let that candelabra fall to the floor!"

Apparently it had done just that as if moved by some unseen force, smashing into fragments of glass shards on the stone floor. Rumours sprang up that nobody had been injured, or - in complete contradiction - that at least three people had lost their lives. The lawyer's reputation was, it appeared, greatly enhanced by the incident. Nobody seemed to pick up on the obvious implication that he must have lied to the court.

Luca Fontana lay down on the double bed and wondered where he could possibly start his quest the following morning. Why on Earth had he suggested to the hotel owner that he was expecting a 'lady colleague' to arrive in a few days' time? The words had just come out of his mouth unbidden. Was it to allay the fear that he might appear to be an eccentric loner in the eyes of the inhabitants of this town? The presence of a woman might help to bestow a sense of normality on proceedings. Or were the words which he had spoken without premeditation the first sign that the curse was already working on *him*? He fell into an uneasy sleep without resolving the riddle.

* * *

He woke up the following morning and went in search of a breakfast room. There was no sign of the owner. There was a bell on the counter which he hit with the palm of his hand. It produced a metallic click which failed to reverberate with anything resembling the sound of a bell. After several failed attempts at drawing attention to his presence, Luca noticed the owner standing in the road outside the hotel stubbing out a cigarette before coming back inside.

"Buongiorno, signore," said Luca with studied cheerfulness. "Any chance of a cup of coffee and a croissant?"

The owner looked at him without returning the smile.

"We have an arrangement with the *Bar Commercio* just down towards the square, *signore.* Just tell them you are staying at this hotel and they'll give you breakfast," he was told.

Luca laid the key to his room on the counter. It was attached to a mini-sized version of a ball and chain. The hotel owner hung it up on the board behind the counter and wished his client a *buona giornata* with a leer – as if he suspected in advance that the visitor had scant chance of finding anything in this town to render his day enjoyable.

Luca Fontana resolved that he would not be discouraged by his first impressions of Collemaga; first impressions were often skewed by the lack of familiarity of the observer. He always trusted in the unpredictable nature of human beings to take him by surprise when he was least expecting it.

With this positive outlook firmly back in place, he stepped through the doorway of the *Bar Commercio.* There must have been at least twenty people in the bar – all male apart from a couple of rather unprepossessing house wives. What scant conversation there was in progress came to an abrupt halt as he walked up to the bar. All eyes were on him.

"What a strange assortment of individuals!" thought Luca. He expelled from his mind an image of the 'mutants' bar' from that scene in Star Wars. He regretted allowing this image to take a hold in his mind, even for an instant, when he noticed that one of the drinkers at the bar – a young man in his twenties - had a club foot. Luca called out a cheery general greeting and smiled amiably at all present.

A voice from one of the tables said something in dialect and instantly everyone mumbled a reluctant *buongiorno.* Luca glanced at the table where the comment had come from and instantly recognised the sleazy young man of the day before, last seen climbing the exterior staircase of his hotel.

"A ubiquitous character!" thought Luca. "I wonder what he said to them."

If he had interpreted the strong local dialect correctly, the man with the thin moustache was saying something like: "Come on, *ragazzi.* This guy's a newcomer." But it had sounded like an exhortation to be sociable rather than an attempt to ostracise an outsider – the foreigner in their midst.

The bar owner was a ruddy-faced, overweight individual who, nevertheless, managed a cheerful greeting.

"They told me at the hotel up the road I could have breakfast here," explained Luca.

"*Certo, signore!*" beamed the bar owner who served him a good coffee and a freshly baked croissant.

"*Due euro cinquanta, signore,*" said the owner with a smile, without producing a till receipt. Any notion that the arrangement with the hotel owner implied a free breakfast was instantly dispelled. Luca handed over the coins with a meaningful frown on his face. The expression was noted and the complicit smile on the bar owner's face was accompanied by a shrug of the shoulders. Luca returned the smile. He had no desire to upset anyone in this town on his first day; besides which, bar owners invariably turned out to be a valuable source of local information in Luca's experience.

Luca Fontana finished his breakfast standing up. He said "*Alla prossima*"* to the bar owner, thereby making it clear that he would be returning despite the lack of a free breakfast. He received a civil nod of the head in reply. Luca had the impression that the bar owner would happily talk at greater length when his establishment had no clients in it.

A handful of people stood up and left just behind Luca. The leavers, he noticed, were screening 'Mr Sleaze' who had stood up and left just behind the others. Although quite unenlightened by his visit to the *Bar Commercio,* he knew that the first scene of whatever drama was being enacted had got underway.

"*Meno male,*" he muttered to himself. "Just as well!"

The sobriquet *Il Porco** suited down to the ground the man who had first pointed him in the direction of his hotel and who might well be running a small-time prostitution racket from *L'Ospite Inatteso*. Luca wondered if he would be trailed by this individual. If that turned out to be the case, he would know for certain that his presence had aroused curiosity in some quarters. He should have confirmation of this without much delay.

What he needed, he decided as he headed towards his parked car, was a sound alibi which would explain his presence in Collemaga. He got into his car, a modest silver-grey FIAT Tipo, and inserted the key in the ignition. He glanced in the wing mirror. Sure enough, he noticed *Il Porco* standing on a street corner at the entrance to the *piazza*. He was trying to look nonchalant as he rolled a cigarette and stuck it in his mouth.

Luca realised immediately that his purpose would be better served if he began his exploration of Collemaga on foot. If *Il Porco's* intention was to follow him – for whatever reason – Luca ought to set about making the man's task easier. He went through the motions of looking for something in the glove compartment before getting out and locking the car. He began walking uphill in the direction of what he assumed would lead to the church and the main square at the top end of the town. He would need to purchase a street plan of Collemaga from a bookshop or a tobacconist's. He sensed rather than saw that he was being trailed at a distance. Sure enough, a brief glance in the curved glass of an old-fashioned chemist's shop window confirmed that *Il Porco* was on his tail. He felt the first thrill of excitement – the initial shiver of an impending adventure and a mystery to be solved.

He spotted the familiar sign of a tobacconist's shop at the far end of the *piazza* near the church. It's distinctive blue lettering on a white background bore the familiar words *Sali Tabacchi Valori Bollati* written beneath the capital 'T'. He wondered how long it had been since Italian tobacconists had ceased to be the official state purveyors of salt. He ought to research it one day – but the custom must have lasted at least up until the fascist era, he assumed. And yet, every tobacconist's sign in the nation still had to show the word 'salt' on the official shop sign. One of the many idiosyncrasies of his complex and contradictory motherland, he assumed.

Collemaga had begun to feel progressively more normal as he climbed up towards the church and the main *piazza*. The tobacconist was well-stocked with row upon row of cigars and cigarettes. Luca obtained his colourful street plan of the town – designed to catch the eye of sightseers and tourists. The latter category of persons seemed to be very conspicuous by their absence, thought Luca. The tobacconist was a pretty, dark-skinned woman in her late twenties or early thirties who asked him pertly – in normal Italian - if he was on holiday in Collemaga. Her tone of voice suggested she was not at all convinced that this could be the reason for his being in her shop. The need to find a credible reason for his presence in this obscure town had become urgent. He turned the conversation back on the young woman, asking about her family. She had a son aged seven, he learnt. A husband was not mentioned.

"I am sure he must be a lovely boy, *signora,*" he said in all sincerity.

"Yes, he is, *signore,*" she replied with a grateful smile at the implied compliment to herself. Yet didn't he detect a hint of sorrow in her eyes as she spoke? He felt a twinge of sympathy for this young mother. Since he liked to smoke the odd cigar from time to time, he purchased a packet of *Toscanello* cigars and a lighter which issued a fierce jet of flame that was proof against any gust of wind. He decided to buy a copy of the local paper, *L'Aquilano.* He was happy enough to part with a ten euro note for his first purchases in this remote township.

"Have you ever visited L'Aquila, *signore?*" asked the tobacconist.

He told her that he hadn't – which was true.

"You should go and see it, *Signor...?*"

"Fontana," he replied. "It's on my list of places to visit while I'm down here. Although I understand it is still a long way off being restored to its former glory after the earthquake..."

As Luca was trying to put away his small change without letting go of the cigars the lighter, his street plan and his newspaper, an A5 sized *volantino** fell out from between the folds of his street map. He bent down to pick it up, glancing at the words printed on a background which showed the town of Collemaga set against the hills and valleys beyond it.

Luca took one look at the flyer and knew instantly that he had found the pretext he had been looking for to explain his presence in this town. At the top of the single sheet of glossy paper appeared the words:

Buy a house in Collemaga for just 1€

Luca showed the flyer to the tobacconist with an enquiring look on his face.

"Is that the reason why...?" she began.

Her eyes showed something akin to apprehension – she was about to warn him off, he was sure.

"Lei è molto simpatico, * Signor Fontana,"* she said. "Just be careful whom you have dealings with in this town."

Luca left the shop thoughtfully. He had smiled at the young woman and had told her not to worry about him.

*"A presto, signore,"** she had added hopefully.

"I'll be back for more cigars, I expect, *Signora...?*

"Just call me Giorgia," she said with a glint in her brown eyes.

"Just call me Luca," he added, trying to sound casual.

The only thing which struck Luca as odd when he was back in the street was that there was no sign whatsoever of his stalker. He appeared to have vanished. Luca felt a stab of something resembling uneasiness - or perhaps it was merely disappointment that the bait had not been taken?

2: *Just a simple tourist...*

Luca was well aware that many rural communes in remoter parts of Italy were selling off uninhabited properties for a token price tag of one euro. It was a State sponsored scheme to try and inject new blood into regions where ageing inhabitants clung on to a way of life that was rapidly disappearing. The scheme was actively supported by the mayors of local communes – often presiding over a populace whose numbers diminished with every new death which struck.

The 'catch', Luca knew, was simply that the house or apartment – often derelict - had to be rendered habitable within the space of two years – and subsequently lived in by couples, preferably with children of school age in tow, for a minimum period of five years before they were legally permitted to put the property back on the market. The scheme was, unsurprisingly, not all that attractive to most Italian families for whom town or city life had become an essential aspect of their lives. Thus, the offer was now open to non-Italian residents too, with or without offspring. Any solution was valid to halt the perennial problem of rural depopulation.

What surprised Luca was the fact that the town of Collemaga did not seem particularly deprived of young children. He had walked past a primary school on his way uphill. The usual calls of lively, undisciplined seven-year-olds and the admonishing voice of their teacher had been clearly audible through the open first floor windows of a classroom. Luca had not even questioned this commonplace sound. He had subconsciously registered the presence of young children with heavy school satchels on their backs trudging uphill as he had left the *Bar Commercio.*

14

He was so used to seeing similar groups of youngsters in Milan that it had not occurred to him that maybe there were less young children on their way to school than might have been expected. But Collemaga only had a population of about two thousand, hadn't it? You wouldn't expect there to be more kids, surely? The older ones would be bussed to larger, neighbouring towns – even as far away as Sulmona or L'Aquila.

Luca dismissed the matter from his mind. The important thing was that he had found a ready excuse to explain why he was spending time in this unlikely town.

He shook his head to clear it of all conjecture. He took proper stock of the gracious *piazza* whose flagstones had recently been replaced or cleaned. It sloped gently downhill towards the town hall, where the Italian flag fluttered in the light breeze next to the European Union flag – total unity thus being officially acknowledged.

At the upper end of the *piazza*, the church tower gleamed warmly in the morning sunlight. He went inside the church whose main doors stood open after the last handful of elderly ladies had dispersed after mass. The equally elderly priest was still pottering about clearing the altar. He picked up the chalice, looking to see if there was any remnant of sanctified wine at the bottom. He took a brief swig, raising the stem of the chalice to an almost vertical position. He wiped the empty vessel with a white linen cloth and completed the post-mass clearing up process. He nodded perfunctorily at the stranger who had stepped inside his church, sticking the first two fingers of his right hand into the holy water stoop before making the sign of the cross – a gesture which Luca could not complete. The parish priest made a mental note that he should pour some more water into the stone basin later on. He had noticed the day before that it was as dry as a bone. He shuffled off towards the vestry leaving the pleasant-looking man in his forties to contemplate the simple beauty of his little church.

Luca knelt down and went through the motions of praying for the continued safety of his family before going outside again. He read the board in the porch where he learnt that the church was dedicated to *San Nicola di Bari,* a bishop dating back to the second century AD, he recalled. He had purportedly been the saint who originally gave rise to the idea of *"Babbo Natale"* – Father Christmas. 'Ubiquitous' was an apt word to describe this saint, thought Luca - aware that the same word had sprung to mind earlier on in relation to *Il Porco.* San Nicola's relics were scattered as far afield as Bari and Venice, according to legend. This early Christian bishop also went under several different names. He sounded as if he was a very versatile saint. Luca thought he should adopt *San Nicola di Bari* as his spiritual guide during his mission in Collemaga.

"Va bene, San Nicola! Let's go and have another cup of coffee and read up all about buying a one euro house," said Luca heading for a bar with a terrace on the opposite side of the square. Above the entrance door, a board announced that the bar was named simply *Bar San Nicola* – which seemed entirely appropriate. He took a series of rapid photographs of the church and the *piazza* on his iPhone. Any observer would assume he was just a tourist – doing what all tourists do ad infinitum. If he ever published an article on Collemaga, he would be able to back up the material with copious pictures.

The late April sunshine was warm on his face. A smiling young waiter had promptly appeared and took his order for an espresso and a bottle of sparkling water. His mobile phone beeped; a message from his wife asking him if he had made any progress and saying that the kids were missing him. He sent a message back which said he hoped *she* was missing him too. The answer arrived immediately: *Va da sé!* That goes without saying! A yellow face with a tear-drop falling from one eye was added to the message to reinforce the words. How significant, thought Luca, that human emotions were, with increasing frequency, reduced to being expressed by an automated cartoon image! He replied saying he would phone her that evening with a progress update.

Luca looked at the *volantino* which was pretty and enticing to the eye but gave little practical information about acquiring a one euro house. The first step should be to ask for further information at the town hall, stated the flyer. He would make the *comune* his first port of call after finishing his coffee. He turned to his newspaper, which covered news from all over the province under the jurisdiction of L'Aquila. As he was flicking distractedly through items of local news, he came across an announcement about the annual *Festa* in Collemaga. It was, he realised with a shock, due to be held in early May – only a few days away. He looked around the square to see if he could spot posters advertising the town's local festival. He could see no sign of any publicity. How odd, he thought.

But with a jolt, he *did* spot the figure of Mr Sleaze emerging from the tobacconist shop where he himself had been less than ten minutes previously. *Il Porco* was prodding the air with what appeared to be an accusatory finger directed towards the interior of the shop.

"Now, what in the name of all the saints is going on?" wondered Luca, thinking about the pretty owner and the cautionary words she had uttered. He was tempted to go straight back to the shop and ask her what the man had wanted, but decided that caution should be exercised because of the proximity of the man whom Luca could still see skulking around near the Church. At no point, it seemed, was the man aware of Luca's presence.

He continued to read the half page of his newspaper devoted to Collemaga. To his amusement, the reporter had gone into well-researched details – the reporter's words – about the reluctance of the local police to issue speeding fines in the town.

The speed limit on the road which takes one towards the upper reaches of Collemaga is clearly signposted at 45 kilometres per hour. And yet the police can often be spotted armed with hand held speed cameras pointed at miscreants doing at least 55. I tried it myself repeatedly wrote the journalist. *Not a single fine issued! Not even an admonishing finger waved in my direction! I asked in local bars – even in the hair-dresser's – to see if they could shed some light. "Ah, the police are wary about the curse," I was told in all seriousness. "They are worried that the curse may be visited upon* them *if they upset anyone in Collemaga."*

Luca contemplated putting this claim to the test – just to see what would happen. Not today, he thought, folding his paper and signalling to the waiter that he would like the bill. The 80 cents tip which he added to the bill was graciously acknowledged by the waiter as Luca headed towards the town hall. *Il Porco* seemed to have vanished again but Luca had the impression that his 'tail' was well versed in the art of skulking. He ambled towards the town hall, admiring its clean façade, and mounted the stone steps leading to the double front doors.

Luca was surprised at the number of *Collemagesi* already occupying the waiting area. He wasn't sure that the word he had used in his mind to denote the inhabitants of Collemaga was the correct one. Maybe it would turn out to be *Collemagenti* – he must remember to ask someone. Luca was surprised that, even in this small *comune,* the town hall had been forced to adopt a system whereby each visitor had to arm him or herself with a numbered ticket issued by a dispenser near the entrance door. "We're a nation of queue-jumpers," Luca thought wistfully about the anti-social tendencies frequently displayed by his fellow-countrymen.

Luca resolved to stand up until his ticket number showed up on the screen. But there were only two town hall staff manning the desks – and at least nine people in the queue before him. It could be a long wait. He thought better of it and decided to take the first free seat vacated. An interminable ten minutes elapsed before the next 'customer' stood up to take her turn. Nobody seemed to be smiling. Whatever secret matters had to be aired by the worthy citizens of Collemaga, they were being discussed in earnest whispers. For a brief moment, Luca considered that the whole process felt more like penitents presenting themselves at the confessional stall.

Barely had Luca sat down, resigning himself to the reality of having to wait all morning before being seen to, when he spotted an alert-looking woman in her early thirties coming down the stairs. She seemed to be looking out for someone. Luca was more than mildly shocked when the woman called out in a clear voice:

"*Signor* Fontana? Is there a *Signor* Fontana here?"

Luca wasn't quite able to explain why he felt he had been wrong-footed; simply because it shouldn't have been possible for anyone to know who he was or, more pertinently, that he had arrived unplanned at the town hall. He himself had only made the decision to come here a few minutes previously. He felt the first intimation of a conspiracy, as if his back had been touched by an invisible, icy finger. But he had little choice. He stood up with a cheerful smile on his face – as if relieved that he would not have to wait any longer.

"Here I am," he said walking towards the woman. He was aware of the glances of suppressed resentment on the faces of those still waiting to be dealt with.

"Will you come this way, *Signor* Fontana? *Le faccio strada,*"* said the woman as she preceded Luca back up the stairs.

"How did you know...?" began Luca. But the woman had evidently been anticipating the question.

"Oh, not a lot goes on in a small town like Collemaga without everybody knowing about it," she answered with a winning smile. "The mayor would like to welcome you," she said.

This information, Luca thought, left a host of questions unanswered. Down-to-earth a person that he was, he could not escape the first shiver of mysticism playing its subtle tricks on his susceptible mind.

As they arrived at the top of the stairs, Luca caught the briefest glimpse out of the corner of his eye of a familiar figure disappearing stealthily down a back staircase. The sense of mysticism vanished in a trice, to be replaced by a sensation of something more concrete but equally sinister; not only had *Il Porco* successfully tailed him that morning, he had even succeeded in anticipating Luca's visit to the town hall. He had the impression that his freedom of action was already something of an illusion. He would have to be on his guard. His project no longer seemed like a diversion in his career. It was as if the opening gambit of a disquieting game of chess had just been initiated. He would have to put on a very convincing act if his true purpose for coming to Collemaga was not to be summarily unmasked.

* * *

"Elpidio Pugliese," said the meticulously well-dressed mayor, standing up and walking round his desk to greet his visitor with a formal handshake. The mayor must have detected a slight rise of an eyebrow on the part of his visitor. "We don't have much control over our parents, *signore,* at that crucial moment in our lives. I would not have chosen such a name for myself had I been in a position to influence matters – and neither am I from Puglia," he added.

Luca made a mental note that he was dealing with an observant and articulate man. His short, stocky frame – he was self-evidently from rural stock - hinted at generations of wiliness and endurance. The mayor of Collemaga should not be underestimated. So why had Luca been fleetingly tempted to blurt out that he, Luca, had been thirty-five when he had himself chosen the name and surname which currently appeared on his 'official' identity card? Just to feel superior? Or to give the mayor the excuse he needed to be suspicious? Either way, Luca should be on his guard about what he revealed of himself. More likely, it was the Collemaga effect surreptitiously at work again, thought Luca, half seriously. But what had stopped him in his tracks, he realised, was the memory of 'Mr. Sleaze' gesticulating in the direction of the young woman in the tobacconist's shop. He must be cautious what he said until he had found out from…Giorgia – that was the name she had deliberately let slip – what had transpired during that man's visit to her shop. *She* did not deserve to be implicated in his covert schemes. Nevertheless, he decided not to mince his words. He would stamp his authority on this conversation. Being on the defensive would not help his cause. He needed to

21

provoke some stronger reaction than mere indifference to his presence.

"I take it you knew *my* name even before I set foot in the town hall, *signor sindaco?*"

Luca detected a fleeting expression of surprise at the directness of the question. But that was all the time it took for the mayor to regain his composure. He flashed a complicit smile in Luca's direction which hinted at an apologetic acknowledgement of the truth behind his visitor's words.

"It would be an insult to your intelligence, Signor Fontana, if I tried to deny it," said the mayor amiably, returning to his desk and sitting down again. "But your arrival in our town was noted yesterday..."

"By that individual who has been on my tail since breakfast time," stated Luca pointedly. "The same man I just saw disappearing down the back stairs as I was being accompanied to your office."

This time, the mayor let out an audible sigh.

"I apologise, Signor Fontana. Luigi does occasionally get carried away by the very minor role he plays in the security of our little community. But we do have to be careful about strangers who arrive here unexpectedly. You must be aware of the unique situation we Collemagasi* find ourselves in?"

A question was implied by the inflexion of the mayor's voice. Luca managed to feign complete ignorance about the mysteries of Collemaga.

"What unique situation, *signor sindaco?*" he asked in complete innocence.

"Ah, Signor Fontana, we truly are the most cursed town in Italy. But it *is* our town, when all said and done."

The passion in the mayor's voice and eyes was generated by deep-seated emotions. Luca was so moved that he did not need to fake his astonishment.

"I had no idea, *signore.* Maybe you could enlighten me?"

Luca did not demur when Elpidio Pugliese picked up the phone and spoke to his secretary:

"Mariangela, please bring us two coffees – and the bottle of grappa."

The same elegant woman who had come downstairs a mere ten minutes earlier to fetch Luca from the waiting area entered the mayor's office carrying a tray. Already Luca was experiencing the ominous illusion that he had been in the town hall for far longer than the twenty minutes he mentally calculated since he had plucked his ticket from the machine and gone to join the queue of locals downstairs. What was happening to his perception of passing time? It was a vaguely discomforting sensation.

At least he had learnt the correct word for the inhabitants of Collemaga.

3:   *The mayor's gambit declined...*

It really was far too early in the day to be drinking grappa, thought Luca. It crossed his mind that the mayor might be attempting to take the edge off his concentration in the hope of lowering his guard. But one look at the way in which Elpidio Pugliese downed the fiery liquid in one gulp dispelled the impression; the mayor needed to fortify himself for this encounter for reasons which Luca could not grasp. To lessen the impact of the liqueur, Luca helped himself to a copious amount of water from the carafe on the tray.

"Too many coffees already today, *signor sindaco,*" he told the mayor in a voice which implied a complicit need to be wary of the Italian habit of over-dosing on espresso coffees before 11 o'clock every morning. The mayor grunted in acknowledgement but still did not attempt to open the conversation. It occurred to Luca that he should not underestimate this inoffensive looking official. It was more than likely that the mayor was playing the devious game of forcing Luca to initiate the exchange of words that would take place, thereby revealing something of his position without the mayor appearing to pry. So be it, thought Luca.

"I suppose you already know the purpose of my visit to Collemaga?" began Luca, who had decided to open up on the offensive. The two men were sizing each other up. Luca had been right. Elpidio Pugliese returned Luca's stare for just long enough to avoid seeming hostile. An ironic smile formed itself on the mayor's face. His grey eyes remained inexpressive.

"Well, *Signor* Fontana, I suppose you could be a government spy. But I think it more likely that you have seen the nationwide appeal to Italian families to help bolster our diminishing rural populations."

It took Luca a fraction of a second to mentally assess the implications behind the mayor's skilful response – the grappa had evidently sharpened his wits. Had Giorgia, the tobacconist, inadvertently revealed to *Il Porco* the fact that he, Luca, had only just found out about the one euro houses? No, thought Luca, she had assumed that he was showing her the flyer as an explanation as to why he was in Collemaga. He still needed to tread carefully however. He did not want to implicate Giorgia in the subtle game which was being played out – with him as the key protagonist. Luca's polemic instincts came to his rescue.

"Do you mean to say that Rome has been covertly sending its agents to Collemaga, *signor sindaco?* Why on earth would they do such a thing?"

Elpidio Pugliese's face registered a flash of respect before he replied.

"To be honest, it has only happened once before, *Signor* Fontana," said the mayor smoothly. Yet, Luca noticed that his eyes darted guiltily from left to right as he was speaking, belying the self-assuredness of his voice.

"You need to understand that we receive generous grants from EU funds – part of an ongoing national project to upgrade rural towns in the south of our peninsula. Of course, we put the funds to good use, as you can see. The piazza and the church have both been cleaned and restored to perfection. We have even opened up our own supermarket so our townsfolk do not have to travel so far to buy their provisions – or spend their money in other towns. Our own little *Magimart* is turning a modest profit."

The mayor had regained his composure by the time he reached the end of the sentence.

"And the spy from Rome...?" prompted Luca.

"Oh yes, him! He did a lot of snooping around and asked a lot of questions. He checked all our accounts and outgoings. But he quickly realised we were operating a totally transparent set-up..."

Elpidio Pugliese's voice tailed off. Was it Luca's imagination or was the shifty look in his eyes back again?

"How long did he stay?" Luca asked innocently.

"Oh, he only needed a couple of days and then he floated off to Rome again we assumed. Nobody saw him leave. Ironically, he stayed in the same hotel as you, *Signor* Fontana."

This time, there was a hint of menace in the mayor's voice – or was it simply a warning? Luca could not be certain. Either way, Luca kept his own counsel and refrained from commenting on the fact that *Il Porco* had informed the mayor about where he, Luca, was holed up. It was time to lighten the atmosphere considered Luca.

"Satisfy my curiosity, *signore* - I was reading in the local paper this morning, that your annual *festa* is taking place in a few days' time. Yet I see no publicity or posters around the town to announce it. Isn't that a bit strange?"

"Ah, I see you are a very observant man. *Complimenti!* Your visit to our town was very well timed. Our *festa* coincides with the day dedicated to our patron saint – San Nicola di Bari. It's a splendid affair, *signore!* The whole town becomes involved, as you will see for yourself – if you are still here, of course..." added the mayor meaningfully.

The ominous note struck – out of the blue - had not escaped Luca's notice. Once again, Luca was unsure as to whether a threat or a warning was implied by the words. Perhaps he was simply becoming paranoid.

"So... the lack of publicity?" pursued Luca.

The mayor of Collemaga let out a chuckle. He was back on familiar territory, thought Luca.

"Would you believe me if I told you that it's part of the mystery of Collemaga we like to cultivate? Tradition has established that we never publicise the event in advance – or even talk about it in public. The inhabitants of our town believe that advertising our *festa* in advance amounts to tempting providence. It's part of the curse that is supposed to hang over our town. Whenever anyone talks openly about our special day, it is inviting bad weather or a violent thunderstorm to occur. Or worse…" concluded the mayor.

"So the town of Collemaga is supposed to have a curse hanging over it, is it?" asked Luca. "How does this manifest itself?"

"Oh, it's just for the sake of tradition that we keep our superstitions alive, *signore* – you know, witches, magic spells, plagues of snakes and so on. Our real problems are far more mundane, I fear; problems of unemployment, low or non-existent incomes, the declining birth rate - all the problems associated with a population which has become too closely knit. We need some new blood in the town," concluded the mayor.

Luca fell silent. The mayor's words had caused a light to switch on in his brain. Of course! An image of the locals in the *Bar Commercio* came to mind – the boy with the clubbed foot. He thought there had been something strange about the place.

"May I ask what your profession is, *Signor* Fontana?" he heard the mayor asking.

"I'm an architect from Turin – I design houses and apartments," replied Luca. What possessed him to lie about his profession – and the town where he lived? Self-preservation, he presumed. Being an architect fitted in well with his excuse for coming to Collemaga. Or could it be the 'curse' manifesting itself again – seemingly putting unpremeditated words into his mouth? He had the sinister

27

feeling that whatever he said now would come back to haunt him later on.

The mayor, however, appeared to be satisfied with his answer.

"Are you married? Children?" the mayor was probing – not very subtly.

"I'm single at present – after a separation. No children as yet." This time, the lie was deliberate. Another flash of illumination had been sparked in his brain. "But you guessed correctly, *Signor Sindaco*. I am here to make preliminary enquiries about settling in Abruzzo. I am curious to know about acquiring a one euro house and doing it up. I feel the need for a new start, far away from the rat-race up north."

The mayor looked pleased at his words, but it was as if Elpidio Pugliese had just closed a book at the end of a chapter. His demeanour suggested that he had formed his own opinions and wished to end the conversation. Indeed, he stood up and came round to shake Luca's hand.

"You would be most welcome to Collemaga, *Signor* Fontana. I shall ask my secretary to explain how you should go about your search for a house. We have an official estate agent in town who deals with these requests. *È una brava persona** – and very knowledgeable about this particular issue."

"*Mille grazie, signor sindaco.* Thank you for your invaluable time."

"Come and see me any time you need help or advice on any aspect of life in Collemaga, *Signor* Fontana."

Luca was officially introduced to the secretary who had ushered him upstairs earlier. She led him to her own office in a business-like manner.

* * *

28

Elpidio Pugliese returned to his office and sat down at his desk.

"I knew I was right to be suspicions about that man," he told himself.

One piece of information which he had made a point of asking Luigi Bonifaccio was about the number plate on Luca's car. "It's got a Milan number plate." Luigi had been categorical.

He picked up his phone and selected the name 'Bonifaccio'.

"Luigi," he said, "move up to level two with our newcomer. My instincts were correct. His account of himself doesn't quite ring true. You know what to do."

He had an image of Luigi Bonifaccio rubbing his bony hands in glee. The mayor let out a sigh, similar to the one of the day before. He secretly prayed that he would be delivered from the onerous responsibilities of being nominally in charge of this troubled community. The sooner the better, he thought, but with little hope that such a day was just round the corner.

Elpidio Pugliese continued to sit at his desk with his head in his hands. He looked as if he was trying to summon up the necessary energy to take the next step. Finally, he let out an even deeper sigh and reached for a second mobile device hidden in his jacket pocket. He did not need to select a contact from a list – there was no list. He simply pressed the green icon on the screen.

A deep, grating voice answered with a brusque *"Sì?"*

"I think we may have another problem visitor," said the mayor.

"So, we shall have to meet up tomorrow," said the voice. The words were spoken in heavy dialect. "Meanwhile, you know what to do… Elpidio."

The call was brought to an abrupt end, leaving the mayor looking powerless and dispirited.

* * *

Luca felt an urgent need to escape from Collemaga at least for a few hours. He had the distinct sensation that the events of the morning had undermined his usual detachment from whatever he was investigating. The overwhelming sensation was that Collemaga was beginning to take over his life in ways that he did not have complete control over. It was so unlike looking into the dark deeds of the Calabrian mafia back in the north of Italy. The difference was, he decided, that back in Milan the mysterious workings of his 'cousins' – at least thrice removed - in the isolated regions of his beloved Italy seemed remote. But here, in Collemaga, he had been plunged into the real world of rural Italy. Yet the sunshine was warm on his body by seven o'clock. He was among people who seemed to obey a totally different set of rules to the 'civilised' inhabitants of Milan. There was a sense of intrigue hanging in the air. He also had to admit to himself the dangerous truth that he had found himself inexplicably attracted to Giorgia – despite only having been in her shop for a few minutes. It was as if meeting this woman had been preordained. He had read something in her eyes which he could not decipher. It was a disturbing sensation which he was unable to dismiss entirely from his mind. The encounter was akin to discovering an unexpected painting hanging in an obscure art gallery. He wanted to go back and have a second look just to see whether the initial appeal would be confirmed by a further visit. A fruitless pursuit, he tried to tell himself.

He had spent the morning with a totally charming estate agent who had insisted that Luca call him by his first name – Aurelio. Aurelio Russo's office was on one of the lower slopes of Collemaga, just off the main road which wound its way to the summit of the hilltop. He had had no difficulty finding the place – indeed his footsteps had seemed to take him to the picturesque side street with unerring precision. The three houses he had been shown were largely intact although desperately in need of modernisation. One of them had a spectacular view over the valley and a shady terraced garden glowing in the morning sunlight. Luca had just stopped himself putting his one euro down on Aurelio's desk and signing the document which would potentially have made him the owner.

"Give me a day or so to make sure this is what I really want to do," he had said almost apologetically to the smiling estate agent, who had not once tried to put any pressure on him. The 'curse' of Collemaga was a benign sorceress who had begun to work her subtle magic on his mind.

The estate agent had insisted on giving him a lift back up the hill to where he had parked his car. It was not far off lunchtime. He would escape from Collemaga for an hour or so and take the road to L'Aquila, where he was bound to find some inviting local *trattoria.*

He looked at his rented car – he never drove his own car when out on the trail – and was instantly struck by the Milanese number plate. He had slipped up when talking to the mayor. His obsession with not giving away personal details had caused him to overlook the fact that claiming to be from Turin would raise the obvious question as to why he was driving a car with a *targa** from a different city. *Il Porco* would undoubtedly have informed the mayor about the car's registration details. However, Luca dismissed the objection from his head – the discrepancy was easily explicable; he had only inferred that he *worked* in Turin. But he would have to be more vigilant during his dealings with officialdom if he was not to be caught out.

Luca had driven to Collemaga from Milan along the main arterial routes, bypassing the town of L'Aquila to his right. He had approached Collemaga via the provincial roads south of the capital city – if only because that had been the route selected on his behalf by the sweetly modulated voice of his satnav.

On this occasion, he had deliberately taken the local *strada statale* out of Collemaga and headed towards L'Aquila with the intention of exploring the surrounding countryside. He could almost detect the note of alarm in the very feminine voice of his satnav, who was telling him the 50 kilometre trip to L'Aquila would take him nearly two hours via this unwisely chosen route -*estimated time of arrival,* stressed Miss Satnav, as if she thought it might be much longer in reality. Luca's hunger won the day and he stopped in a village called Pontefalco – a mere ten kilometres from Collemaga. The earthquake-shattered city would have to wait for another day.

He drew up outside a modest looking *trattoria* with the inviting name of *La Buona Forchetta,** whose owner, his wife and two children were just finishing off their own lunch as Luca stepped over the threshold. Three pairs of eyes stared at him in disbelief. The owner of the fourth pair stood up with a welcoming smile on his face. A man of about Luca's age with an unkempt salt-and-pepper moustache, which had trapped fragments of the fish stew, announced himself as Bruno Vespini. He wiped the moustache with the back of his hand with an apologetic grin on his face.

"Did you want to have lunch, *signore?*"

"If possible, *signor* Vespini. I'm starving."

"Bruno," corrected the owner. "Would you prefer fish or meat?"

"Well, fish, it smells delicious but…"

"We have plenty left, *signor…?*"said Bruno Vespini with an interrogative inflexion of the voice.

Luca supplied his name and added that he was happy to be called plain Luca. The owner disappeared into the kitchen while his wife smilingly stood up and prepared a table for him. The two children, a boy and his younger sister, continued to mop up the sauce on their plates with chunks of bread, eying the newcomer with well-concealed resentment at being deprived of their second helpings.

Bruno Vespini had waited patiently for Luca to relish every mouthful of the fish stew before sitting down with his client. He placed a tray with two coffees and a bottle of local liqueur on the table.

"So you enjoyed my *acqua pazza,** did you, *Signor* Luca?"

"Best I've ever had!" replied Luca in all sincerity. *Congratulazioni, Bruno!"*

Thirty minutes later, Luca took his leave with a firm promise to return one day soon. Even the children gave him a grudgingly friendly nod as he left the trattoria.

* * *

Luca had talked to Bruno Vespini at some length before taking his leave. He mulled over what he had gleaned about Collemaga. The owner of the trattoria had not seemed like a man who would make up stories merely to impress his customers. Luca had been sufficiently disturbed to cause him to pull into a rough-and-ready layby and make a phone call to a friend of his who worked for the Ministry of Finance in Rome.

"*Ciao*, Luca. What are you up to these days?" asked his friend, Giacomo. Luca outlined the bare essentials of his latest investigation.

"I'll tell you all about it next time I'm in Rome. I'm not sure where this is leading me just yet."

"How can I help you?"

"I need to know if you ever caught wind of a visit by anyone from your department who was sent to investigate financial irregularities in a particular *comune* in Abruzzo. There might have been large sums of European money involved."

The line fell silent for ten seconds, prompting Luca to ask: "Giacomo? Are you still there?"

"Yes, I was recovering from shock. You wouldn't by any chance be talking about *quel paese,** by any chance? The town beginning with 'C' which no-one ever mentions by name?"

"I guess so, Giacomo. I sense that it has struck a chord in your mind."

Luca's friend, Giacomo, drew a deep breath.

"We did send a young man to check up on how certain funds were being spent. The sum amounted to not much short of three million euros. It seemed a straightforward task so we sent one of our brightest young men there – about two months ago. Mattia De Angelis, his name was."

"Was?" Luca picked up on the past tense.

"He never returned. His family are still pushing the *Carabinieri* to investigate fully. He was even on that Rai 3 programme called *Chi l'ha visto?** – you know, Luca, the one which investigates cases of missing persons when the police haven't come up with any obvious leads. He has just vanished off the face of the earth."

It was Luca's turn to fall silent.

"I suggest you think twice about whether to stay in...that place, Luca," advised his friend.

"Thanks, Giacomo. I'll let you know what happens. If you don't hear from me, then send out the sniffer dogs," said Luca attempting humour. Inside, he felt apprehensive. He could simply go back to the hotel in Collemaga, pack his suitcase and return to Milan - and his family.

The owner of the *trattoria*, Bruno Vespini, had hinted that someone 'from Rome' had disappeared without a trace. "Just rumours, of course," he had added. "If you're serious about buying a one euro house in this part of Italy, then you should consider looking in and around our town. We have a similar scheme here and there are 17 000 of us living in Pontefalco. We have more amenities here – shops, supermarkets, a secondary school, even a clinic and a cinema. It's much nearer to L'Aquila too – and our inhabitants are not afraid to call their town by its name."

Luca arrived back at his hotel and lay on the bed mulling over the events of the day. He decided to spend one more night in Collemaga – if only because he couldn't face driving back up north in the dark. He heard footsteps descending the iron staircase above his head. With energetic resolve, he looked in the wardrobe – which smelt of stale mothballs – and took out a stained spare pillow from one of the shelves. He clambered resolutely on to the desk and stuffed the pillow up against the high window. This action made him feel better. He did not like the idea that *Il Porco* could spy on him whilst in the privacy of his bedroom – even for one more night.

He sat on the bed and took out his mobile phone. It was high time he called his wife and children to tell them that he was coming home. As he was on the point of pressing the icon to make the call, he was surprised to hear a discreet knock on his door.

35

*"Chi diavolo...?"** he muttered, getting up to open the door.

The younger and prettier of the two 'girls' who lived on the floor above was standing forlornly on the threshold - looking pleadingly at Luca.

4: The girl from Morocco...

*"Mi dispiace, signore,"** she began in halting Italian. *"HE* made me come down. I didn't want to..." Her Italian seemed to fail her but the appeal in her eyes was self-evident. Luca did not go through the pretence of displaying moral indignation. She was little more than twenty years old and, it had to be said, a very appealing young woman. Compassion easily got the better of his sense of judgement. His wife regularly accused him of 'being ruled by your heart rather than by any one of your brain-cells' – adding, on good days, that this was the reason why she had married him. He stood to one side without a smile on his face and ushered the girl into the room with a sweep of his left arm. Without hesitation, or led by habit, she headed for the bed and sat perched uncomfortably on the very edge. The look of relief in her eyes was plain to see.

"Come ti chiami?" Luca asked kindly.

"Marianne Lagrange, signore," she said simply. *"Sono marocchina sai? Mio papà è francese."*

Luca was frowning. An obvious thought had just occurred to him.

"Donc, tu parles français, Marianne?" asked Luca.

In the blink of an eye, she was transformed into the girl that still lay beneath the surface of her make-up. Her face lit up with a smile as she ran towards Luca and wrapped her arms round him – as if she had just rediscovered a long-lost elder brother - or a father, he reminded himself. The warmth of the contact with her body disturbed Luca, who valiantly dismissed extraneous thoughts from his mind. He was relieved to identify more paternal feelings taking over after the first few seconds of being aroused by the pressure of her breasts against his body.

"Vous parlez français, monsieur!" she stated with undisguised joy in her voice. "Now at last I can tell somebody how I am really feeling in this horrid little town..."

Her next gesture was telling. She pulled away from Luca abruptly and glanced up in alarm at the window above the desk. She saw the pillow blocking the view from the iron staircase and giggled in amusement. Luca had no need of enlightenment as to the motives behind her relief that 'goings-on' in that bedroom could no longer be observed. He could easily imagine that *Il Porco* was perverted enough to be a common *voyeur* – or even take pleasure in filming the activities of hotel guests if he thought a bit of blackmail was in the offing.

Luca put the television on and turned the volume up just enough to cover the sound of their voices. He thought it unlikely but feasible that the room was bugged, but it was better to be safe than sorry. This precaution, in addition to the fact that the girl would be speaking in French, should be enough to prevent their conversation being intercepted or understood.

"Make yourself comfortable, Marianne. I can imagine you need to unburden your soul a little bit now you've found a friend," he said kindly.

She asked Luca if she could have a glass of water. He took two bottles of mineral water from the rudimentary refrigerator. Making herself comfortable for Marianne involved perching herself on the bed with her legs crossed. Luca put a pillow against the headboard and leant against it with his legs outstretched. Somehow the situation did not seem incongruous. Besides which, there was virtually no other furniture in the room apart from the desk and the wardrobe.

"How come you speak such perfect French, *monsieur?*" asked Marianne.

"Ah well, my wife is French, you see. Marie-Louise, she's called. Plus I had a very good French teacher when I was at high school."

"Do you have any children?" asked the girl in such a natural way that he had no objection to telling her about his family. It was an ice-breaker and Luca had the distinct impression that Marianne was motivated by an unconscious desire to evoke her own missing family back home. It was hard to gauge what emotions she must have suppressed in order to survive a life of enforced sexual slavery, he supposed.

Gradually, Luca managed to steer the conversation to where he wanted it to be. He asked her very gently how she had ended up in a town like Collemaga –under the heel of Luigi Bonifaccio. She put her hand out and gripped Luca's left arm tightly. There were already tears of anger and despair forming in the corner of her eyes. Her hand remained locked on to Luca's arm while she poured out her heart and soul in one long breathless flood of words.

During his life as a journalist, Luca had frequently been told tales about girls from Africa who had been spun colourful yarns and been persuaded to abandon their homeland with vacuous promises of a 'prosperous' new life in Italy – a country desperately short of waitresses and child-minders they were led to believe – but who had ended up as prisoners in the country's flourishing sex trade. But it was the first time he had personally met a victim who had been caught up in the trammels of one among many such morally depraved criminal networks. He felt overwhelming pity and rising anger taking hold of him as he studied the girl's desperate, tear-stained face.

"But how come you fell a victim to such deceit in the first place, Marianne?" he asked the girl when she had finally stopped to draw breath.

"My family are poor farmers who live out in the countryside, *monsieur.* My father makes and bottles wine but he doesn't make enough money out of his skills and it's often difficult to raise enough cash to look after my three younger brothers and sisters…"

"Please call me Luca," he interjected. Any formality between them seemed quite inappropriate after her pitiful account of her abduction. She looked at him and smiled a grateful smile.

"Luca," she repeated quietly, as if trying out the name to see how it would feel.   *"Merci, monsieur Luca,"* she added gratefully.

"But you're a bright girl, Marianne," continued *Monsieur* Luca. "Why don't you just go home… escape from this awful situation?"

"But how can I do that – without my passport and only a handful of euros in my purse?" she stated pitifully. "HE keeps my passport. HE keeps most of the money I make, *ce type louche!*

She showed him her brand new Italian identity card – the type issued to foreign visitors, only valid as long as one stays on Italian soil. Luca nodded in understanding. She was a virtual prisoner of the 'Sleazeball' – an expression she had just translated precisely into French.

"I call him *Il Porco,* Marianne."

She smiled in a conspiratorial manner – a moment of warmth shared with someone who was on her side in her desert of isolation.

"Why are you here in Collemaga, *Monsieur* Luca? Are you on holiday?"

She had asked the question with a hint of anxiety in her voice. The unbearable thought that his stay might only be brief had just struck her. Luca looked thoughtful. He had to decide on the spot whether to take her into his confidence. He would need to choose his words carefully. It struck him only in that instant of time that the girl's chance arrival outside his bedroom door would make it impossible for him to leave the following morning without abandoning her to her fate at the hands of Luigi Bonifaccio.

Even though she was unaware of it, this encounter with Marianne had subtly altered the perspective of his mission in Collemaga. It was no longer simply a matter of satisfying his own personal curiosity. He felt a shiver of apprehension which he was quite sure Marianne detected in a fleeting change of facial expression. She was looking at him anxiously. Luca took a deep breath, knowing that his next words would be cast in stone – assuming he wished to retain his integrity and self-respect for the rest of his life. He let out an involuntary sigh.

"I'm a journalist, Marianne – freelance. My original idea was to investigate why this town has the reputation of being cursed. Then I was going to sell the story to a newspaper or magazine…"

"Then I came along and complicated your life," she stated almost inaudibly.

Luca smiled kindly, moved by the pinched look of anxiety which her face had assumed.

"Don't worry, Marianne. When I leave in a few days' time, I shall take you with me back to Milan. We need someone to look after our two children so my wife can go back to work. I can't leave you alone here, can I?"

She flung herself at him, put her arms round his neck and hugged him. It was a spontaneous gesture and quite clumsy because of the awkward way they were sitting on the bed. Once again, Luca had to consciously guard against the sensations of arousal which contact with her body engendered. She was obviously aware of the effect on him through the slight stiffening of his body and withdrew the contact reluctantly.

"*Excuse-moi,* Luca, *je suis désolée.* I was just afraid it would finish up as it did with that other young man who was here a few weeks ago…"

Luca's mind was alert in an instant. "What other man, Marianne? Thank you for saying the *other* young man, by the way."

Marianne grinned for the first time during the conversation. Luca noted quite incidentally that her teeth looked yellowish – another aspect of his rash promise which insinuated its way into his mind. She would need a visit to his dentist. This extraneous thought served as a reminder of the commitment he had just undertaken – without consulting his wife. If she only accused him roundly of being too impulsive, he would consider he had got off lightly.

"He was just a boy really," continued Marianne. "But he was sweet and gentle with me. I think it was his first time. I felt I was helping him overcome his shyness."

"Did he tell you his name, by any chance?" asked Luca. "It could be important."

"Only his first name – Mattia. He said he was in Collemaga on government business…"

Marianne was looking anxious again – seeing the intense interest that her chance comment had aroused in her newfound friend.

"What's wrong, Luca?"

She had finally dropped the '*monsieur',* he noted.

"Because he never made it back to Rome, Marianne - he seems to have disappeared. His family have reported him missing to the police."

Luca had occasionally wondered if dark-skinned people ever turned pale when they were frightened. His last words spoken to Marianne provided him with living proof that it was possible.

"Luca," she whispered fearfully, "he may still be alive – somewhere in Collemaga. There's this big house…"

"What makes you say that, Marianne?"

"I heard *HIM* talking about it over the phone once when he thought I wasn't listening."

"Can you tell me anything else about this house?"

Marianne was looking round fearfully. Once again, she glanced nervously up in the direction of the triangular window where Luca had stuffed the pillow. Luca was sensitive enough to realise that she was no longer in a frame of mind to be communicative. She was looking at her watch and then at Luca.

"It's the house that belongs to the *fattucchiera,* Luca…"

Luca remembered this ancient word for 'The Sorceress' in one of the articles he had read about Collemaga.

"I have to go, Luca. *He'll* become suspicious if I stay any longer. How will I know when you're ready to…?"

She was so desperate not to say the words 'rescue me' that she just dried up. But the look of longing on her face was heart-rending. They discussed exchanging mobile phone numbers but Marianne told Luca that *Il Porco* regularly checked all the calls and messages on her phone. It would be too risky, she explained. In the end, Luca scribbled his number on a piece of paper for her. She was still looking anxiously at him.

"Give me a few more days, Marianne. I won't let you down, I promise. I know..." Luca had had a simple idea. "When you notice the pillow has gone from the window up there, you'll know I'm ready to leave the following morning."

Marianne's face was beaming at the simplicity of this covert signal.

"But you mustn't tell *anyone* – even the other girl who works with you...sorry, you know what I'm saying."

"Oh, Fatima!" said Marianne scornfully. "No way! She would just go and blab it all to *HIM*. She couldn't keep a secret if it meant saving the world from a nuclear war."

Luca laughed out loud at the image she had created. He looked at her again with renewed affection as he walked towards the door to usher her out.

"I have really enjoyed your company, Marianne. And I'm so glad to have found a new friend in this town..."

Luca did not immediately understand why Marianne had not followed him to the door. She was looking at him apologetically.

"Luca, I'm so desperately sorry, but..."

Of course! He was being slow on the uptake. She was reluctant to ask him for money, but she could not go back upstairs empty-handed or she was lost.

Luca retrieved his wallet from his jacket pocket.

"Here, Marianne. Give him €50 – but keep that one for our journey!"

She stood on tip-toe and kissed him on the cheek, but her lips brushed his as if by accident. *"Grazie mille, Luca"* she whispered and she was gone.

* * *

Luca was mulling over the events of the day. He could not believe how drastically the situation had altered. Obviously, he had discovered the reason why this hotel was called *L'ospite Inatteso,* he thought ironically – Marianne had indeed been a totally unexpected guest.   It was a good half hour later when he remembered that he had not phoned home since he had arrived the previous day. There was little point in putting off the moment although he was tempted to procrastinate on the pretext that he should watch the news first. He knew that what he had to tell his wife, if he were to give a proper rendition of the day's proceedings, would evoke a strong reaction – even outright condemnation. Marie-Louise tended to see matters strictly in black and white and she was not one to hang back if she wished to speak her mind – always in French when roused. She only deigned to speak Italian when dealing with routine matters such as what she should buy on her next trip to the supermarket – or when addressing her neighbours and the children's teachers.

The land-line phone in Milan rang for nearly a minute without being picked up. Luca was about to breathe a sigh of relief. But Marie-Louise answered just as he was about to cancel the call.

"Ah, Luca, I knew it was you," she began.

His wife was in one of her feisty moods, he could tell.

"I was reading the kids their bedtime story," she added in a tone of voice which implied that the familiar task involving their offspring was several notches higher up her priority list than picking up the phone promptly to talk to him. Furthermore, Luca noted, she was speaking very decidedly in French – not deigning to give him any linguistic advantage in the exchange which would follow. However, this tactic could equally be adopted by him – by reverting to Italian.

45

"Mi dispiace, amore," he began. "I'm truly sorry I haven't phoned you before this evening. But you cannot imagine the speed with which events have been unfolding down here. Would you believe me if I told you I have been looking at houses which only cost one euro?"

There was no audible reaction from the other end, so Luca boldly continued to tread the path which would get the more dubious aspects of his first day's research out in the open without further delay.

"And this evening, I've had a long and revealing talk to a young Moroccan woman who is forced to work as a *ragazza squillo** in the town. She…"

"T'as fait QUOI?" exclaimed Marie-Louise in total disbelief. "I trust this exchange did NOT occur in your hotel room, Luca!"

"I was in our local bar earlier on," he replied evasively, merely relieved he had managed to avoid telling an outright untruth. He went on to tell her in a convincing enough manner what part the girl had played in his investigation. There was no way he could tell her about his rash promise to bring the girl back to Milan with him – let alone the fact that he had parted with over a hundred euros. He knew his wife well. He would have to wait until she had accepted what she quite reasonably saw as his neglect of his family as a result of this mad expedition to the deep south of this 'foreign' country.

"And what may I look forward to being told after tomorrow's investigative activities?" his wife asked in a tone of heavy sarcasm.

In for a penny, thought Luca.

"Oh, I'm going to try and discover where the Witch of Collemaga lives," he said.

Marie-Louise was not going to grace his reply with any intelligent comment.

"I have to say goodnight to the children. *Bonne nuit,* Luca."

"Give them my love, Marie Lou. *Ti amo, amore.*" he added hopefully.

She might have reluctantly replied *"Moi aussi,"* before hanging up. Luca could not swear to it.

It was late and he was feeling tired enough to fall asleep instantly. He thought he could make out a woman's voice singing somewhere above his head. If he remembered correctly, it was a popular French song he had heard his wife singing. Marianne, feeling happy for the first time in ages, he assumed.

His pre-sleep mind was active with the images of that eventful day. But he subconsciously detected an underlying sensation which echoed the one he had experienced in the mayor's office. It was a trick of the mind even more potent than the previous one -he fell asleep with the dream-like conviction that he had spent most of his life in Collemaga.

5:   *The die is cast...*

Luca was disturbed to discover that he felt disappointment on waking up the following morning – aware that his pre-slumber imaginings had dissipated with the rising sun. 'Normal' time had re-established itself in Collemaga. Furthermore, he had no clear plan of action in his head and not the remotest idea of how the day would pan out. His pre-slumber escape into another time warp had retreated to his subconscious mind – a place where more subtle influences could begin to wreak their magic spells.

He showered, shaved and got dressed because that is what his body habitually dictated he should do at that time of day. The only immediate obligation was to find a place where he could drink his cup of morning coffee. He was not sure that he could face the *Bar Commercio* again.

As he reached the bedroom door, he noticed a white envelope had been pushed under it during the hours of darkness. Curious yet on his guard, he fumbled with the flap. He found a 100€ note in it and a message scribbled in French.

Mon cher Luca. Thank you for everything. I felt so bad that I took money from you last night. You were so kind to me. I had to give HIM the €50 note. Gros bisous. M. xxx

Luca felt tears pricking his eyes. The simple honesty of the gesture from a girl desperate for money gave him the impetus he needed to regain a positive outlook on his stay in this town. What did it matter if he never wrote a single journalistic word about Collemaga? He had done the right thing by giving hope to a young woman in deep trouble. Anything else could be considered a bonus. Then he recalled that Marianne had slipped in a few significant, fearful words about, Mattia, the young man from Rome whom she claimed might still be alive. He wished he had

48

questioned her more closely at the time. But she had mentioned Mattia's name in connection with a house which belonged to *la fattucchiera* – the sorceress. That must constitute some sort of lead – the identity of the local witch should be common knowledge. Furthermore, a modern-day *maga* should not constitute a serious personal threat...

"What? Not even a witch who might have been involved in the disappearance of the young State employee who had been 'snooping' around Collemaga?" said a warning voice inside his head. He remembered the look of suppressed terror on Marianne's face when she had told him in hushed tones about Mattia.

He sighed and headed for the *Bar Commercio* – convinced that he would learn more there than walking up the hill to the bar on the *Piazza di San Nicola.** There was no sign of the hotel owner anywhere. It was gone half past eight, he noticed. It was well past his usual first coffee moment. The relative lateness of the hour meant that there were fewer people in the bar than the previous day. However, Luigi – *Il Porco* - was there sitting opposite the girl called Fatima. He directed a knowing leer in Luca's direction. Luca had to control the desire to go and punch Luigi Bonifaccio's nose. Seeing the look on Luca's face, he stood up and told the girl to get her backside off the chair. Fatima accepted the insulting words without demur. Marianne had been right – she was too slow-witted to take offence at the way she was being treated. Luca felt a stab of pity for the girl, but there was little he could do for her at this stage. She had in all likelihood become dependent on Luigi to the extent she could no longer envisage any other way of life. As they were walking towards the door, Luigi made a gesture with his hands to the effect that Fatima was also available if he wanted. The gesture implied that she would be a lot cheaper too. Luca took one menacing step

49

towards Luigi, who pushed the girl hurriedly through the doorway. *Il Porco* had a self-satisfied smirk on his face – content that he had succeeded in riling Luca; revenge for blocking his view of the bedroom with the pillow, Luca supposed.

The barman had placed a croissant on the counter and was making Luca a coffee without being asked. Luca nodded at the barman and turned his attention to the one remaining client, who was reading a newspaper. Luca recognised the hotel owner, who looked at him with an ill-concealed expression of mild scorn.

"So will you still be needing an extra room for that 'friend' of yours you mentioned when you arrived, *signore?*" he asked with a complicit smirk on his face.

Luca controlled the surge of renewed anger. He had to play a careful game from now on. No doubt Marianne's visit to his room was common knowledge in the *Bar Commercio* by now.

"She seems to have been delayed, *Signor* Frassica," replied Luca, stifling his annoyance at the outrageous over-familiarity displayed by the surly hotel owner. Luca even managed to return the complicit grin accompanied by a surreptitious wink.

Luca took two bites out of the croissant before downing the coffee – which was good – in three gulps in quick succession. He handed the bar owner a €10 note as he took a shot in the dark:

"I'm told that Collemaga has its own *fattucchiera, signore.* Does she live in these parts?"

The bar owner's face had frozen. He was looking nervously at the hotel owner who had torn a page of his newspaper in surprise at Luca's unexpected question. The hotel owner gave a surreptitious shake of his head – a gesture that Luca had intercepted out of the corner of his eye.

"We know nothing about any witch, *signore*," answered the bar owner in a voice that did not correspond to the words he had uttered. He looked appealingly at Luca in a manner which implied that he should not pursue the subject. The hotel owner, Dario Frassica, stood up and left, shooting a warning glance in the bar owner's direction.

"I'm sorry, *Signor...?* said Luca.

"Enzo – Enzo Materano."

Luca had intuited the day before that the bar owner seemed to be more amenable than his clientele. He hoped his usually infallible intuition had not deserted him. He held out his hand to the man, who shook it almost guiltily.

"My name is Luca Fontana, Enzo. I'm sorry if I was being tactless just now. I was merely curious about what someone in the bar up the road told me yesterday. He seemed to think I might find the notion of the existence of a local *maga* entertaining."

Luca had deliberately implied that his 'informer' had been a man from another part of the town. It was obvious that *Il Porco* had been spreading the news about *one of his girls* visiting Luca's room the evening before. He was mindful of the danger of implicating Marianne.

Enzo's next words would shed an altogether more disquieting light on the obscure little township whose secrets he had come to unearth.

"There is nothing amusing about our local sorceress, Signor Luca. That Luigi guy, who you wanted to lay into just now, is her illegitimate son. You must be careful what you say and do in this town."

Luca was staring in astonishment at the bar owner, unable to find appropriate words with which to reply.

"And you did *NOT* hear that from me," added Enzo pleadingly.

* * *

Luca instinctively headed for his car – just to check it was there waiting for him. It represented his sole means of evasion if his research came to nothing - or if matters got out of hand. He was increasingly aware that menacing elements had crept into the equation. He might have to make good his escape – *their* escape, he corrected himself – sooner rather than later. He was reassured to find that his car was parked in the *piazza* a few metres downhill from the *Bar Commercio.* But he could not ignore a niggling sense of vulnerability brought on by the awareness of how remote he was from his normal world. Above all, he identified the bar owner's revelation as the real source of his unease. Were Luigi Bonifaccio's sleazy back-street tricks being presided over by some more malevolent force? By his own mother, in point of fact! Surely he was exhibiting the first symptoms of paranoia?

Luca felt in his jacket pocket for the cigars he had purchased the day before from Giorgia's homely tobacconist shop. A cigar would calm his nerves and enable him to take stock of his discoveries in the half hour of meditation which each cigar always afforded him.

But not here in this sunless little square, he decided, as he headed further downhill, instinctively making for the house he had viewed the previous day with its secluded, sunny garden. It had awoken the dormant desire to possess a dwelling with its own outside space – not just a terrace attached to a city apartment on the fifth floor of a seven storey block of flats.

To Luca, it appeared to be one of those defining moments in life – an instant of time when instinct or impulse took over from reason. Only later on would he analyse what happened between the moment when he opened the latch on the flimsy wooden gate leading to the secluded garden - and the unexpected arrival of the estate agent with another potential client.

He was sitting on the stone bench which he had noticed the day before. The air was filled with the humming of bees and the sweet perfume of honeysuckle somewhere in the garden – sounds and smells so absent from city life. Even the day before, he had had the impression that the bench was beguilingly inviting him to make himself comfortable. The sun, warm on his face, had travelled imperceptibly on its slow arc around the Earth. Time was measured only by the slowly diminishing length of his cigar.

That was the moment when a flash of inspiration struck him; why should he wait to rescue his protégée, Marianne, until the day when he was ready to depart? The solution was simple - he would drive Marianne to the neighbouring town of Pontefalco in secret and leave her with the family who ran the *trattoria* where he had had lunch. That way he could safely leave Marianne for a few days while he returned to Collemaga. Nobody would attribute her disappearance to any intervention on his part if the manoeuvre was carried out at night time.

He was still enjoying the breath-taking view across the deep valley of the River Senna when he heard the voices approaching from the other side of the house.

"Merda!" he muttered to himself. Too late to take evasive action!

The estate agent's face registered mild shock as he came into sight. Luca stood up with a guilty smile and an apologetic shrug of his shoulder.

"I'm sorry, *Signor* Russo," he said to the estate agent. "I thought it would be a pleasant way to make up my mind about the next step I should take regarding this house."

"I suppose I should point out, *Signor* Fontana, that you are trespassing. By rights, I should report you to the *Carabinieri.*"

Luca did not reckon, however, that the estate agent was convinced by his own threat. However, the lady who accompanied Aurelio Russo was looking put out at the presence of a rival purchaser. She coughed pointedly.

"Oh, I'm sorry," said the estate agent. "This is *la Signora* Janssen. She's from The Netherlands."

The Dutch lady showed no signs of wishing to shake Luca's proffered hand.

"I'll just finish my cigar as I'm here, *Signor* Russo, and then I'll make myself scarce."

Luca was alarmed to find he had no intention of giving ground to the surly lady from the far north of Europe. He had as much right to be in this garden as she had.

"Not quite true," the other half of his brain informed him.

"I'll come and see you in your office later on this morning, *Signor* Russo. Would 11.30 be alright?" he suggested, looking meaningfully at the Dutch lady.

The lady spoke Italian with a strong accent – suggesting to the estate agent that she had seen enough of the garden and that perhaps he would show her round the house instead.

"*A presto, Signor* Fontana," said the estate agent happily enough. Having two people chasing after the same property often led to a rapid sale.

The second half of his cigar promoted a very different internal debate. He had the distinct impression that he had come to a decision. After all, the house itself would cost him much less than the change he had in his pocket from the bar owner up the road. He did briefly wonder how his wife would react to his decision. That was a bridge to be crossed later on. In any case, if he ever needed to hide from the *'ndrangheta* – a very likely scenario in view of his prime mission in life – where better region of Italy could there be to hide in than Abruzzo? He sighed with contentment as he smoked the rest of his cigar.

* * *

The deed had been done, papers signed. The house was virtually his. The initial cost of €1 plus €3500 for the administration fee had been paid via credit transfer from his own personal account. If matters got out of hand and he had to escape from Collemaga in a hurry, he could easily recoup the outlay from the proceeds of his article. Aurelio Russo had been delighted. Luca would have to formally present himself at the Town Hall to sign the registration documents, the estate agent explained.

"I shall tell our mayor you are on your way, *Signor* Fontana. I'm sure he will want to congratulate you in person," the estate agent had informed him.

Luca had spent a good hour with the estate agent looking round the three storey house – which even had a wine cellar in the cool basement – a feature that he had long dreamt about. He reckoned he would only have to spend €30 000 over the two year period during which he was legally obliged to make the house habitable. Up north in Milano he would have had to part with three times that amount to have the same work carried out.

As Luca climbed the steps to the town hall just before lunchtime, he congratulated himself unreservedly on his impulsive decision; he had at the very least established his credentials in the eyes of the mayor – and any other parties in Collemaga who might have vested interests.

* * *

A smiling mayor personally came down to the foyer and ushered Luca upstairs to his office. Yet Luca retained the distinct impression throughout their brief encounter that Elpidio Pugliese was more relieved than overjoyed at the prospect of Luca's sudden conversion. There seemed to be some inner conflict going on, judging by the mayor's unconscious body language. Wherever Luca went or in whatever activity he indulged in in this town, there always seemed to be elusive 'undercurrents'. But the inevitable cups of coffee appeared on a tray with a plate of *Abbracci** biscuits – the same biscuits which his own children dunked enthusiastically into their cups at breakfast time, he noted with a twinge of nostalgia.

He was about to share this intimate item of information with the mayor - in the spirit of conviviality which should have been apparent between them at this stage of proceedings – but he remembered just in time that he had claimed to be childless the day before. How near he was, yet again, to slipping up and falling foul of his own inventiveness. Yesterday, he had felt the need for caution, which had been replaced by a different and more dangerous sensation that he had embarked on an adventure. He should be wary, he reminded himself, not to allow his sense of euphoria to cloud his judgement.

"We are very glad to welcome you to Collemaga, *Signor* Fontana," the mayor was saying. "As you are obviously an entirely dependable and intelligent man, I shall entrust you with the documents you will need to sign regarding the conditions of purchase and so on. We can discuss any issues tomorrow or the day afterwards, when you have had time to peruse them."

"Of course, *Signor Sindaco,*" said Luca, reasonably.

"You will see that the contract recommends that local builders be used – to support the town's economy but, of course, you will be free to…"

The mayor's mobile phone made an intrusive jangling noise, which could not be ignored. The mayor looked worried as he looked at the screen. In fact, Luca was sure he had turned a shade paler. A gritty male voice began to speak without preamble – in a thick dialect. Nevertheless, Luca had the instinctive sensation that *he* was the subject of this exchange of words.

"The individual concerned is about to pay me a visit," said the mayor. The grating sound of a sneering laugh was accompanied by further incomprehensible words.

"Sì sì – la faccio sapere, signora…"* The mayor hung up, looking uncomfortably at Luca.

"I'm sorry to interrupt our conversation, *Signor* Fontana. We must meet up again soon. I have to attend a meeting right now."

The mayor ushered him to the door and shook him perfunctorily by the hand, avoiding direct eye contact.

* * *

Luca decided to drive back to the neighbouring town of Pontefalco and talk to the agreeable owner of the *trattoria* about his plan to rescue Marianne. He could hardly turn up with the French girl out of the blue – especially as the manoeuvre would have to take place in secret in the early hours of the morning.

He did not give a moment's thought as to how he would explain Marianne's situation to Bruno Vespini. He had not seemed the sort of man likely to be squeamish about the niceties of Marianne's predicament – and Luca was intending to reward the man for any temporary inconvenience.

But Luca had another matter on his mind as he drove rapidly towards Pontefalco. When the mayor had brought the phone call with the person with the sneering voice to its conclusion, he had addressed 'him' as *SIGNORA!* The speaker had been a woman. In a flash of perception, Luca had understood that the person on the other end of the line was *la fattucchiera* – the town's sorceress. He could still feel the cold shiver that had shot up and down his spine in that instant of grim enlightenment.

6:   *Un rincontro 'casuale'* *(A 'chance' encounter)*

"She's reputed to be a hermaphrodite," Bruno Vespini was telling Luca with grim relish. "And that is one of the milder things they say about her!"

Luca had spent the best part of an hour relating to the owner of *La Buona Forchetta* everything that had transpired since they had met two days previously – finishing up with the sinister exchange between the mayor and the woman – the sorceress - with the voice of a man.

Luca was hungry and the sweet smell of cooked lamb emanating from the kitchen was irresistible. He had held Bruno spellbound with the story of Marianne Lagrange, but had not yet spoken to him about his temporary solution to her problems. He thought it would be more tactically effective if he allowed the details of her plight to sink in before he broached the subject of her concealment within the walls of the *La Buona Forchetta.* Besides which the place was rapidly filling up with diners – local farmers and a handful of businessmen; in sharp contrast to his first visit when he had arrived later on in the day.

Luca exercised his reserves of will-power and drank only water with his lamb stew. He ate very slowly and had a dessert to follow. Most of the diners had left and gone back to work by the time he was presented with a coffee and a liqueur.

Luca's strategy of waiting until the restaurant was empty again turned out to be an unnecessary precaution. He tentatively outlined his plan for her rescue with fingers crossed under the table. He added that he was more than willing to pay Bruno for any inconvenience caused.

"It would only be for a few days, Bruno. But I would like to stay in Collemaga until their *festa* on Thursday – so I can include it in my essay."

"She can help us by working as a waitress – and take the kids to school too. I would not dream of taking your money to help out a girl in trouble – especially not *that* kind of trouble, Luca. It's a great idea. In fact, if for any reason you need to stay on after the *festa,* I would be more than happy to let Marianne remain for longer."

As events were to transpire, Bruno's words would turn out to be prophetic.

"You really are stirring up a hornets' nest, aren't you, Luca! Just be triply cautious about whose nose you put out of joint. You may well be underestimating the risks involved in upsetting the balance of power in *that* town..."

"I will be careful, Bruno. But I believe you are right – I have only scratched the surface of Collemaga up till now."

Bruno Vespini walked to the door with Luca and shook him warmly by the hand.

"You're a good man, Luca Fontana, and a courageous one too!"

"My wife thinks I'm simply an impulsive fool who tempts providence at every new turn that my life takes."

"She could have a point. Take care, Luca! I shall expect you some time in the early hours of tomorrow morning," said the owner of the *La Buona Forchetta* with an expression on his face which clearly said: 'If all goes according to plan...'

* * *

Back in Collemaga, Luca realised that he would need to devise a plan to alert Marianne as to their imminent departure. He parked his car in the usual - almost empty – square near the hotel. As soon as he stepped inside his bedroom, he instinctively knew that something had changed but it took several seconds before his conscious mind caught up with his first instinctive reaction. Somebody had removed the pillow covering the window. His first superstitious reaction was to think it was some conjuring trick, or a sign from above that his plan had 'official' blessing. He shook his head to expel such fanciful thoughts. Somebody had been in his room and removed it. If it was the chambermaid, it would be only the second time during his visit that her services had been apparent – the bed-making had been notably haphazard so far. Luca had searched in every draw and looked in the wardrobe to make sure that the pillow had not simply been replaced, before he took further action. There was no sign of it. Luca stormed out of the room in search of the hotel owner – whose absence had been even more marked than that of the chambermaid.

By banging loudly on the counter for several minutes, he had apparently alerted the hotel owner, whose moody footfall could be heard descending the wooden staircase.

"Somebody's been into my room today and removed that pillow I deliberately put up to stop me being spied on by... anyone on the outside staircase," he added in a controlled manner. "Have you got an explanation for this intrusion into my right to privacy, *Signor* Frassica?"

To Luca's surprise, his forthright response to the missing pillow had shaken the owner's confidence. Whilst trying to maintain his habitual indifference to his one and only 'normal' guest, it was obvious from the shifty manner in which his eyes glanced to left and right that Dario Frassica was nervous.

To Luca's surprise, he heard a second set of footsteps descending the staircase. The owner uttered some impatient words in dialect in the direction of the stairwell. The footsteps halted. But Luca had cottoned on. It was the shoes and legs of Fatima – the other girl – that Luca could just make out. Fatima turned round and walked stolidly upstairs again.

Luca put on a knowing, lascivious smirk – to indicate that he had fully understood the situation. Dario Frassica had to take second best choice to satisfy his libido. The message was not lost on the owner of *L'Ospite Inatteso*.

To Luca's surprise, Dario Frassica looked pleadingly at Luca, as if to enlist his help.

"Please, *signore* – let things settle down for a day or so and I'll let you have a cushion or something back again to cover up that window."

The man was obviously completely under the heel of *Il Porco* – or whoever it might be who was attempting to manipulate the course of events. *His* events, he pointed out to himself.

He nodded at Dario Frassico, feeling almost sorry for the man. Now he would have to find a way to tell Marianne that her rescue would take place that night. It might well be the case that she was unaware that it was not him who had removed the pillow from the window – their agreed signal that the time for her escape had arrived. He couldn't take the risk of passing on messages through anyone else. With his firmly held belief that fate would always come to his rescue, he decided to walk up to the square at the top of Collemaga. He wanted to visit Giorgia again – one of the few people in Collemaga he felt certain represented normality. He had an overwhelming urge to tell her that he had taken the step of purchasing a house. Why this feeling of compulsion? He had an awful suspicion that he knew what the motive was behind the simple excuse which his mind had invented to justify the visit. It did not bear analysis. Luca inevitably felt a sense of alarm at the way in which his subconscious mind so often took the lead in determining the course his life should run.

His disappointment was intense when he stepped inside the tobacconist's shop to find a large, surly man with a black beard which covered the whole of his face sitting motionless behind the bar. He did not deign to acknowledge Luca's presence but rather stared at him resentfully.

"Good afternoon, *Signor....?*" he began. The man nodded but did not show any other sign that he wished to communicate.

"I was expecting to find *la signora* here," Luca ventured.

The eyes, the only feature visible on this hirsute face, treated Luca to a hostile stare.

"School, picking up the kid. Back in ten minutes," stated the barely visible mouth, speaking in dialect.

Luca was not prepared to wait that long, let alone buy anything he didn't need merely to justify his presence in the shop. He left the man with an apologetic gesture and a courteous *'buonasera'*. He walked dejectedly down the hill again wondering who the man could be. Surely he couldn't be...? He preferred not to speculate on the man's connection to Giorgia.

Luca did not immediately recognise the woman walking up the street holding the hand of a small boy. He was about to step to one side onto the road to let them pass when he recognised Giorgia. She was smiling radiantly at him, obviously having recognised him some seconds ago. She was standing close to him, facing him squarely. She turned her cheek slightly, instinctively expecting a *bacio* on each cheek, whilst her eyes never left his face for an instant. Luca found he had placed a hand on her sleeve as he drew her marginally closer towards him to exchange the brief kiss.

Giorgia did not look embarrassed at all – the gesture had been entirely spontaneous, a tacit recognition of how they felt about each other. But, he noticed, a mother with a little girl was studying them closely as she sidestepped on to the road. Collemaga was a very small town.

"And this is Marco," she was saying. But the expression on her face had altered subtly. There was a silent appeal in her eyes, which Luca understood as soon as he looked at the expectant face of the seven-year-old boy. The two holes for breathing were the salient feature of his face, with only a partially formed nose to support them. Luca understood everything in a flash, but not soon enough for the seven-year to detect the fleeting reaction on the face of his mother's 'new friend'; instinctively his hand had covered his face. Luca did not pause to think; he squatted down at the child's level and raised his hand for a 'high five' handshake – which the boy responded to with a smile of gratitude. Luca was looking at the tousled black hair, the smiling mouth and above all the intense brown eyes. Yes, he *was* a beautiful child.

"Ciao, Marco! I'm so pleased to be your friend," he said in all sincerity.

The trio continued to walk back up the hill, the boy hand in hand with his mother. Luca, on her other flank, was happy for her shoulder to be touching his upper chest intermittently in time with the rhythm of their steps. Luca recognised the familiar signs - the slight electric shock at the sensation of physical contact between two beings between whom there existed the early warning signs of mutual desire. He did not attempt to resist it.

"I was looking out for you, Giorgia," he lied. "There was this man in your shop who told me…"

"He's just a cousin," said Giorgia hurriedly. "Marco's father isn't here anymore. Nino just looks after the shop for me when I'm with Marco."

The couple had reached the *piazza* and the little group paused in front of the shop.

"You will come inside with us, won't you, Luca?"

The invitation was delivered in a deliberately flirtatious tone of voice accompanied by an ingenuous smile. Only Giorgia's eyes were pleading with him not to say 'no'. Luca placed his arm briefly round her waist as the little group entered the shop.

Neither of them had noticed the surreptitious presence of a certain individual some fifty or so metres behind them. He had a self-satisfied leer in his face.

* * *

In a cramped apartment behind the shop, Giorgia sat Luca round the kitchen table while she prepared a teatime snack for her son. Luca was surprised how rapidly his mind had accepted the little boy's deformity – and chatted to him as he had done to his own children when they were still Marco's age. It was certainly not the right moment to talk to Giorgia about the underlying implications of this minor affliction, he thought. Indeed, it seemed unlikely that they would ever broach the subject.

"Incidentally, Giorgia, I noticed that *that man* – I call him 'Mr Sleaze' by the way – paid you a visit just after I left you two days ago. He seemed to be making aggressive gestures in your direction. What did he say to you?"

Giorgia had laughed with a pleasantly trilling laugh at the expression *Il Porco* -which seemed such an appropriate expression to describe Luigi Bonifaccio.

"I see you have already come across the shadier aspects of this town, Luca. He's the town's nosey parker, the grass. He wanted to know exactly what you had spoken about when we first met. I told him you were looking for a one euro house – I hope I didn't say anything out of place."

Luca shook his head reassuringly.

"I had the impression that you had not really thought about an excuse for being in Collemaga until you saw that little flyer. You clutched at the idea on the spur of the moment. Am I right?"

Giorgia's brown eyes were shining mischievously as she challenged Luca.

"I think you are a very smart lady, Giorgia."

Luca was seized by a desire to stand up and kiss her on the mouth but contented himself by reaching across the table for her hand and squeezing it gently. Giorgia only let go of his hand after a reluctant five seconds. The gesture was the first sign that the attraction between them was mutual. It was enough to produce a wide-eyed look from Marco, who had his mouth full of a Nutella sandwich.

The die was cast.

"So why was *Il Porco* making those threatening gestures at you as he left the shop?"

"He told me to find out as much as I could about you, Luca. I put him in his place and told him that if it wasn't *my* business to ask you about your reasons for being here, it certainly wasn't *his*. He doesn't like people who stand up to him."

"Please don't get yourself into trouble on my behalf, Giorgia. Luigi Bonifaccio is not a pleasant character at all. I know who his mother is, by the way," added Luca, testing the waters.

Giorgia's face was a picture – a mixture of apprehension and admiration.

"You certainly *haven't* been wasting your time, have you?"

Luca told her about the house he was intending to purchase down the bottom end of the town. She looked at him with mouth agape as he told her how he had been captivated by the three storey building with its rocky, sweet-smelling garden.

"I am so happy that this means you won't be leaving us behind for ever, Luca. But *please* be careful, won't you! I don't want you to fall foul of the darker elements of this town."

It was apparent she wanted to reach across the table and take *his* hand, but she seemed to control the impulse.

"By the way, Luca, why *have* you really come here?" she asked, looking him straight in the eyes, with an audacious smile on her face.

Luca drew in his breath sharply. The moment when he would have to trust Giorgia had arrived. He instantly dismissed the possibility that she was acting as a spy for Mr Sleaze. It just didn't fit her character. So he told her the truth.

"A freelance reporter, eh?" she said. "I would never have guessed *that*. You must be so careful, Luca. This place has dangerous undercurrents. You really do run the risk of stirring up a hornet's nest..."

"Funny you should say that, Giorgia. Somebody from another town near here used exactly those words to me only this morning."

"So please take us both seriously, *caro* Luca."

A silence fell round the table. Marco had finished eating and asked his mother if he could leave the table. He could be heard going up a flight of stairs to where the bedrooms were. Luca broke the silence with a few carefully chosen words.

"I have only been here a few days, Giorgia. But events have already taken me by surprise. I have a very different perspective of this town today than when I arrived."

He took a deep breath in the expectant silence.

"Something important has happened, Giorgia. I met you…"

It was she who stood up and walked towards him – and kissed him rapidly on the lips, uttering a sigh of pleasure.

Luca's mobile buzzed, breaking the spell. There was a text message from Marianne, which said simply: *Alors, on part cette nuit?**

Luca decided that it was not the moment to tell Giorgia what he intended to do that night. He would tell her tomorrow – when he was safely back in Collemaga.

7:   *The abduction of Marianne Lagrange...*

Luca was preoccupied by a sense of guilt as he walked down the hill towards the *L'Ospite Inatteso.* He knew the reason for his guilt, of course; he was allowing himself to become involved with another woman in order to fill the growing emotional void he had been experiencing at home over the last year or so. But he had two children, of whom he was very fond. It wasn't fair on them. Such arguments always worked well for a time before emotions which usually remained buried more deeply inside him began to resurface. He was debating whether to telephone his wife, Marie-Louise, that night to tell her that he had – theoretically at least – gone through the motions of buying a second home, even further away from her beloved France than Milan. He even identified a possible hidden motive for buying the house – it might precipitate Marie-Louise's oft repeated threat of 'taking the children back to France', where, she claimed, they would receive a better education and grow up in the countryside. Her parents lived in a spacious house outside a picturesque town called Villefranche-de-Rouergue – with the river Aveyron running through the town centre. His sense of culpability was intense.

Luca had intended to walk down and check his car before going to his room, where, he knew, his confused thoughts would have time to multiply exponentially before it was time to embark on the next phase of his mission in Collemaga. A casual check on his FIAT Tipo would undoubtedly have saved him moments of anguish later on that night. Back in his bedroom, he resolutely retrieved his lap-top from its ingenious hiding place and concentrated on beginning the article which would soon, he hoped, appear in the Italian press. He should also take photos of the town before he left – especially during the *festa* in a few days' time.

Round about nine o'clock, he remembered to make a phone call to Giacomo, his friend in the Ministry in Rome, whom he had been meaning to call since he had spoken to Marianne.

"Giacomo… *Disturbo?*"

"Yes, you are, Luca – as usual. But I'm quite used to it. *Dimmi!*"

Luca told him about his conversation with Marianne and particularly about her fearful comment concerning the missing 'boy' from the Ministry, whose name was Mattia.

"Marianne seemed to think he was alive and being kept somewhere in this town, Giacomo. It might be a sound course of action to alert the police in Rome. I suspect that the police force in Collemaga might not be entirely willing to leap into action."

Giacomo sighed audibly but promised he would deal with the matter the following morning.

"I'll let you get back to your family, Giacomo," said Luca apologetically. He switched on his postage stamp sized TV set high up on a shelf in his room – with the sound turned down low – and realised from the voices he had heard in the background during his phone conversation with his friend that he was watching the same channel. He never found out exactly what the drama was about; it remained a background noise as he typed busily in an attempt to remember every element of his story about Collemaga so far. He had arranged with Marianne by way of a terse text message that their departure would take place in the early hours of the following morning. Nevertheless, he had dozed off fully clothed when he heard an urgent scratching sound from the other side of his bedroom door.

Marianne was smiling with her lips but her eyes looked wild with anxiety.

Luca looked round the room checking that he had not left anything behind. A fleeting movement – nothing more than a shadow – had caught his eye. It was so brief that it hardly registered. He looked up automatically at the now uncovered window. Had there been a face up there for less than the time it had taken to blink?

He turned the light out as he stepped quickly into the corridor, lit by a single dingy light bulb at the head of the stairwell. He mentally shrugged off his suspicion. He could hardly turn back now. Marianne was carrying all her worldly goods in one small rucksack.

"Come on, Marianne," he whispered. "Say goodbye to the *Ospite Inatteso,* once and for all."

Luca had already checked that the main hotel door could be opened. The owner simply left the key in the lock so he would not have to see off any guests who departed at the crack of dawn.

They approached the *piazza* where Luca's car was parked without exchanging a word – each conveying the tension that the other felt. Luca was brought to a standstill as soon as he saw his car. Despite the square being relatively empty of cars, his own car was neatly hemmed in by two old FIAT cars which, he assumed, had been deliberately positioned to prevent him getting in through either door.

"Porca miseria!"* he swore under his breath. How could this have happened? It was uncanny – as if someone had intuited what his intentions had been.

Marianne's face was a picture. To Luca's amazement, she had smiled mischievously as if this setback was all part of the adventure.

71

"If they think *this* is going to be enough to stop us leaving, they'll be very disappointed," she whispered fiercely. "Unlock the car, Luca. I'll get in through the boot."

Luca's FIAT was an estate car version so, he thought, it might be possible for a small person to get in and climb over the seats.

"Give me the keys, Luca," she said. "I can reverse the car out of the space once I'm inside."

Somehow, it had not occurred to Luca that his *protégée* would be able to drive.

"I have driven a car – once before," she added reassuringly, correctly interpreting the expression on his face.

Luca was amazed at her agility. She had dumped her rucksack on the ground and taken off her padded anorak before squeezing through the narrow space between the rear head-rests, her jean-covered legs disappearing as she landed on the back seat of the car. Within the space of ten seconds she was seated in the driver's seat and had inserted the key in the ignition and turned the engine on. There were a few tense moments while she worked out where the reverse gear was situated. She backed the car rather too jerkily into the road with the engine revving.

Luca looked up at the buildings and noticed a curtain moving in one of the windows on the top floor. So much for secrecy, he thought as Marianne, smiling triumphantly, shifted with athletic ease into the passenger seat.

"Brava, Marianne!" he said as he headed out of town into the open countryside. He knew that he had initiated a process which would have serious consequences for himself – and his project. Pandora's Box had been opened.

* * *

That someone was following them quickly became apparent. Luca had continuously glanced up at the mirror to check he was not being paranoid. He had even deliberately taken a wrong turning and had had to turn down a farm track, reverse and head back towards Pontefalco. They had passed the pursuing vehicle – a nondescript old Peugeot – heading towards them. Marianne had cottoned on to what was happening immediately.

"It's not *HIM!*" was all she had said, looking fearfully at Luca.

It took their pursuer some forty-five seconds to adjust to the sudden crisis. But there was no doubt in Luca's mind that it was his car that was the prey. It was hanging on doggedly about five hundred metres behind them and closing in again bit at a time.

"I'm sorry for the trouble I've caused you, Luca," said Marianne in a little, subdued voice.

Luca looked sideways for an instant and managed a broad, reassuring grin.

"Ne t'inquiète pas, Marianne,"* he told her. "This is not the first time in my life I've had to lose a trail. It's usually the mafia on my tail – and this guy's an amateur. But we shall have to make quite a detour to shake him off – or her I suppose..."

There had been something about the face he had glimpsed during the split second in which the pursuing car had flashed by that had suggested flowing blond hair. Who could possibly have reacted so quickly to the situation back in Collemaga and to have been able to follow him with only a few minutes' notice? It was uncanny – and disturbing.

Marianne was looking nervous and in a state of deep thought. Luca realised that she must have been thinking along the same lines as him.

73

"I'm so sorry, Luca," she began after a few minutes. "I think it might have been my fault. I left my phone by my bedside while I was packing my clothes – after you sent me the message. I share a room with the other girl, Fatima. She usually sleeps like a log – or appears to be doing so. I went to the bathroom at some point. Maybe she read your message while I was out of the room. It was only just after midnight..."

That's it, thought Luca, enlightened. It was Fatima's face he had fleetingly caught sight of framed in the window. She must have managed to warn *Il Porco* that something was afoot. He may be a piece of low-life excrement, thought Luca, but he was also a survivor. He must have guessed what Luca's intentions were.

"Don't worry, Marianne," he said seeking to reassure her. He did not wish her to carry a sense of guilt at the moment of her release from her bondage of slavery. "Just hang on to anything – and make sure your seat belt is secure."

Luca pressed his foot down hard on the accelerator and followed the few sign posts for the nearest town. He was sure he was not travelling in the direction of Pontefalco. Never mind, they could re-orientate themselves after they had lost the pursuing vehicle. It was essential from his point of view – and Marianne's safety – that their pursuer had no clue as to their intended destination.

He was entering a small town called Capestrino – still many kilometres away from the nearest main town, Sulmona, Luca noticed on the sign post. This place should prove to be right for the manoeuvre he had in mind. Marianne gasped in surprise when Luca, without appearing to slow down, switched off the car lights completely – leaving only the pallid light given off by the infrequent street lamps to ensure he did not collide with anything.

"Look out for a petrol station – or a supermarket car park." Luca commanded his companion – a difficult task in view of the speed at which they seemed to be speeding through the deserted town.

"There!" said Marianne, "take the road to the right. There's a sign pointing to an API petrol station down there."

Luca took the street indicated by Marianne. He had to swerve across the road at the last minute as he spotted the row of pumps in the dim courtyard. Sure enough, there were a couple of deserted cars which had been parked on the edge of the garage forecourt. He switched off the engine. The silence outside was absolute in the sleepy little town.

"We should get out of the car just in case someone managed to follow us," said Luca.

They hid behind the bushes at the rear of the petrol station from where they could still observe their car. In the distance, Marianne's sharp ears caught the sound of a car travelling fast along the road which led out of the town – the road they would have taken had she not spotted the sign for the filling station.

"*Brava,* Marianne!" whispered Luca putting an arm round her shoulders in a gesture of reassurance. She merely placed her head against his chest and sighed at the sense of comfort which she felt.

Nevertheless, Luca insisted that they stayed where they were for what seemed like an eternity.

"Whoever it was, they are almost sure to realise we are behind them and come back to have another look," stated Luca.

Just before dawn arrived, early morning traffic began to be heard as postmen and market stall holders set out for work.

"I think we're safe now," Luca said to Marianne, who was beginning to shiver from cold or from nervous reaction. "We should retrace our steps now and see if we can find another route to Pontefalco before it gets light."

"I never thought my escape would prove to be so difficult, Luca," she said in a shocked voice as the gravity of the consequences of their escape began to sink in.

Once again, Luca put a reassuring arm round her shaking shoulders as he led her towards the car.

"I know it sounds like a corny advert for hair shampoo, Marianne – but I believe you're worth it!"

Then she burst into tears of utter relief.

* * *

The satnav did not, to Luca's relief, send them back along the route by which they had arrived at that spot but indicated they should continue along the road where the API petrol station was situated.

"That's good," said Luca, "less risk of running into whoever has been tailing us."

Marianne's reply to whatever Luca said on the rest of the journey seemed to consist of variations of the words 'thank you'. They arrived at Pontefalco after only fifteen minutes of travel along a winding road. But they had entered the town from a different direction and it took Luca another fifteen minutes to find the *trattoria* La Buona Forchetta. A radiant blue light was beginning to illuminate the mountain tops and cast a subdued light over the still sleeping town. Luca drew up a hundred metres away from the *trattoria*.

"I'm just making doubly sure nobody has been following us," Luca explained to a very subdued Marianne.

After fifteen minutes they walked along the street and knocked discreetly on the closed doors of the restaurant. The door was opened after a tense few seconds to reveal the owner, Bruno Vespini, fully dressed but looking somewhat haggard - as if he needed some sleep in the near future.

He ushered them both inside without a word and shut and locked the solid double door behind them.

He shook Luca's hand and said: "I bet you were followed, weren't you...?"

Luca nodded and said simply: "Yes".

The owner then turned to Marianne, took her hand in both of his and said: "You're safe now."

She was evidently making a big effort to suppress a fresh outburst of tears at the kindness which lay behind this man's words and gesture.

Bruno made them all a coffee which was drunk in silence. Bruno's wife appeared, in her dressing gown and introduced herself as Lisa.

"Come on Marianne," she said. "I'll take you to your room. You look quite drained."

Marianne stood up and picked up her rucksack and began to follow Lisa automatically. She seemed to realise after a few steps that Luca would no longer be there when she woke up. She ran back and hugged him, pressing her face into his chest as Luca stood up to return the embrace.

"Please don't get into trouble because of what you have done for me, Luca," she pleaded in French, perhaps intuiting that her saviour might have taken a bigger risk than either of them realised.

"I'll be back in two or three days and then we'll sort you out, Marianne," he said, giving her an extra hug of reassurance.

After Marianne had been led upstairs, Luca explained in great detail everything that had happened since they last met.

"Don't worry, Bruno," he explained as he told him about the house purchase. "I haven't yet signed the final agreement document – but I really did need an alibi to explain my presence in Collemaga."

"But I gather you like this house, don't you, Luca," stated the perceptive owner of the *trattoria.*

Luca shrugged his shoulders by way of admission of guilt. But he told Bruno Vespini nothing about his encounter with Giorgia. That was another issue altogether in Luca's mind and he wasn't yet ready to share that aspect of his stay in Collemaga with anyone.

"At least, you won't have to worry about Marianne, Luca. I can tell we are all going to get on well together," he reassured Luca, who had realised that he should not delay any longer his return to *'quel paese'* - as Bruno still insisted on calling Collemaga.

They parted company like old friends.

"*Grazie infinite, Bruno.* I thank you for your humanity and your great generosity of spirit."

Bruno dismissed the compliment with a wave of his hand.

"*È normale, Luca.* You would have done the same for me."

8: Facing the music...

On his journey back to Collemaga, Luca was suffering mildly from the usual sense of alarm he felt whenever he had committed himself to some rash course of action. He didn't doubt for an instant that he had acted correctly in rescuing Marianne from the clutches of Luigi Bonifaccio. But what had seemed like an adventure the night before would, he was fully aware, have a direct impact on his own project. He had made an enemy of at least one person – not to mention the shadowy figure of his mother. Luca could not imagine what the reaction of *Il Porco* would be, but he guessed the consequences would prove to be compromising, to say the least.

On arriving in Collemaga, he deliberately parked his car along the main road which wound up the hill to the piazza at the top end of the town. There were a number of 'official' parking spaces, marked with the usual blue lines, just off the road. He observed ironically that the police station was nearby, but doubted that this would guarantee the safety of his car in any meaningful way.

Getting out of the car, he sensed a change of atmosphere but put this down to his state of mind. He walked along the backstreets towards the hotel, clutching his lap-top computer, which he had had the foresight to remove from his bedroom the previous night. He might have imagined that the atmosphere in Collemaga had subtly altered since his night time expedition, but there was no room for doubt as soon as he stepped inside the Bar Commercio. The bar owner, Enzo Materano, looked at him reprovingly. He was shaking his head in disbelief as he served Luca his usual coffee and croissant. The few remaining clients looked shiftily at Luca and headed for the door as if they suspected he was the carrier of some fatal disease. His escapade of the night before must already have become common knowledge. Luca handed over a €5 note. Enzo Materano put the change on the counter, shaking his head some more, as if to say:

"What have you gone and done?"

His eyes expressed reprobation but Luca was convinced he could detect a hint of guarded respect there too. Finally, the bar owner spoke:

"*Signor* Luca, you should get into your car and leave this town without looking back – if you know what's good for you."

Luca managed a complicit smile and replied:

"I thank you for your concern, Enzo."

The bar owner shrugged his shoulders resignedly. He had done his duty as a human being but doubted his advice would be heeded.

Enzo Materana's attitude was one thing, but the look of outright dread on the hotel owner's face was in a different category altogether. The man obviously wanted to warn Luca of some impending danger but he was too scared to utter any words of caution. Luca was certain of only one thing; he had no intention of spending another night under this roof. He headed for his bedroom. Looking up at the uncovered window on the staircase, he was astonished to see the face of Fatima looking at him. She had a look of horror on her chubby face. She made a kind of pointing gesture with her forefinger in the direction of the bed. Surely she wasn't suggesting...? Was she hoping that he would rescue her too by dint of offering him her body? She must have heard a noise on the stairway because when Luca looked up again, she had vanished.

That was the moment when Luca spotted the sheet of paper on the one and only armchair.

Any thought about subtle reprisals on the part of Luigi Bonifaccio was transformed into a tangible threat. In bad handwriting, *Il Porco* had written:

Signore, you will find three snakes in your bed. L.B.

Luca's initial reaction of disgust gave way to the desire to laugh out loud at the puerile idiocy of the words, penned in elementary Italian. Nevertheless, he felt compelled to cautiously lift up the corner of the duvet to ascertain whether Luigi Bonifaccio had really gone to such extremes to avenge the loss of his best 'asset'. The shock of seeing not three but only two snakes on the sheet brought him back down to earth. The zigzag black lines down the reptiles' backs indicated they were vipers. They squirmed at being exposed to the light but remained lethargically where they were.

Luca considered the simple step of vacating the room, but his outrage was such that he refused to give way to his natural aversion to the creatures. He remembered some novel he had read as a teenager in which this identical trick had been played on the main protagonist in the story. If Luigi Bonifaccio imagined he could get away with this devious game of mental torture, he could think again. In the story, Luca recalled, there had been only two snakes, but the fear that there was a third one lurking somewhere in the bed was far more sinister than the threat from the two visible reptiles.

Luca's anger far exceeded the perceived risk of what he undertook in the next minute. He gently removed the pillow from its pillowcase, deftly picked up the nearest snake just below its diamond-shaped head and dropped it into the pillowslip. He shared with most people an aversion to touching snakes and his heart was beating wildly. The second viper, sensing danger, had begun to wriggle. Luca had to force himself to make a clumsy grab at the snake before it escaped. He seized it too low down below its head. The snake was writhing angrily as he dropped it into the pillowslip, snatching his hand away and closing the top tightly. He was sure the snake's fangs had punctured the coarse material only centimetres from his hand. He knotted the material tightly and marched towards the reception desk, waving the writhing pillowcase defiantly in the owner's face. The hotel owner recoiled in terrified disbelief at the transformation which had taken place in his seemingly conventional guest – quite apart from his fear of the contents of the pillowslip.

"Somebody's idea of a joke, I suppose!" said Luca, trying to instil scorn into his trembling voice. "I would like to settle my bill – and you are fortunate I'm paying you at all after the shoddy hospitality on offer. The only reason I am willing to part with my money is because you are obviously under the spell of this weird town – and some of its inhabitants. But *I* am leaving immediately."

"Thank you, *Signor* Fontana," stammered Dario Frassica, by now in complete awe of this man as he prepared the modest bill and handed it to Luca.

"And you had better check with Luigi Bonifaccio whether there really was a third snake in the bed before you attempt to change the bed linen," added Luca for good measure as he handed over the cash.

Luca only returned briefly to his room to retrieve his trolley suitcase into which he slipped his personal computer. He marched out into the sunless back street with defiant strides.

Out of sheer curiosity, Luca briefly turned round to see the pillowcase stirring where he had left it on the counter. Dario Frassica already had his mobile phone pressed to his ear. Luca could imagine all too easily who the hotel owner was speaking to.

Luca headed instinctively for the piazza at the top end of Collemaga. As his anger died down, he noticed that his whole body had started to shake – a nervous reaction to his potentially perilous encounter with Luigi's snakes. What had happened in the hotel bedroom had been born of an instinctive refusal to be intimidated by the machinations of a low-life pimp. But in the aftermath of his impetuous gesture, he detected the quasi numinous fear of creatures whose existence predated mankind by millions of years. He had not only defied a man whose moral values were off the scale of all that was civilised but had had a close encounter with a different life-form which existed in a parallel universe to the one he was accustomed to dealing with. He felt shaken.

Luca made his way to the bar near the town hall. The same lad in his early twenties who had so genially served him on the previous occasion came out promptly with the same radiant smile on his face. Could it be the case that there were some citizens in Collemaga who were still unaware of his night time escapade?

"Bring me a grappa please, *giovanotto.*"

Luca was aware that calling the waiter 'youngster' had offended him. The ready smile had momentarily disappeared.

"I'm sorry," he said. "I didn't mean to sound patronising. May I call you by your first name instead?"

"Stefano," the young man said, the smile restored.

"I'm Luca, by the way."

"I'll fetch you your grappa, *Signor* Luca," said the waiter. "I am sure you deserve it."

Luca privately shook his head. He was wrong – even this young waiter must have got wind of what he had done the previous night.

Stefano returned and placed the little glass on the table in front of Luca.

"It's a special grappa, *Signor* Luca – on the house!"

"Well," Luca thought. "At least one person approves of me in this town."

As he fondled the stem of the glass after the first few sips of the fiery liquid, Luca tried to fathom out the motives behind *Il Porco's* unexpected game with the vipers. It was a very unusual reaction in the circumstances, considered Luca. Had it been intended as a show of strength, an attempt to scare him off? Or was the man merely driven by frustration and anger? Maybe the snakes were his obsession – Luca had seen on television that, in this part of Italy, snake-handling often formed part of a traditional display of prowess. Local festivals often involved people parading through the streets with poisonous snakes entwined round their shoulders – in defiance of the risks. Snakes were supposed to be a symbol of the power of the nether regions of Hades – to be tamed by those courageous enough to handle them fearlessly. Maybe he would see Luigi Bonifaccio performing this act of bravura during the *festa* in Collemaga – due to take place in the next few days. Luca wondered if *Il Porco* had been taken aback by his act of defiance that morning. There was certainly no sign of him skulking about the town.

Sitting under a sun umbrella outside the bar, Luca looked nostalgically towards Giorgia Calvera's tobacconist's shop. A steady stream of customers were entering and re-emerging minutes later – in greater numbers than usual, he imagined. Maybe reports of his exploits of the previous night were circulating. He wanted to see her again and the impulse was suddenly irresistible, but he did not want to have to face the hirsute 'cousin' again and then be forced to make an unnecessary purchase just to save face. To his surprise, he saw the elderly parish priest coming out of the church followed by a handful of equally elderly ladies who had just attended early morning mass. Luca mused sadly that even Jesus himself, at the Last Supper, had managed to assemble a gathering of twelve for the occasion – and they had nearly all been in their twenties! To Luca's mild astonishment, the priest ignored the ladies and headed straight for Giorgia's shop. He reappeared only seconds later in the company of Giorgia herself. She was smiling and nodding at the spritely old cleric. Her figure, even at a hundred metres away, aroused that nebulous feeling of magnetic attraction which he had not felt for years. He stood up in the hope of attracting her attention. She looked over towards the bar. She was making an urgent gesture for him to come over. He began walking across the piazza – having forgotten completely about his turquoise trolley suitcase which remained standing neglected by the table he had just vacated.

The barman came out and called over to him.

"Signor Luca?"

Luca felt himself blushing and waved at the barman as if to reassure him.

"Just going to buy a packet of cigars," he called out.

The top of Giorgia's head barely reached the level of his chin, whereas his wife was as tall as he was. Giorgia's smile was warm and sincere as she practically pushed him inside the shop and locked the door behind her twizzling the sign around to *CHIUSO** to repel any unwanted invasion by further customers. She kissed Luca on the mouth, her smile shaping itself to his lips.

"You are going to sleep here tonight, Luca," she said simply. "It's probably the only safe place left in the town right now."

"Ah, so you've heard...?" he began.

"That piece of news has been round Collemaga at least three times already this morning, Luca. The last I heard, I was told you and your car had dematerialised in a blinding flash of light as you were driving through some town. I took that bit with a pinch of salt however. Luca, you are *pazzo* – quite crazy!"

But the light in her eyes was full of admiration.

He kissed her and this time, the warm sensation lasted for an eternal five seconds. She broke away as she saw another customer approaching her shop. She deftly swivelled the sign round to *APERTO* again and opened the door to usher Luca out on to the pavement.

"By the way, Luca, the parish priest asked me to tell you that he wants to see you urgently – in the confessional, he said!"

Again, she was smiling in that half-mocking way, but the promise of intimacy in her eyes was unmistakable.

"*A presto, signore.* Take care of yourself," she added for the benefit of the new customer who was entering the shop.

Luca went to retrieve his suitcase and insisted on paying the barman for his grappa despite protestations.

"It was a very superior *grappa,* Stefano. And very much needed," explained Luca to the young bartender as he gave him a handful of coins.

"*Grazie.* See you soon, *Signor* Luca."

Feeling conspicuous, Luca re-crossed the square trailing his suitcase behind him and headed – puzzled – towards the open doors of the church. The priest was lurking in the shadows behind the holy water stoop – once again replenished.

* * *

"Good morning, father," Luca began. "I understand from Giorgia that you wish to see me."

The look of nervousness on the old priest's face was unmistakable.

"Yes, but not by the door, *signore.* Somebody might come in unexpectedly…"

"Would that *'someone'* be an individual called Luigi Bonifaccio, by any chance?"

"Signore, you haven't been with us for very long. Otherwise you would not be taking this matter so lightly."

"I take it you know what I did last night, father?"

"Yes, it was a very Christian thing to do, *signore…"*

"Please call me Luca – especially as I understand from Giorgia you want to hear my confession."

"No, *signore…*Luca - that was just Giorgia's sense of humour at work. But I don't want to discuss matters with you standing here. Please, if you don't mind, may we talk in private? If anybody comes in, we won't be overheard in the confessional. And if you are seen coming out of the confessional, *HE* might believe you're feeling contrite about…what you did last night."

So that was it, thought Luca. The priest must be yet another person to be cowed into submission by Luigi Bonifaccio – or his illusive mother. The priest obviously felt he would be protected if he was safely ensconced behind the screen which separated him from this 'transgressor', who seemed to be flouting all the rules which prevailed in Collemaga.

Feeling his kneecaps pressing against the hard leather cushion, Luca had unpleasant memories of his early adolescence when his mother had made him go to

87

confession once a week. "You know you've been having indecent thoughts about girls again, Luca," she would unfailingly accuse him every Saturday before he went out with his classmates. He had been reduced to 'inventing' lurid accounts of his wayward thoughts for the benefit of the priest hiding anonymously behind the grille through which it had been impossible for a teenage Luca to gauge his reactions. Thus he began – almost out of habit – by saying to this old priest: "Forgive me *padre* – for causing you all so much trouble since my recent arrival in this town – *mea culpa!*" he said, beating his chest in mock contrition.

He thought he detected a smile on the priest's face distorted by the wire grille.

"Young man, you arrive in Collemaga just like Jesus Christ casting out the money-lenders from the Temple. I feel it is *I* who should be confessing my sins of omission to *you.*"

"I'm sure you have not done anything drastically wrong, *padre...*" suggested Luca.

The priest sighed deeply.

"It's what I *haven't* done, *signore.* I have lacked the courage to defy the forces of evil in this town. I have pretended that the problems do not exist. I have told Luigi that what he is doing is immoral, that he has no right to use girls just to make money out of their bodies. He just sneers at me – knowing that his mother will back him up. Do you believe in Satan, *signore?*"

"Luca," he reminded the priest.

"Lucifer, you mean, don't you, *signore?*" said the priest, entirely misinterpreting his penitent's interjection.

Luca laughed in a most un-confessional-like manner. "Luca, is *my* name, *padre.* And yes, on balance, I do believe in the powers of evil. They often seem to carry more weight in the affairs of mankind than the forces of good."

88

The priest realised belatedly how he had missed the point. He managed a chuckle and a dignified apology. But he continued speaking in the same vein as before.

"Yes, Luca, you are right – and as I get older and older, I feel less able to summon up the Holy Spirit to come to my aid."

"You could help *me,* father, by telling me a little about Luigi's mother – who is the *fattucchiera,* or so I'm told."

"How much time do you have, Luca?" asked the priest wearily.

"Until I can no longer bear the pain in my knees, father. I confess I have lost the habit of kneeling down in recent years..."

"Then I will be brief, Luca," replied the priest apologetically. But, Luca noticed, he made no attempt at suggesting they should leave the confessional booth and sit on a 'comfortable' chair in the nave.

"You have probably heard – or read about – the story of the lawyer way back last century, who declared publicly that the candelabra would crash down if he was not telling the truth?"

Luca made an affirmative noise.

"Well, our *fattucchiera* is descended from him. Nobody ever uses her first name and all the parish records are inexplicably missing. In earthly terms, she must be only about forty-five years old. But, rumour has it, in her house – which is perched on a cliff top at the very edge of this hill – she prances about like a teenager. Her cellars – this is just a rumour – go well below ground level, carved out of the rock below."

The priest paused, as if reluctant to continue.

"My knees, father!" prompted Luca.

"She is, I believe, what one might call 'sexy'. But she is evil personified. She has claimed – to me personally – that she has carried out black masses regularly over the years at the time of the summer solstice. *Her* beliefs, she informs me, go back to the beginnings of time and are far more potent than the wishy-washy precepts of Christianity. She delights in torturing me mentally with her satanic powers."

"But what about Luigi, her supposed son?" asked Luca. "She must have had him in the normal way?"

"Not according to her, Luca. She claimed to me once that she had had intercourse with the devil – who commanded her to produce an heir."

"Well, if that young man has been begotten by Satan, father, I think his powers must have become massively diluted," Luca ventured.

"Don't underestimate those two, Luca," continued the priest. "Especially not her - she plays games of mental torture with her victims. She wheedles and manipulates you with false kindness. And just when you begin to think she is a person with feelings after all, she will crush you to pieces."

"What can you tell me about a young man called Mattia De Angelis – who has apparently disappeared without trace, father?"

There were alarming sounds coming from the other side of the screen, as if the priest was gasping for breath. Luca felt he had pushed the old priest too far. He stood up and made as if to come round the confessional to where the priest's door was located. But the priest beat him to it.

"I've told you all I can, *signor* Luca. You must go and talk to the mayor – make him understand that you want to get to the bottom of what is really happening in Collemaga. I shall pray for you that the Holy Spirit will manifest himself through *you* rather than through this weak vessel," he said beating his own chest as if in castigation.

"I thank you, father. I am sorry if I have caused you any distress."

"Just be wary Luca. You are a good man – I feel it in my bones. But, mark my words, she will get you in her clutches before too long…"

"You mean, after my very Christian act of last night, father?"

"That too – but she has many other motives for maintaining her rule of terror in this town. You will never have had such a challenge to your courage and resistance - as you will discover when you meet *HER* face to face."

With the old priest's warning ringing in his ears, Luca left the church feeling shaken - but mainly feeling thankful that he was no longer kneeling down. It was hard to imagine that an encounter with this woman, apparently endowed with physical charms, could be more threatening than his encounter with the snakes. His suitcase felt like an unnecessary impediment to his freedom of movement, but he had little alternative but to trundle it around after him like a reluctant poodle.

9:   *And in the darkness bind him...*

My name is Mattia. I only remember it because I scratched it on the wall with a ballpoint pen when they first locked me up in this room. No windows – and only one light bulb which they turn off completely several times a day – or is it the night? They allow me out to go to some stinking toilet with a wash basin once every now and again.

What is my surname? It used to be De Angelis as far as I remember. I don't know how long I have been here. They give me some awful food once or twice a day – I don't know what time it is. My watch has gone. My phone has gone. I know they are giving me some drug – it's in the food. It is slowly eating away my brain cells. There is this awful man who brings me the food down – I am sure I am underground, buried alive. The food is always cold. The man is lanky and sly and has a thin moustache and mean lips. He smirks at me as if to say: "You are going to be here until you die." I wish I could die. It would be better than staying alive. I want my family, my mum and dad and my little sister. They must be sure I am dead by now...

He hears footsteps approaching along the stone corridor. He is not sure how long it was since he was given food – but it wasn't that long ago. That could only mean one thing. He feels dread and his heart is thumping. What he fears is that it must be once again time for the skinny man whose breath stinks of smoke and hashish to force him upstairs to see that ghastly, terrifying woman whom Luigi addresses as 'mamma'.

"My mother wants to talk to you, Mattia."

He cowers in the corner of the cell but it offers him no protection.

"No, no, no! Please, not now."

"Mother wants to see her guest again. It's been a long time. Come on. Hurry up. You can't keep mother waiting. She's got something nice for you to eat," Luigi insists.

Luigi grabs Mattia roughly by his arm and forces him up the stairs to the house above. Mattia is whimpering quietly to himself.

And there she is – perched on a high padded chair as if it was a throne. She smiles an exaggeratedly beguiling smile as Mattia enters, showing a set of pearly white teeth which look ready to devour whoever comes too close. Her hair is long and raven black, framing a face which reminds Mattia of Morticia – of whom as a child, he was always terrified. Her grey eyes seek out the fear in his own eyes. But Mattia dreads the moment when she will open her mouth and speak. It is a seductive female voice, sullied occasionally by the hint of a rasp.

"Come in and sit down near me, Mattia. Don't look so scared –I'm in a good mood today. Here, have one of these lovely candied fruits. Go on, they won't bite you, dear boy."

Mattia's hand reaches out to take the offering, fearing that the plate will be snatched away as his tentative hand takes one of the tempting sweets.

"Now, Mattia, bring your chair nearer to me. That's it… a bit closer. That's better. Now I can touch you. Tell me again about your little sister. You must really be missing her by now. Come on, tell me, dear." The voice is coaxing but the cold grey eyes shine with a life that is satanic, tempting him, drawing him in, giving him a tiny gleam of hope.

Mattia begins, stuttering a few words at a time. "She's called Silvia… twelve years old… she has dark hair and…"

"When's her birthday, Mattia? We must send her a birthday card – from you and me."

"In December, but I want to go home…"

"And so you shall, dear Mattia. Just as soon as I decide the time is right."

The words are said so sincerely that Mattia's hopes are raised – just like on the previous occasions. He hears that man sniggering somewhere behind him.

"Gigi," the witch is saying. "Don't laugh. We want to let Mattia go free, don't we?"

"Sì, mamma. We want to make him happy," replies Luigi obediently.

"But first of all, Mattia, you have to make ME happy, don't you?"

These were the words Mattia has come to dread more than any words he has ever heard in his life. He was mugged once by a knife-wielding ruffian in Rome. The mugger's voice had been sinister, persuasive. But it was nothing to the fear that this woman could instil in him – and he feels powerless, degraded and sickened. She is already unbuttoning her white blouse to reveal a well-rounded breast.

Mattia vomits on the floor. Something he has never done on the three previous occasions. The transformation on the woman's face is diabolical, revealing all the pent up hatred inside. Her mouth is turned down in frustrated anger.

"Get him out of here, Gigi. The little worm!" she yells at her son. "He wants to be free. Show him the door to freedom."

"Sorry, madam," Mattia manages to stutter in the woman's direction. "I'm sorry. I couldn't help it. Please forgive me!"

But the cycle is complete - the gentle voice, the sweet words, the promises of freedom have all been abandoned. Now he feels the cruel dismissal which leaves him more dejected than on all the previous occasions put together. Total despair creeps ever closer after each exposure to this terrifying being.

He is being frogmarched by Luigi along the corridor which leads to his cell. Now he is forcing Mattia to climb a stone staircase which leads steeply up to a door through which he can see daylight. Mattia has never noticed these steps before.

"Dai, Mattia! That's your door to freedom," says Luigi in inviting tones.

Mattia climbs upwards, almost running. He can't believe his good fortune. He flings the door open and almost takes one step beyond the threshold. There is a sheer drop to the valley below where the river meanders along below the town of Collemaga.

10: In which the mayor of Collemaga opens up...

Luca headed for the town hall. He needed to push matters forward with his house – he had plans for the house which he hoped would involve Giorgia. He was equally eager to gauge the effect of his rescue of Marianne on the mayor, Elpidio Pugliese. He may have unwittingly complicated this man's life. Of his usual 'stalker' there was no sign – in itself a sinister portent.

He went directly upstairs to confront the mayor's secretary, not feeling in the mood to sit around downstairs to wait for someone to take notice of his presence. He was aware that the half a dozen or so inhabitants of Collemaga, mainly womenfolk, were staring at him with a strange mixture of apprehension and curiosity. One woman, who looked as if she might be a mother, actually grinned sheepishly in his direction as he trundled his suitcase upwards to the floor above. She obviously thought better of it and looked away again guiltily, glancing round to see if any of the others had noticed her reaction to Luca's presence.

The secretary put on an air of busy efficiency as she was confronted by Luca marching boldly into her office.

"The mayor is exceptionally busy this morning," she announced peremptorily without giving Luca time to even make the request.

"I can well imagine that he might be, *Signora...?*"

Luca remembered that her first name was Mariangela. But it would be improper for him to address her so informally at that point.

"Di Pietro." She supplied the name readily enough. "Are you thinking of leaving us so soon, *Signor* Fontana?" she asked, eyeing Luca's suitcase. Her tone of voice suggested that she considered this might be a sound idea.

"I'm afraid you won't be getting rid of me quite so easily, *signora,*" Luca replied with a smile. "I haven't quite finished buying my house yet."

Mariangela Di Pietro found Luca's determined stance unnerving.

"As I said, *Signor* Luca, the mayor has left me strict instructions not to be disturbed by *anybody* this morning..." Her voice tailed off, discouraged by Luca's lack of reaction.

"I don't think I am just 'anybody' at this juncture of time, do you *Signora?* I have come to see the mayor and I intend to wait right here until he will see me," stated Luca with menacing quietness.

In the end, the secretary stood up and headed for a concealed door that Luca had not noticed the previous day.

"I'll tell the mayor you are here, *Signor* Fontana, but I know the mayor very well. He does not react kindly to being disturbed when he is involved in other more pressing matters."

"I am not appealing to his kindness," retorted Luca with a terseness in his voice which visibly shook the secretary's well-practiced armour of officiousness.

She went into Elpidio Pugliese's office without knocking and closed the door behind her. She re-emerged a mere fifteen seconds later. Her whole demeanour had undergone a metamorphosis. She was regarding Luca with a deferential smile on her face. The abrupt transformation reminded him of the game he used to play with his son and daughter at bedtime where you hide your face behind a pillow and emerge suddenly from behind it with a completely different expression to the one before.

"The mayor would like you to have lunch with him, *Signor* Luca," she said, even inadvertently calling him by his first name. "Would it be acceptable if you were to come back here at midday?"

97

Luca performed an ironic bow of acknowledgement in the secretary's direction as he turned and walked towards the door followed by his suitcase.

He was surprised to catch the words *"E bravo, Signor Luca!"** coming from Mariangela Di Pietro's mouth, almost inaudibly, as he left the office.

"Interesting!" he thought. "So she too approves of what I did last night."

* * *

Luca had a couple of hours to kill before his unexpected lunch appointment with Elpidio Pugliese. Things were certainly on the move, even if he could not be certain in which direction.

He thought he should go and check up on his car parked along the road leading up to Collemaga from the valley below. He was relieved to find the vehicle intact. He glanced over the road to where the *Carabinieri* station was. He was being observed by one of the two police officers in residence. The officer, probably of the lowest rank, was staring at him suspiciously as he stood on the steps leading up to the entrance. Was there a hint of hostility in the way this officer was subconsciously fondling his pistol holster? The man, in his thirties, was developing a paunch and his face looked blotched from drinking an excessive amount of beer during his off duty hours. The sad decline of someone who leads a monotonous life-style, thought Luca. Nevertheless, he had detected a hint of resentment in the officer's stance which gave him pause for thought. Luca speculated on the likely motive behind the glare – a single man in a small town, who was not obviously attractive to women...? He understood why this officer might feel resentful towards him.

"Gli ho tolto l'osso di bocca!" Luca said under his breath. The image of a dog whose precious bone has been taken from its mouth seemed ironically appropriate.

But it was enough to make Luca think it would be wise to re-park his car later on in the day – maybe just after dark when he was not being 'observed' from the police station. Just as a precautionary measure.

Luca headed towards the *Bar San Nicola* where, unusually, there were a number of local men having a noisy discussion standing round the bar. He decided to take a table outside and wait for Stefano to come out and serve him. He knew that the lad had noticed his arrival, but he had not run out to greet him as he had done on previous days. He understood that Stefano was inhibited by the presence of the male customers, who had fallen silent on Luca's arrival. After a few minutes, the group of men began to disperse. The expressions on their faces as they walked past the seated Luca were telling. They studiously avoided looking in Luca's direction, walking past him hurriedly. Embarrassment was the principle emotion that Luca detected on their faces. Only one man looked at him. He bore a look of resentment on his face that was clear to see.

Only when the last customer had melted away down a side street did an anxious Stefano appear on the scene carrying a coffee and a glass of water on a tray.

"Well, Stefano, what was all *that* about?" ventured Luca in an attempt to break the ice. He could see that the young barman was embarrassed by his presence and was not sure how he should react to the man who had seemingly overturned the town's *status quo* in the space of one night. "As if I couldn't guess," added Luca with a reassuring smile.

"*Signor* Luca, you have done a very rash thing. Do you realise you are playing with fire?"

"Well, Stefano, it certainly won't be the first time. Now I understand that a number of men in the town might have looked for a bit of consolation from that young woman. But it was hardly a pleasure for her to be at the beck and call of every lascivious old man in this town seeking relief for their sexual urges whenever they felt like it. Don't you agree?"

"Oh, I think what you did for Marianne was incredibly courageous, *Signor* Luca. And so do many people in this town – the women especially but even many of the men. That group of men in the bar were angry because you've…"

"…robbed the dog of its bone - yes I know, Stefano. And I am unrepentant."

"*Bravo, Signor* Luca. But I am more concerned about *your* well-being now. You have opened a can of worms – a Pandora's Box…"

"Beautiful metaphors, Stefano! You should be a teacher, not a barman."

"*Grazie* Luca - that *is* my intention. I'm going to university next year. But getting back to your situation in Collemaga, you have not been here long enough to understand how this town works. There are malevolent elements at work which are all too easy for an outsider to underestimate…"

Luca's phone was ringing discreetly in his pocket. Stefano took his leave so that Luca could take his call.

"Take great care, *Signor* Luca. You don't fully understand what you are up against."

Luca nodded at him in acknowledgement as he looked at the screen of his phone. It was the owner of the restaurant where Marianne was hiding. He felt a stab of apprehension. After such a short time had elapsed, it was unlikely to be a reassuring call.

Luca listened carefully to Bruno Vespini – while his coffee grew cold.

"What did he look like, Bruno? Was he a shifty man in his thirties who smelt of doped cigarettes?

I understood immediately who he was, Luca – the son of the fattucchiera. He fitted your description exactly.

But did he see Marianne?

I don't think so – but she was coming downstairs to get a cup of coffee.

Did she see him? Was she visible to anyone standing near the bar?

She never got further than the first two top stairs. She came up and knocked on our bedroom door. We were already up and I'd been down to the bar to open the main door and switch the coffee machine on. She was shaking like a leaf. But what she said was almost amusing. She said she could 'smell' him as soon as she reached the third step. I think her sense of smell might have saved her...

Did you go back down to the bar yourself?

Of course. That's when I realised who it was.

What happened next, Bruno? Did you...?

I asked him what the hell he was doing in the bar so early. I told him we normally only serve locals at that time of day. He said he was looking for someone.

"Well, you're looking in the wrong place," I told him. "There's only my wife and two children here."

Luckily my two kids came downstairs at that moment because they had heard a strange voice. They sensed the atmosphere and just stood staring at him in an unwelcoming way. I'm sure they realised instinctively that – what did you call him? Il Porco? - was the man whom Marianne was escaping from. Kids are very acute when it comes to strangers. I didn't offer him a coffee and so he just sidled out.

Thanks Bruno. Make sure Marianne stays out of the way.

You don't need to worry on that score, Luca. I am more concerned about your safety now. I told you you must never underestimate that evil couple – I mean his mother too…

I believe you, Bruno. I have been told the same thing by too many people now to take the matter lightly. Listen Bruno, I'm going to speak to my friend in Rome and ask him if I can give his number to people I can trust – including Marianne. I shall send you his number later on today – just in case anything should happen to me.

That sounds like a very good idea. I guess Il Porco is doing the rounds of every bar and restaurant – in Pontefalco and the neighbouring towns. He's a mean character and he is hell bent on finding his prey again.

Once again, Bruno, thank you for what you are doing. I'm going to stay on for the *festa* the day after tomorrow and then I'll come and rescue Marianne.

The call came to an end leaving Luca in a state of anxiety for his *protégée*. He swallowed his cup of tepid coffee and asked Stefano for another one. Stefano took one look at Luca's face and brought him a *grappa* to go with the coffee. Luca remained where he was long after the grappa had gone simply because he felt he was on safe territory. He retrieved his computer from the suitcase and spent the intervening hour or so before lunch writing up his account of the 'most cursed town' of Collemaga. Should he try and contact his friend Giacomo Mainardi in Rome? No, he decided. He should be safe for now. After lunch with the mayor, he hoped he would have something more concrete to convey to Giacomo.

The church clock struck midday while he was still typing. He stood up and covered the short distance to the town hall just as the clock chimed for the twelfth time.

* * *

Elpidio Pugliese looked anything but relaxed as Luca was ushered into his office. He looked wildly around the room as if he was afraid some invisible presence might be lurking in a corner. The invitation to lunch was not going to hinge on the quality of the food, thought Luca. He felt impelled to say a few words to break the tension.

"Where are we going to have lunch, *Signor Sindaco?*" he asked.

The mayor looked at him askance – as if this simple question had completely missed the point of their rendez-vous.

"I am taking you to my house, of course, Luca. I can't be seen in public with you, you must understand. And for goodness sake, drop all this formality. I know Elpidio is an unusual name, but it's the only one I possess."

"I'm so sorry to have upset the applecart in this town, Elpidio. And I'm even more sorry that you have become involved..."

"Come on, Luca, let's go. I have a great deal to say to you – after we have enjoyed my wife's cooking. She has been out to kill the fatted calf, so to speak. You'd better not turn out to be a vegan or anything outlandish like that..."

"No, fear of that, I can assure you."

To Luca's surprise, the mayor led him out of the town hall via the back staircase – the same one used by Luigi Bonifaccio when affecting his stealthy departure from the mayor's office two days previously. The mayor's car – suitably black – was parked in a reserved spot. To Luca's astonishment, Elpidio Pugliese ushered him into the back seat with the request:

"I'm so sorry to put you through this indignity, Luca. But I cannot afford to be seen in your company just yet.

Would you mind lying flat out of sight – just while we get out of town?"

So he was to be driven into the countryside by this nervous individual. The thought flashed through Luca's mind that this could be a trap. Maybe the forces of evil had ordered his abduction. Elpidio seemed to sense Luca's hesitation – he was definitely a very alert human being, thought Luca.

"Have no fears, Luca. This is just between you and me. I hope you will understand me better by the time we take our leave of each other. Now, come on please, I shan't feel at ease till we are well clear of this place."

Luca put his suitcase in the car – lying flat on the floor – before he slid onto the back seat. He had not even found a comfortable horizontal position before the car shot out of the car park and headed down the hill past the police station at something approaching 100 kilometres an hour. Luca could not help but smile at the unexpected nature of their car ride.

"*Va bene, Signor* Luca. I apologise for subjecting you to this farcical ride. We've almost arrived. You can sit up normally now."

The car pulled into the drive of a country house within striking distance of another village. The mayor had a modest but traditional villa surrounded by a flower-filled front garden. His wife – Luca assumed it was her – was standing by the front door ready to welcome him. The owner of the villa was looking almost relaxed.

Introductions were made on the doorstep.

"This is my wife, Eleonora – her parents were thoughtful enough to provide her with a normal Italian name at her birth. Elly – this is Luca Fontana, the man I've been telling you about."

"It's a pleasure to meet you, *Signora.* You have a lovely house."

"It's my sanctuary, Luca," stated Elpidio with the first real smile that Luca had been treated to by the mayor since his arrival in Collemaga. *Prego,* after you, Luca."

Luca stepped over the threshold with the strange feeling that he was being treated to a modest kind of hero's welcome – an impression confirmed by the mayor's wife.

"You could turn out to be the answer to our prayers, *Signor* Luca."

He was beginning to feel like an Old Testament prophet sent by some divine hand to save a besieged people.

"I'm sure I do not deserve such an accolade, *signora.* I only hope I do not let you down," replied Luca – even more mystified than ever.

"Let's have lunch first, shall we, Luca?" said the mayor. "Business only after eating, in true Italian fashion."

Most of the meal was eaten in silence – out of respect for the quality of the cooking. Starters had been skipped in order to be able to appreciate fully the *Abbacchio** lamb stew. Luca did briefly comment on the sweet taste of the meat.

"Local lamb – fed on mountain herbs," stated Elpidio succinctly. "You can't beat it."

Over a more relaxed dessert, Luca learnt that the couple had a grown-up son and daughter, both of whom had emigrated to Rome for the necessity of pursuing a career.

"It's a relief for us that our children are independent, Luca," said the mayor. "They have one child apiece – and they come home to visit us as frequently as a busy life allows. Since you don't have children as yet, Luca, you can't appreciate what a comfort that is…"

The mayor was looking intensely at Luca, as he had spoken these words – almost as if it had been a challenge. Luca had been neatly trapped by Elpidio's words. He would have to decide instantly whether to break his habitual rule of saying nothing in public about his private life – or risk betraying the trust of this man who seemed desperately to want to open up to him. There was no choice to make.

"Elpidio – I have not been entirely straight with you. I am married and we have a son and a daughter. My wife is French and has spent most of our married life telling me she wants to move back to France. So my family life is a little uncertain – entirely my fault, I have to confess..."

The mayor seemed strangely satisfied with Luca's response – for motives which Luca could not fathom.

"Let's go to my study, Luca. Elly, could you please bring us...?"

"Coffee, *amore?* Of course, I will," she replied simply. "Go and talk business you two."

"Thank you for that delicious meal, Eleonora. It's the tastiest lamb I have ever eaten – just perfection!" said Luca in all sincerity.

* * *

Luca was ushered into the study crammed with books and documents, Luca noted. Many of the titles on the shelves were classic Italian literature – from Dante to *I promessi sposi.** Luca took a seat at the large table where the mayor's array of electronic devices and printers were much in evidence. Elpidio walked over to the bookshelf and selected a hardback book which looked about ten years old – before e-books had invaded the literary world. He placed the book on the table in front of Luca without a word. There was, however, a knowing look in his eyes.

"I take it that this *is* your book, Luca," he stated simply, "despite the author's name being different."

Luca's respect for Elpidio Pugliese's wiliness increased ten-fold.

The book was entitled *La Storia della Mafia Calabrese.* It was the first book he had written some eight years previously – before he had adopted his assumed name of Luca Fontana. It stated that the author was married with one newly born daughter. On the inside of the outer book cover was a photo of himself, looking younger but unmistakably him.

Luca looked at the mayor with a wry, apologetic grin on his face.

"Shall we get down to business, Elpidio?"

11: Cards on the table...

"Might I equally assume that architecture is not the principle activity in your professional life, *caro* Luca?"

"You may, Elpidio. And I apologise for underestimating your intelligence from the outset."

"So what is your angle precisely?"

"I'm an investigative journalist. I was taking a break from writing about the *'ndrangheta*. My wife was very categorical that I should stop investigating the mafia's role of invading every corner of public life in the north of Italy – and across the rest of the world, come to that. They even have a strong presence in Australia too, did you know that? Thanks to the well-established presence of a multitude of Italian immigrants. Marie-Louise is very concerned about the safety of our family – I have a young son too, as well as the daughter you already knew about from the book cover."

"I'm amazed that you have managed to avoid serious reprisals so far, Luca, judging by the revelations in your book – which I have just finished reading, by the way."

"There is an aspect about my writing which may be counter-productive," continued Luca. "I might have escaped being bumped off simply because I am reinforcing the sense of terror which they instil in the population at large. To their twisted criminal minds, I am paying them a compliment by acknowledging the cruel grip they have over so many sections of our society."

Unexpectedly, Elpidio Pugliese treated Luca to a broad grin.

"So you decided to turn your talents into looking into the plight of the simple folk of Collemaga instead, did you? Thinking it might be a safer option?"

Luca nodded and shrugged his shoulders in silent acknowledgement of the accuracy of the mayor's observation.

"Wouldn't it be ironic, Luca, if your intervention in the affairs of this small town stuck up in the mountains of Abruzzo turned out to be more perilous than your dealings with the mafia?"

"Are you suggesting that Luigi Bonnifaccio – and his mother – pose a greater threat than the *'ndrangheta?*"

"The mother, our *fattucchiera,* yes, certainly! The Calabrian mafia is a huge organisation which can protect itself with the greatest of ease. But in Collemaga, you are challenging just a handful of individuals whose sole power base is here - in our town. You pose a direct threat to their survival – and they will react to events in no uncertain terms."

Luca was still only partially convinced that his life was in danger. The mayor could read the scepticism by the expression on Luca's face.

"You should back off immediately, Luca my friend, if you value your own life. Even your valiant abduction of that young Moroccan woman has caused a major threat to their reputation and stability."

"All that has happened to me so far is that individual called Luigi Bonifaccio playing a very infantile prank on me with a couple of snakes..."

"Yes, you rattled that individual's self-esteem very effectively, Luca. By the way, the vipers had probably been milked of their venom – that's a kind of side-line activity that Luigi indulges in. It brings him in a bit of money selling the venom to some pharmaceutical company that manufactures the antidote."

Luca shook his head in wonderment.

"No, it's the mother whom you should worry about. She's a terrifying individual who wields real power in this town."

"And yet, I gather, you consider that I can help you save Collemaga – judging by what your wife said before lunch."

Elpidio Pugliese let out a deep and disconcerting sigh, but otherwise remained silent for what seemed like ages.

"Publicly, I dare not be seen to condone what you have done," he resumed. "I have become too embroiled in the set-up in this unfortunate town. Entirely through my own weakness, it has to be said. But you are an outsider, Luca. You can bend the ear of people in Rome, maybe. You are obviously very determined - and courageous, it seems to me. I wish for nothing more than to be free from the clutches of this wretched woman. She is akin to Lucrezia Borgia in her ability to manipulate people – and twice as ruthless. She truly believes that she is gifted with satanic powers. I want to be mayor of a normal, uncomplicated community – even with all its inherent problems..."

Elpidio could not suppress the note of appeal in his voice.

"By inherent problems, Elpidio, you are referring to...?"

"Let's just say we need an infusion of new blood in this town. It was why I was initially agreeably surprised when you came to my office wanting to buy a house..."

"On that score, *Signor Sindaco*, I have no intention of letting you down," Luca rashly blurted out. "But if I am to help you with this other matter, I shall need something much more concrete to go on."

Elpidio Pugliese let out another profound sigh.

"This is the moment I have been dreading for years – yet I am relieved that the moment has finally arrived," he said quietly. "To be honest, I always thought I would be confessing my involvement in all this to a high court judge. *Ecco* - I'm glad it's you I'm telling."

He took a deep breath and began talking:

"You cannot imagine how unnerving it is having dealings with *her,* Luca – our *fattucchiera,* I mean. Her son leaves one irritated and slightly nauseated. If indeed he *is* her son – as he tells everybody. But the mother is 'another pair of sleeves'* altogether. To start with, her voice is unsettling; often she speaks like a man. She claims to be a hermaphrodite. She can equally assume a totally convincing, seductive female voice. She reminds me of the mother in The Addams Family to look at. In a sinister kind of way, she is very attractive – I don't know whether you are acquainted with the Addams family, Luca?"

Luca merely nodded – not wishing to interrupt the flow of words.

"Her name is Margherita, by the way, but nobody dares call her that – I call her Morticia to myself. I expect you have read up about the lawyer who lived in Collemaga last century – the one who caused the candelabra to come crashing down in the courtroom?"

Luca nodded again.

"Well, Morticia is a descendant of this man. She inherited most of his money and, more importantly, all of his property – which means she owns almost half of the town. She lives off the rent from these properties, which give her a modest income. The 'rent collector', in case of default of payment, is Luigi..."

"I call him *Il Porco,*" Luca could not resist interjecting.

Elpidio managed a brief smile before resuming rapidly, as if any break in his narrative would cause him to lose the will to continue with his confession.

"She manages to keep a tight hold on every aspect of life in the town – especially on the little secrets that people would rather keep to themselves. That way, she can use the information to cajole or blackmail whoever she wants to subjugate to her will. For all his seemingly base nature, *Il Porco,* as you so aptly call him, is very adept at using the internet to hack into people's private lives. What he can't learn from his computer, he finds out by wheedling information out of anyone he can by coaxing or flattery – and by the mere mention of his *'mamma'.* Any man who used one of his 'girls' was an easy target for blackmail. And you took the prettiest of the two of them away from under his very nose! It's a very precarious life in Collemaga, Luca, and ultimately self-destructive. The whole town lives under a cloud of mutual suspicion. Very few people are totally immune..."

"But how about you, Elpidio?" interrupted Luca. "Surely she can't have a hold over you...can she?" ventured Luca when the mayor seemed to be hesitant about how to continue. The mayor appeared to be deeply embarrassed. His face was suffused with a blush of guilt.

"Ah, Luca...if only that were true!" he began. "I've been the mayor here for nearly nine years. I have done my best to be a conscientious mayor as far as possible. But the truth is that I have no rivals to contend with. I'm coming to the end of my second five year stint of office. I'm sure you know that mayors in Italy cannot hold office more than twice..."

Once again Luca acquiesced with a simple nod of the head.

"There could be a mayoral crisis next year. There is nobody 'neutral' who wants to put themselves forward as a candidate. They are too aware of who is really in control in our town. *Dio ci aiuti,* Luca –God help us - the next mayor of

Collemaga could even be Luigi Bonifaccio! Can you imagine that?"

"But, Elpidio, how did you fall under the spell of this woman – nine years ago?"

Elpidio was breathing heavily again. Obviously he had reached the point where he could no longer avoid the crucial part of his story. He could not bring himself to look at Luca in the face but began addressing his words to a picture of the Apennine mountain range on the wall opposite.

"I was a farmer for most of my life – living here in this house where our two children grew up. The house was nothing like it is now. I was quite an important figure in the agricultural world back then – I was the local representative of the farmers' union, Coldiretti. I had some standing in the eyes of the community – I'm not being immodest, Luca," stated Elpidio, with a brief appealing look in Luca's direction before he redirected his gaze towards the Apennines.

"Then the idea came into my head to put myself forward as mayor of Collemaga – even though our house here is much nearer Cimabianca than Collemaga. The mayor in office was nearly sixty-five and rumour had it that he was weary of being constantly under the sway of ... that woman. So I thought I would step into his shoes and show the inhabitants I wasn't afraid of some woman who passed herself off as a *fattucchiera.* I had not really crossed her path up till that point, Luca."

"Go on Elpidio," murmured Luca encouragingly.

"There was another candidate for the office of mayor – a primary school teacher and a communist. He had often openly criticised our sorceress both in public – especially in the *Bar Commercio,* which he frequented – and also in the local press. It was obvious to me that he was a strong contender. I was arrogant enough at the time to assume that my standing in the community, where so many of the population are farmers, would be enough to guarantee the success of my candidacy. That is when I was contacted by our resident witch for the first time – and invited to her house."

A brief glance in Luca's direction to make sure that Luca's attention had not strayed. The latter was staring intently at him.

"Well, she began in her most seductive female voice to tell me that she was strongly in favour of my candidacy as mayor – telling me in flattering and insinuating words how the town was in need of a 'real man' to be in charge of the town – rather than a wimp – and a communist one at that. As I said earlier, she can swap from a male voice to a female voice without warning – it is a very disconcerting experience:

You should also know, Elpidio," she said to me during our 'intimate discussion', *"that your rival has been accused of molesting his pupils when he was teaching in Sulmona. It's on record. I'll let you have the newspaper report before you leave…"*

She had gauged how ambitious I was and knew that I would somehow use this information to discredit my rival – which I did, in public. And, of course I was elected mayor. The teacher in question had to leave Collemaga under a cloud of shame – poor guy. He was completely innocent of the accusation. The witch had only given me half the story…"

Elpidio had fallen silent again. Luca knew that some other revelation was about to come to light. The mayor's reluctance to continue was painful. At that moment, Eleonora knocked discreetly on the study door and deposited a tray on the table. She had guessed that a bottle of grappa might be required as well. Elpidio ignored the coffee altogether – but gave himself a healthy dose of the grappa. As soon as his wife had left the room again, he leant over the table and spoke earnestly to Luca in hushed tones, the painting of the Apennine Mountains finally abandoned.

"Luca, I had an affair with a woman in Collemaga round about that time and she became pregnant. The Catholic Church teaches us that abortion is a mortal sin – and I agree. It is! Oh God help me, Luca, I made it happen. It was the worst thing I have ever done in my life. I went to confess to our parish priest for the first time since I was an adolescent. But I then came to realise just how evil *that woman* is when I tried to block some scheme she had devised which involved her son, Luigi.

"Do I have to remind you, Elpidio, that you have caused the death of an unborn child? Some people here might consider that to be murder."

It was the first time I had heard her 'male' voice and it added an uncanny, satanic power to her words – as well as setting me wondering how on earth she had found out. From that point on, I was putty in her hands.

You get the picture, Luca. So I won't bother you with the many other incidents as a result of which she has been able to guarantee my permanent acquiescence. I'll skip to more recent events. When all this is over, we can sit down together and fill in the gaps if you like."

"I can assure you, Elpidio, that my own perception of what I am doing here has undergone a transformation. I simply do not have the same agenda as I did when I first arrived in Collemaga. So do not be concerned that what you tell me now will find its way into my next book!"

Luca's obvious sincerity was rewarded by a look of deep gratitude on the mayor's face. It enabled him to move on to the next part of his story.

"A couple of years ago, I was contacted by the agency in Rome responsible for awarding European grant money to towns in rural areas where the need to restore the often medieval fabric was greatest - often untouched for hundreds of years. Our grant amounted to almost three million euros. The *fattucchiera* was present at the council meeting – as she always is. She insisted that she should be in charge of the renovation of the church and all the buildings round the main *piazza* – as well as the renovation of the *piazza* itself. She has a mafia-like hold over all the building contractors in the town. No other builder's tender stood a chance. As you can see for yourself, the job was carried out professionally, but the estimate for the work carried out was considerably higher than her real outgoings. She guaranteed my silence by insisting that I should 'share in the town's good fortune' as she put it. Her workers were responsible for carrying out all the renovations to this house, Luca, including the roof which had been leaking for years…"

The mayor was looking guilty again. Luca had to reassure him in some way.

"When the time comes, Elpidio, I shall be happy to tell the authorities that we could never have proceeded if it had not been for your complete cooperation."

"*Grazie mille,* Luca. Do you really believe you can set in motion…?"

"I make no promises – simply because…well, you know yourself how the government in Rome inevitably drags its heels over any matter that can be shelved. But, I am hopeful…" Luca stated. "So, what you are telling me is that, directly or indirectly, a significant percentage of the European funding to give Collemaga its facelift ended up in this woman's possession?"

"That is correct. I myself authorised this payment. It all looks good on paper but I reckon she has something like €450 000 left over from the original payment for the works carried out – even taking into account the modest amount of money spent on renovating my house."

"Are the transaction details officially recorded, Elpidio?"

"Yes, I have all the necessary documents locked up in a vault in the cellar of the town hall, Luca. Not even the *fattucchiera* has a key to that," said Elpidio. "It is kept in a safe place that nobody else knows about – except Eleonora, my wife, in case anything should ever happen to me."

"Did Mattia De Angelis see these documents during his visit, by any chance?"

"Yes, he did. They look *bona fide* to a relatively uninitiated person. The lad really shouldn't have been entrusted with such a task – he was very inexperienced in the ways of the world," said the mayor bitterly. "It was all too easy to persuade him that everything was above board. Nevertheless, I think he remained suspicious. He was quite an intelligent young man."

"Well, it gives me something sound to go on," said Luca.

Now, I really must get back to Collemaga..." said the mayor looking nervously at his watch.

Luca and Elpidio stood up together and the secrecy of their conversation was sealed with a spontaneous handshake.

But there was still one element of the mayor's account that Luca needed to put to the test.

"By the way, Elpidio, while I think of it, can you shed any light on the disappearance of Mattia?" Luca shot at him.

The mayor was looking genuinely puzzled by the question.

"I assume he went back to Rome, didn't he?"

"No, he never made it back to Rome. He has been reported missing by his parents. Marianne – the young *marocchina* – was convinced that he is still imprisoned somewhere here in Collemaga. She reckons she overheard some telephone conversation between *Il Porco* and someone he was calling. She really is a smart girl."

Elpidio Pugliese had turned pale.

"If that *is* the case, Luca, then heaven help him. If he is in the hands of that woman, then he would be better off dead. But yes, now you mention it, his disappearance was suspiciously abrupt."

The pair headed for the main door where the mayor's wife was waiting. Luca held Eleonora's proffered hand in both of his as he thanked her for her hospitality and reassured her that he would do everything in his power to resolve the situation – and play his part in returning Collemaga to the status of a normal commune. Elpidio and Luca began the return journey to Collemaga. Once again, Luca had to lie flat out on the back seat. Luca volunteered to get out of the car well before the town's boundaries.

"I'm happy to walk back into town, Elpidio. I can walk off my excellent lunch."

The mayor did not even attempt to reject his guest's face-saving offer. He looked at his guest with a wild smile, which revealed his inner turmoil – tempered with a grain of optimism. The mayoral car shot off with inordinate haste yet again, a split second after Luca had retrieved his reluctant suitcase from under the back seat. Luca did not tell Elpidio that he had been invited to stay with Giorgia that night. He would keep his relationship with Giorgia a secret if at all possible.

Luca trudged up the main road trundling his suitcase behind him. He would be very glad to be able to leave it somewhere safe, leaving him free to walk around the town without looking like some refugee tourist with nowhere to stay. He had reached the *Carabinieri* outpost. He took one look at his car. The front wheel had been removed and replaced by a block of wood under the suspension housing.

12: *In un posto 'sicuro'?* *(In a 'safe' place ?)*

Luca suppressed the initial sensation of panic at the sight of his disabled car. The all too frequent shocks encountered whilst dealing with the *'ndrangheta* had endowed him with a philosophical acceptance of apparent setbacks. Such trivial seeming occurrences were often a sign of progress. He had got the invisible powers of Collemaga rattled. Nevertheless, it was a salutary warning that the time for complacency was over.

"What self-respecting car-wheel thief would stop at stealing just one wheel?" he reasoned, "even when immediately opposite a police station."

It was obvious that this minor act of vandalism had been carried out according to orders from certain quarters, to warn him – or prevent him from carrying out some other heinous offence. Perhaps *Il Porco* thought Luca was about to abduct his second girl? Or more probably, it was intended to prevent him leaving the town in a hurry. This potential motive for the theft of his wheel should really put him on his guard – it substantiated all the warnings he had received from friends and well-wishers.

There was only one obvious culprit. After locking his suitcase in the car boot as a temporary means of freeing himself from this encumbrance, Luca marched defiantly over the road towards the *carabiniere* station. On the door, there was a notice which stated in two simple words: *Fuori sede.* Despite the notice implying that the occupants of the police station were 'out on police business', Luca banged loudly and repeatedly on the unresponsive front door.

An elderly lady was hobbling by, stick in one hand and a meagre looking shopping bag in the other. To Luca's astonishment, she looked at him with a wicked grin on her face.

"Try that side door, *signore*. You'll almost certainly find someone inside – even if they are pretending to be off duty," she informed him waving her stick at an unobtrusive entrance door set back from the main façade of the building.

She had a twinkle in her eye as she stumbled off down the street, obviously pleased to have been able to inflict some minor act of revenge on the local constabulary.

Luca's irruption into the rear office of the police station had an alarming effect on the officer who only hours previously had been eying Luca up-and-down in the street and beating his truncheon threateningly in the palm of his left hand. The officer's blotchy, alcoholic complexion was heightened by a blush of severe embarrassment. He had shot to his feet on Luca's unexpected incursion, revealing that his trouser flaps were unfastened. He had been staring at his computer screen. From where Luca was standing, he could just make out the image of a naked couple on a bed. The police officer had glanced fleetingly towards the rear of the office. An oily blanket had been thrown carelessly over an object which looked exactly the size and shape of a car wheel. Luca congratulated himself on the accuracy of his deduction.

Nevertheless, the flustered police officer made a feeble attempt at covering up his predicament.

"What right do you think you have, *signore,* to burst into a closed police station in this manner? I shall call my commanding officer from upstairs and we shall throw you out on to the street."

Luca had assumed his most cynical smile.

"Please do invite your commanding officer to come down stairs, *tenente...?** I am sure he will be very pleased to know you are using the police computers to look at pornographic material."

The officer was glaring at Luca – anger and discomfort equally apparent.

"We're supposed to check up on these things..." he muttered unconvincingly.

"I have just spent five minutes banging on the front door of this place. Why did you not come and open the door immediately instead of lurking in this back room?" snapped Luca. "For all you knew, it might have been an emergency!"

"It's my off-duty time," he protested feebly, still struggling to button up his trousers. "How did you know about the side entrance?" stammered the officer, still wondering how this notorious visitor from the north of Italy had been able to invade their hallowed preserve with such ease.

Luca looked scornfully at the officer.

"Sit down, please, *tenente!* You are embarrassing both of us. Now, you will kindly tell me what you were thinking about when you removed my front wheel. And no, there is no point in denying it was you. I can see it over there behind you. You are here to uphold the law – not indulge in acts of petty vandalism."

"I was ordered to do it, *Signor...?*" stammered the officer in subdued tones.

"Fontana. And was it your senior officer who ordered you to remove my wheel? No, I imagine not!" said Luca, not waiting for a reply. "I would guess it was that sleazeball called Luigi Bonifaccio who gave you the order. Am I right?"

The officer nodded not even able to look at Luca directly in the eye.

"I will put your wheel on again, *signore,* just as soon as..."

"Oh, there's no hurry, *tenente.* I have no intention of going anywhere just yet," stated Luca as he headed casually for the door. "Just bear in mind that things are going to change radically in this town in a very short time. The present regime is coming to an end. Just remember *you* will be held accountable."

Luca felt that such a thinly veiled threat would not do any harm at this stage – even though he had no real basis as yet to make such an assertion. He strode out through the side door without a backward glance – his second defiant exit since his arrival in Collemaga, he reminded himself.

The police officer belatedly managed to do up his trousers. His embarrassment had given way to an ugly scowl which contorted his features. He would avenge his humiliation at the hands of this outsider. "Just you wait and see, *Signor* Fontana!" he hissed. He was talking to himself. Luca was already out of ear-shot.

* * *

A quick visit to the *Bar San Nicola,* just to kill a bit more time before he headed for Giorgia's shop. It was late afternoon and it would look too conspicuous if he was seen entering the shop and not re-emerging afterwards. Stefano seemed instinctively to know when his favourite client needed something stronger than a coffee. In the end, Luca took out his computer and spent the intervening hours of daylight updating his account of the day's events. He had to adapt his description of Elpidio Pugliese to suit the radically altered circumstances. He spared no punches, however, when describing his visit to the police station. He had not persuaded that individual to part with his name – so he was simply referred to him as *Il Tenente* – the lowest ranking title in the *Carabinieri.* At least, the man was granted the privilege of a capital T!

There were more than the usual number of clients in the bar and the square was slowly filling up by seven o'clock. There was an unusual air of expectancy about the town – Luca had to remind himself that the next day, Wednesday, was the eve of the *Festa.* There were still no obvious signs of preparation. He queried this with Stefano next time he called him over for a refill.

"No, Luca," said Stefano, reinforcing what he, Luca, had already been told. "It's traditional not to prepare for the carnival until the after dark on the eve of the *festa* -so as not to tempt providence to send us bad weather for the actual festivities," explained Stefano.

Luca supposed that this myth was easy to uphold. The *festa* was held in early May and it must be very unusual for it to rain at that time of year. With such meteorological certainties playing their part, it was a safe bet to believe in God's good will towards the inhabitants of Collemaga – or Satan's.

"Does the *fattucchiera* take part in these festivities, Stefano?" Luca asked.

"Oh yes – she plays a *very* prominent role, Luca. You will be able to see for yourself," replied the young bartender.

A hesitant frown crossed his face as he spoke these words. Almost as if he had experienced some dark premonition. But he added nothing in words – and Luca had let it pass. Had he felt a shiver of apprehension as he noticed the fleeting expression of uncertainty cross the lad's face?

Enough! He paid his bill and walked slowly across the *piazza* towards Giorgia's place. He was wondering if it *was* technically *her* property – or if it was rented from... His turquoise trolley case seemed to be making a conspicuously loud rumbling noise as he pulled it over the cobbled surface. If he was too early, he had thought of a pretext as to why he should enter the shop. An everyday chore that was long overdue.

To his joy, Giorgia was there behind the counter. But apart from a brief gleam of pleasure in her eyes, she ignored his presence. There was another customer in the shop – the parish priest, who appeared to be buying up a year's supply of lottery tickets. He, at least, gave Luca an unguarded smile of recognition.

*"Buona sera, padre,"** said Luca. "I wish you good fortune with those."

"I buy them on behalf of all our parishioners, *Signor* Luca. It's a collective endeavour. They trust me with their money, you see," the elderly priest added with a grin.

"Well, I repeat, father – best of luck. I hope you all win the jackpot."

"And I hope you will be successful in *your* venture, Luca," added the priest enigmatically as he headed for the door.

"What does he mean by *that?*" Luca asked Giorgia. By way of response, she disappeared through a door behind the counter, beckoning him to follow her with a seductive wiggle of an index finger.

Luca got no reply to his question. Giorgia's brown eyes were agleam with humour and something akin to lust as she wrapped her body round his and kissed him on the mouth. After countless seconds, she drew away laughing.

"You left your trolley case in the shop. Maybe you should go and retrieve it, Luca."

The forlorn object was rescued and finally put out of public view in the apartment behind the shop.

"I'm going to close up the shop in thirty minutes," said Giorgia. "Can you manage to last out that long? When you

125

see the shop lights go out, I'll take you inside round the back of the house – it's not so conspicuous..."

Another customer pushed open the door. Luca cut in quickly as if he was a normal customer.

"Can you put some credit on my phone, *signora?* Make it €50 please," said Luca, handing over his WIND top-up card.

"Buona notte, signora – e grazie a Lei!" Luca said as he left the shop with a curt nod at the man who had just entered the shop. Luca barely glanced in Giorgia's direction. He stepped outside into the gathering dusk, adrift in this town for yet another thirty minutes, before... who knows what might happen?

* * *

He explored the network of narrow, maze-like streets behind the main square where he had never set foot before. There seemed to be only two or three street lights shared between the sum total of all the streets he traipsed along. One imposing dwelling, more like a *castello* than a house, with its elegant turret pointing to the heavens, was set well back from the street itself. It must have been perched high above the valley below judging by the expanse of sky visible behind it. The sun's last rays setting in the east endowed the building with an eerie glow.

In a flash of inspiration, Luca *knew* who this house belonged to. He found himself walking faster than usual back towards the main *piazza* with its familiar sights and sounds. Still fifteen minutes to go! Luca sought sanctuary in the church and sat on a hard wicker chair. There were a number of phone calls that he should not delay making as soon as he had ceased wandering around like an itinerant ghost; a church did not seem the appropriate place to make

126

them. Strange how remnants of childhood memories endowed a sense of awe in one's mind as soon as one was inside a church! One of the calls should be to his distant wife and children. He found himself kneeling on the prayer mat with his head in both hands. Was he praying to the invisible spirits to guide him and give him strength? Was it guilt because he knew he was going to be unfaithful to his past life during the coming night? He fell into a deep reverie for a few timeless minutes. He was startled out of his wits when he felt a gentle tap on his shoulder – accompanied by suppressed giggles from the row of chairs behind him.

"A very sound preparation for the ordeal which you'll have to face tonight!" said Giorgia Calvera, her eyes shining with humour. Her son, Marco, was smiling at him too, sharing the joke.

* * *

Giorgia had cooked a light meal for the three of them, apologising for the delay before going to bed.

"I neglect Marco too much as it is, Luca. I can't send him to bed on an empty stomach too."

"Marco does not look like a neglected person to me," stated Luca.

"I'm not," said Marco attempting to cope with a mouthful of *Fusilli alla Puttanesca** and smiling at the same time.

Luca had apologised for his lack of appetite, explaining that he had eaten copiously at lunchtime. Giorgia took one look at Luca's face and understood that it would be pointless asking him for details.

"Besides which," Luca ventured, "I sleep better on an empty stomach."

Giorgia gave him a look which clearly stated that he was being over-optimistic if he thought that sleep was on the agenda. As if to emphasize the point, Luca was treated to the sight of Giorgia stretching her arms in the air with a sigh of anticipated pleasure – a gesture which thrust into view her olive-skinned breasts.

Luca smiled and shrugged his shoulders in resignation.

"Come on Marco, I'll take you up to bed as soon as you've had your dessert," said Giorgia.

To Luca's – and Giorgia's – surprise, Marco came round the table and gave Luca an affectionate *bacio,* as if he was already part of the family.

"Buona notte, Luca," said Marco, adding with his own childlike perception of what his mother had in mind for Luca. *"E sogni d'oro** – if you have time!"

Luca gave the seven-year-old boy a kiss on the forehead, cupping the back of his head gently in his hand.

"And sweet dreams to you too, Marco," he said. "See you in the morning."

Giorgia returned after fifteen minutes.

"I always make sure he's asleep before I leave him, Luca," she explained. Without any premeditation, she came and sat on Luca's lap, with her arms wrapped round his shoulders. She was smiling and her eyes were alive with anticipation.

"Before I end up in paradise and forget about earthly matters altogether, Giorgia, I want you to take these phone numbers and keep them somewhere completely safe. If anything unexpected happens to me over the next few days, you will need to contact these two people immediately."

Giorgia was looking at him solemnly. She was taking in his words in deadly earnest. Luca handed her a piece of paper on which he had written the names Giacomo

Mainardi, Bruno Vespini and Marianne, accompanied by their respective mobile numbers.

"And remind me who I'll be dealing with?" she asked pointedly.

Luca felt something stir deep within him. She had not come out with any trite words such as: 'Nothing is going to happen to you' or 'I'm here to protect you, Luca'. It gave him a sense of reassurance that the woman with whom he could safely assume he was about to have a relationship was not superficial or falsely romantic. Had he found his *anima gemella** at last?

"Bruno is the restaurant owner who is looking after Marianne for me – the young Moroccan woman, whom I..."

"Oh yes, everybody in Collemaga knows about *her*. *Bravo,* Luca! You did a daring and very courageous thing. I understand he tried his favourite snake trick on you. Later on I want to hear all the details. And the other man?"

"Giacomo Mainardi. He's a close friend of mine. He lives in Rome and he is a high-ranking civil servant who works for the Ministry of Finance. He is the one to contact immediately if anything happens to me in the next few days..."

"At least, you are *expecting* to get into trouble now, Luca. It just might make you act more cautiously from now on," said Giorgia, instinctively holding him tighter to her body.

Luca paused.

"It may well be the case that I shall have to expose myself to danger – just to ensure that everything that is wrong in Collemaga really comes to light."

"That sounds like a premonition, *amore...*" said Giorgia almost to herself.

It was the first time she had uttered the word *'amore'.* It seemed to signal the end of talking for the present. As if already conjoined, they stood up and moved towards the bedroom at the back of the house – obeying the hidden instinct that had brought them together a few days beforehand.

* * *

The church clock was striking two o'clock. It marked out the passing of earthly time throughout the night – simply because the mechanism was so old that nobody had devised a way of silencing it. It had merged into everybody's sleep patterns.

Giorgia and Luca lay together holding each other silently in a warm embrace. The time for words was still a few glorious minutes further away along the road which would eventually lead back to reality.

Luca was struggling with his thoughts – he did not intend to intellectualise what had happened, so soon after they had finally ceased making love. But it had been so different, so spontaneous, so uncontrolled, so mutually entwined...

Was it some English philosopher or wit who had stated that 'comparisons are odious'? Luca felt almost outraged that this piece of wisdom had first been coined by a non-Italian. But he was faced now with the living proof of the truth which those words embodied.

They had climbed to the azure summit together. There had been no conscious order to the steps they had taken together before diving into the deep warm waters which had engulfed them in a timeless tide of passion. No recriminations, no hasty separation of bodies as soon as the act was over..."

"Grazie, amore mio," said a sleepy voice from somewhere inside the intimate space which cradled them. "That was so beautiful."

"Grazie a te, Giorgia. I have never in my life…"

"Shhh!" said the voice placing an erect index finger firmly over his lips.

13:   *Una sosta...* *(A pause...)*

Luca and Giorgia had lain awake for another hour before the need for sleep had finally prevailed. Luca's life had taken so many twists and turns in the last twenty-four hours that he only realised at that point of time how much Giorgia was still unaware of.

"The sensible thing for you to do, *amore,* would be to get into your car and drive away from this town as fast as possible. But the only trouble with that is that I could not bear to part with you now..."

Giorgia felt her lover's body stiffen ever so slightly, instantly alerting her that something must have happened that she knew nothing about.

"Apart from the fact that I have no desire or intention of leaving you, Giorgia, such a course of action is no longer as straightforward as you might imagine."

After a few seconds into his description of his visit to the police station, Luca was amazed to feel his partner's body shaking with suppressed laughter. She had buried her face in the soft skin of his stomach in order not to laugh out loud. In the end, the giggling could no longer be suppressed.

"That's the funniest thing I've heard in ages," she said still chuckling over the account of the police officer with his flies undone, watching porn on a police computer. But she gasped in outraged indignation when Luca informed her that his front tyre was propped up against the wall in a back room of the police station.

"He's a nasty piece of work, that young *carabiniere* officer, Luca. He's completely under the thumb of that woman who calls herself..."

"La fattucchiera," Luca completed the sentence for her. "Yes, I gathered that."

"The older officer is a lot more honest – but he just tries to keep a low profile. He's not far off retirement. And that pair represent the full extent of the official arm of the law in Collemaga. But how did you manage to break into the police station and catch the other one in the act...?"

Luca told her about the feisty old lady with the shopping bag.

"Oh, I know who you mean – she's called Elisa Creti. She's been calling out the police for all sorts of minor offences against her person over the years. Nowadays she takes more direct action – presenting herself at the police station in person. They send her away with a flea in her ear, telling her she's imagining it all. She would have taken great pleasure in making trouble for our two upholders of the law."

Giorgia yawned for the first time – sleep rapidly catching up with her.

"You must tell me about Luigi and the snakes tomorrow – later on today," she corrected herself. "I've only heard the version that the gossips have been spreading about the town – someone even claimed that you captured the snakes and tied them up inside a pillowcase..."

Luca pulled her towards him and whispered in her ear:

"That is just how it was, Giorgia."

"Sei pazzo, amore,"* she said gaily.

But Luca had one more question to ask before she fell asleep in his arms.

"Giorgia, may I ask you? Do you own your shop and this house or does it ...?"

"It belongs to *her*, Luca - as do nearly half the properties in this town – including the new mini-supermarket at the far end of Collemaga."

"I am in the process of buying an old house just down the road, Giorgia. It needs renovating inside but it's as

133

sound as a bell and has a beautiful garden. That excuse I had to invent in the shop on the spur of the moment has become a reality. The house deeds will be in both our names..."

"But how could you possibly have known that we would...?" Giorgia began.

"I knew it as soon as I first set eyes on you," said Luca simply.

"*Ti amo, Luca,*" said Giorgia and fell asleep until well after the time that she usually opened the shop. It was her own son who came into the bedroom and shook his mother's sleeping form.

"*Buongiorno, Luca. Hai dormito bene?*"* Marco asked in all innocence.

The die is cast, thought Luca – with no misgivings, but with more than a tinge of guilt about his abandonment of his life in Milan. He really must make that phone call to his wife without delay.

* * *

"*Mamma,* can Luca come and fetch me from school at lunchtime? Or is he still too sleepy?"

"I'm sure he would love to take you and fetch you from school, *amore.* But we need to keep him hidden for a few days. He might be in danger from...some people in Collemaga. And we don't want anybody to know he's staying with us. It's our secret. Please don't say anything to the kids at school – or your teacher."

"I get it, *mamma. L'acqua in bocca,** I promise," he said making a zip-it-up gesture with thumb and forefinger across his sealed lips.

* * *

When Giorgia returned from the school, she had to open the shop hurriedly because a number of puzzled individuals, whose regular habits had been disrupted by the closed sign on the door, were gathered outside the shop exchanging doom-laden scenarios to explain the absence of their purveyor of vital cigarettes and scratch cards. They had even discussed calling out the two *carabinieri* officers, but immediately dismissed the idea in the knowledge that the latter would have taken longer to react than it would have needed to organise a posse of citizens to scour the whole town.

When Giorgia had managed to clear the backlog of customers, she joined Luca in the back of the shop. Luca was looking at Giorgia almost fearfully. Inside, he was half expecting the effects of the powerful emotions of the night time to have worn off. Giorgia took one look at him and understood at a glance.

"I hope you realise what happened to me last night, *amore.* To us, I mean."

They stood in the confined space of the living-cum-dining room and embraced in silence.

The shop doorbell rang – another customer.

"What about that surly, hirsute gentleman who I saw behind the counter once, Giorgia? Isn't he...?"

"My second cousin, very far removed, do you mean? He won't be coming back while you are here, *amore.* If you want to make phone calls, why don't you go upstairs to Marco's room. You won't be disturbed by the doorbell. The shop is usually busy at this time of day."

She kissed Luca on the mouth and ran out into the shop.

"Don't ever leave me, *amore,*" she said over her shoulder as if it had been an afterthought.

Luca heard her exclaiming to the customer:

"Good morning, father. You're looking very pleased with yourself today."

Luca went upstairs as Giorgia had suggested. He needed to concentrate on his phone calls. He was saved from making his first call - to Bruno Vespini – when Bruno's name appeared on the screen as the phone rang. Luca's heart missed a beat. If the restaurant owner was phoning him, that could only mean that Marianne was in trouble.

"*Pronto!* Bruno?" he said more abruptly than he intended.

"Luca, I'm sorry to disturb you but I thought I should tell you. We've had to move Marianne away from Pontefalco. We've had a visit from some blond woman who said she's from Collemaga..."

The woman who was driving the car which followed him from Collemaga on the night of the abduction? wondered Luca.

"She was claiming that she employed a Moroccan girl called Marianne as a child-minder-cum-house-maid. She claimed with amazing surety that she understood the girl was staying with us. I don't know how that witch has narrowed down her search to our little corner of Pontefalco. But, as I told you, she is a very dangerous woman."

"But what about Marianne?" interrupted Luca, impatient to know whether his *protégée* was in danger.

"Oh, don't worry, Luca. My wife, Elena, drove Marianne down to Sulmona after dark yesterday evening. She has a sister who lives there with her husband and two young kids. Our two children went with her too. She hid Marianne on the floor of the car until she was sure they were not being followed. Marianne is very shaken but seemed happy enough to be even further away from that individual. What

136

did you call him? Luigi, the sleazeball? Marianne sends you a *gros bisou,* by the way. I guess that's a kiss..."

"Thank you yet again, Bruno. I am sorry to have caused you so much trouble. I have been severely underestimating the threat to myself – and to you and Marianne. I should be able to come and see you in a day or so. But I want to be sure you've got that phone number of my friend in Rome – Giacomo Mainardi. If you haven't heard from me within three days, please give him a call. He will know what to do."

"I have his number safely on my phone – and on my wife's too, Luca. Now, for goodness sake, take care of yourself."

Luca's heart rate had increased at this unexpected piece of news. Just how many people was he up against, he wondered.

The need to contact Giacomo in Rome was pressing. Naturally, Giacomo did not reply, but a sweetly modulated female voice announced that the 'desired person' was unavailable and would the caller care to leave a message etc etc. It was frustrating. He should have phoned Giacomo the previous evening. But there was nothing to be done now except contain his soul in patience. He resigned himself to leaving a terse message to call him back as soon as possible. He hoped that the anxiety in his voice would convey the urgency of the call.

He could think of no excuse as to why he should delay calling Marie-Louise, his wife. "Maybe, I'll make myself a cup of coffee first," he thought. But he knew he was simply delaying the moment out of sheer moral cowardice. He strengthened his resolve and dialled her Italian mobile number. It too, informed him the person he wished to speak to had obviously gone into hiding to avoid talking to him.

He cut the automated voice off impatiently. Carried along by his resolve to get the conversation over and done with, he rang the landline number of their apartment in Milan. There was no answer. Could she have gone to her parents' home in Villefranche-de-Rouergue and simply stayed on there? He suppressed the ignoble hint of optimism he felt that Marie-Louise had unilaterally decided it was time for them to go their separate ways.

One last try! He dialled the French landline number of his wife's parents. It was his mother-in-law who answered with a curt "Allo?" As soon as he asked if Marie-Louise was with them, the mother became even more abrupt. Her tone of voice implied that the presence of her daughter and grand children in their house was entirely due to a dereliction of duty on *his* part. He was forced to admit to himself that this was the case.

"Yes, Luca, of course they are here! Where else would they be? Marie-Louise is out with the children. She is trying to organise places for them in the local school. I'll tell her you called."

"Maybe you should tell her it might not be safe to return to Italy just yet. I am involved in a situation which could become difficult, Arianne..."

"Marie-Louise will stay with us for as long as she likes. *She* is always welcome here – as are your two adorable children," she stated, rubbing salt in the wound.

"Thank you, Arianne," said Luca. But she had hung up without uttering another word. Some of his brain cells, despite his strenuous resistance, even dared to suggest to him that Marie-Louise took after her mother to an alarming extent.

There was little else he could do. He curbed his desire to go downstairs and seek out Giorgia. He could hear the shop door-bell announcing a new customer with incessant regularity. He took out his computer and forced himself to concentrate on his revised account of Collemaga. With the sun streaming through the little upstairs skylight window in Marco's bedroom, it was hard to believe the town was 'cursed' in any sense. It had brought him nearer to finding a soulmate than he had ever been in his forty-two years of life on planet Earth. His false sense of security came entirely from feeling 'safe' in Giorgia's presence, he reminded himself. He tried phoning Giacomo again – but with the same frustrating result as before. Never mind, there was always his home landline to try later on that evening.

"Che palle*!" he muttered. He was painfully aware of the need to shore up his rear flank - just in case events in Collemaga took a more sinister turn.

* * *

Luca was deeply disturbed when he came downstairs shortly after midday on hearing Giorgia's voice as she came back from picking up Marco. She was speaking in soft, consoling tones. Marco had been crying. He was still sobbing pitifully as he clung on tightly to his mother's hand.

As soon as he saw Luca, his hand instinctively covered his face, looking downcast and ashamed. He ran upstairs without speaking.

"A couple of boys have been making fun of him – because of his nose," said Giorgia almost in tears herself. She came towards Luca seeking comfort.

"Marco is a very sensitive boy and I think he might be intelligent too, Luca - certainly more than most of his classmates. Some of the children have minor deformities but Marco's is the most apparent. Sometimes these boys just turn on him. There's one girl called Monica who always sticks up for him. But on occasions, he just can't take any more. Like today..."

Luca was looking thoughtful. He was thinking how rapidly one discovers that any change of direction in life inevitably involves taking on new commitments towards new human beings. True to character, Luca did not baulk at the unexpected challenge. He did not even bother reminding himself that Marie-Louise usually accused him of being merely rash and precipitate.

He placed his hands on her shoulders and held her glance.

"You are looking *very* serious – for such a newly liberated man," she managed to say with a sardonic smile and with that note of teasing familiarity which Luca was rapidly coming to love.

"When things settle down..." he began. But they were interrupted by the arrival of a defiant looking boy of seven. In that short interval, he had painted his face so that it resembled a whiskered cat. Luca smiled at Marco and his mother smothered him with kisses.

"Stop, *mamma,*" he said, "you'll wash off all the paint."

On the spur of the moment, Luca knelt down to be on a level with the boy and held his hands.

"When things settle down," he repeated, "we will take you to Milan to a doctor I know. And he will give you a new nose – you will even be able to choose what it looks like!"

"Is that a promise, Luca? You're not just saying it to cheer me up, are you?"

"It's a promise, Marco."

The look on Giorgia's face was a still-life picture of loving admiration. She did not need to verbalise her feelings.

Luca merely nodded at her in confirmation of what he had told her son.

And so the rest of the day proceeded in tranquillity.

"Have you smoked all those cigars you bought yet, Luca?" Giorgia asked him.

"Only two," he replied. "I haven't had time to think about them."

"You could go out and smoke one in the little courtyard at the back if you want to help pass the time. It's almost invisible from the neighbour's house."

"I never smoke when there is a chance I shall be kissing the woman of my dreams later on," he said attempting to mimic Giorgia's ironic tone of voice.

"How thoughtful of you, *Signor* Luca," said Giorgia with heavy sarcasm. But her eyes conveyed a different message.

* * *

"By the way, Luca," said Giorgia as the three of them were tucking into a dish of *Pollo alla cacciatora** that evening. "I forgot to tell you earlier. You have a fan and a convert in this town – apart from Marco and me that is."

Both Luca and Marco were looking at Giorgia expectantly.

"Don Sandonato – the parish priest!"

Marco giggled unexpectedly.

"He was in the shop this morning talking as if you had worked a miracle on his behalf. He won €100 000 on the lottery tickets he bought yesterday while you were in the shop. You remember, don't you? He'll have to share the money out between another eight or nine parishioners – but he is quite convinced it was your presence in town which has changed his fortunes."

Another one – apart from the mayor – who seemed to be convinced that he was some kind of saviour who could put their troubled world to rights, thought Luca laconically.

"By the way, how did your confession go the other day? Did he absolve you of all your past misdeeds?" asked Giorgia.

"Ah, Giorgia. I fear it was I who had to listen to *his* confession."

"That can't be right," said Marco. *"You're* not a priest, Luca."

"Thank goodness for *that,* at least!" stated Giorgia with feeling.

"That was delicious chicken, by the way, Giorgia. Your *mamma* is a good cook too, isn't she Marco?"

"Yes, Luca - but that was her special dish because she loves..."

"Basta, Marco," said Giorgia decisively.

A short time later, Marco went happily up to his room. He had given his mother a hug and, for the first time, bestowed a wet *bacio* on Luca's cheek.

"Grazie, Luca. I wish you were my *papà!"*

"I hope I shall be your best friend instead, Marco," replied Luca, filling the emotional gap with words which he hoped would be adequate.

* * *

Luca and Giorgia talked for ages before going to bed. They mutually decided they should concentrate on sleeping that night.

"It doesn't matter if you don't want to answer, Giorgia. But who *is* Marco's father?"

"Someone who has gone away – far away, Luca," was all Giorgia said by way of explanation. "Let's just say, I made a bad judgement. But then, I have never regretted having Marco – and now I couldn't live without him. Life is so strange. But *you* must understand what it's like, *amore.* I'm sure you don't regret having two children either."

"Yes, you're right. Life *is* strange – and very complex. Although at the moment, I would just like it to be simple," said Luca.

"It's the *festa* tomorrow," Giorgia reminded Luca, in an attempt to redirect the conversation. "After midnight, they'll start making all the preparations. You'll see tomorrow morning – you won't recognise the town. It gets transformed into a magic world – just for this one day every year. Everyone tries to forget the underlying problems that Collemaga faces."

"I suppose the *fattucchiera* must take part in the festivities?"

"Oh yes, Luca. You'll see for yourself. But it's all pageant and tradition – none of the sordid everyday reality which blights the town – where nobody can trust even their own neighbours. People come all the way out here in their droves – even from as far away as L'Aquila. Especially since the earthquake in 2009 – coming here takes their minds off their own grim memories of that night in April so many years ago."

"I can't wait to see this *festa*," said Luca.

"It's really very spectacular. We even have a thirty minute fireworks display at midnight."

"But who finances it all?" asked Luca. "No, that was a silly question. The answer is all too obvious, isn't it?"

"Yes, it *is* obvious! There is *no* aspect of this town entirely free of that woman's stranglehold," stated Giorgia bitterly.

"But if we cannot be seen together just yet, how are we going to enjoy the *festa* tomorrow?" asked Luca.

Giorgia's laughter trilled out in the crepuscular darkness in the bedroom.

"Just you wait and see, Luca. Nobody will recognise us – and in any case, I don't care if they do! You are my hero – and you're going to save us all from *la fattucchiera!*" Her laughter was infectious.

The last thing that Luca did was to try phoning Giacomo in Rome. Repeated attempts at calling the mobile number had failed. In the end he called on his friend's land line. It was Giacomo's wife who answered.

"Is Giacomo alright, *Silvia?*" Luca asked anxiously. "I really must speak to him urgently."

"He's had to go to Turin, Luca. His train gets into Rome about midnight tonight. He's had to replace his mobile phone because he was having problems with the screen. It'll be the same old number – but the new phone hasn't been registered with the telephone company yet."

"Please tell him I called, won't you Silvia? There are important developments I need to talk to him about..."

"I'll make sure he phones you tomorrow without fail, Luca. Don't worry!"

"*Grazie mille,* Silvia. *Buona notte!*"

At least Luca now knew why he had not been able to contact his friend. But what a fateful moment in which to be having mobile phone problems, Luca thought unfairly – as if Giacomo himself was to blame for the lack of communication between them.

"Sorry, Giacomo," he said to himself by way of silent atonement to his closest friend and ally. "I must be more anxious than I care to admit..."

Luca joined Giorgia in bed where they talked quietly for some time. Despite what they had decided about concentrating on sleep, they happily disregarded their own advice.

Just as well, thought Luca, who had a subconscious premonition that there would be an interruption to their intimate life before the following day had run its course. He did not share his private fears with his partner on this occasion.

14: *La Festa di Collemaga...*

"I know you're worried deep down inside, *amore.*"

Giorgia's last whispered words before she had fallen asleep the previous evening still rang in his ears. But, in the morning light, the threat seemed nebulous. What could *'they'* do as long as their newly formed family unit of three stuck together?

After a hasty and very early supper consisting of scrambled eggs, Giorgia and Marco went up the stairs leading to Marco's loft bedroom. They were whispering and giggling in conspiratorial manner whilst looking at Luca and exchanging secret nods and shakes of the head. Luca had been ordered to stay where he was in the living-cum-dining room. Giorgia had closed the shop at one o'clock and had not re-opened it.

"We want to surprise you, *amore,*" was the only explanation he had received as they headed upwards.

Luca had vaguely noticed a steep, narrow staircase, more like a ladder that led up to a level even higher than Marco's bedroom – a loft immediately beneath the roof, he assumed. The couple had obviously headed up to the very top of the house. He could vaguely hear them rummaging about for a good twenty minutes. The pair of them could be heard descending to the level of Marco's bedroom. After that, a disconcerting silence fell.

Luca made a quick phone call to Giacomo – but there was still no reply. He wanted to phone Marianne too but decided he ought to become domesticated and wash up the few plates and saucepans that had been left on the table. He placed his mobile on the table, intending to phone after his domestic chores had been accomplished. While his back was turned standing at the sink, he was startled by the sound of Giorgia and Marco's voices dramatically announcing their re-appearance.

The transformation was total and disturbing in its abruptness. They were both wearing carnival masks and full length costumes. Giorgia had become a raven-haired snow queen with milky white skin and cold, unsmiling blue lips. She wore a coronet which looked as if it was made of icicles. But it was Marco who provided the greatest shock – he had been transformed into Pinocchio. He was wiggling his head from side to side to emphasise the long nose that formed part of the face mask.

"Look, Luca" he said in a muffled but happy voice. "My nose has grown!"

Luca could only laugh and applaud their magical metamorphosis, but the poignant irony of Marco's choice of costume left a stab of sorrow for this loveable child's real-life plight.

"Well, nobody is going to recognise *you* two," he said. "But what about..?"

"Just you wait and see what we've got in store for *you,* Luca," said Pinocchio, pre-empting Luca's query. They beckoned him to follow them upstairs.

Giorgia and Marco had erected a tailor's dummy on the landing and dressed it with a costume which looked just like any one of the Three Musketeer's - complete with a mask which sported a black moustache that turned up at the tips. A black top hat with a white feather sticking out of it completed the disguise. The dummy was too short and the breeches trailed limply on the floor where a pair of pointed black shoes was waiting for Luca's feet.

"Size 44, Luca?" asked Giorgia. "I would guess that's your size."

Luca nodded and looked at his 'disguise' in great amusement.

147

"Now, you've got to put it on, Luca," Marco told him, revealing his childlike impatience at wanting the three of them to get out on to the streets of Collemaga.

* * *

The three figures had crept out of a back door through an unlit courtyard at the rear of the house. A narrow street brought them back out on to the main square in front of the shop – the same back street that led down to the house of the sorceress, Luca noted mentally.

"Let's go down to the far end of the town first, Luca," suggested Giorgia. "We can walk in a big circle and then come back up here for the procession. The grand finale always ends up in the *piazza*."

As with all carnivals held in the south of their peninsula, the everyday aspect of the town had been transformed by lofty white latticed arches attached to lamp posts or to the walls of the houses by anything that was capable of having a wire wrapped round it to support the wooden arches. Brightly coloured light bulbs lit up the arches, which descended all the way down the hill. Luca had always been amazed, during his visits down south, at how such a transformation could be wrought in the space of a few short hours. It was one of the extraordinary aspects of Italian life which rendered his motherland unique in Europe. What was different here was the atmosphere. A sinister expectation of a conflict between two opposing forces hung in the air.

The doors of the church stood wide open and the subdued lighting inside the church came from nothing other than a bank of lighted candles. The figure of the elderly parish priest could be seen bustling about in the interior, attending to a wooden crucifix nearly as tall as himself, which he appeared to be polishing and cleaning with devotion.

"I've never seen him do *that* in previous years," remarked the Snow Queen puzzled. Maybe this year's carnival was really going to be different.

One street stall which had been erected in the main piazza, sold cheap figurines of the Virgin Mary and another saint which, Luca supposed, must be of San Nicola of Bari. But a rival stall next to it had attracted a greater number of people; it was selling black candles, devilish face masks and – Luca had to look twice in disbelief – upside down crosses hanging from a knotted cord. There were other black art mementos depicting demons and devils suspended on the end of chains or in the form of broches.

"Surely, I can't be seeing what I think I'm seeing, Giorgia," he whispered over Marco's head, his voice sounding muffled through the mask.

"It's supposed to be just a token show of evil, Luca – a hint of black magic which nobody takes too seriously these days - just a shadow of our medieval superstitions!"

Luca was thoughtful for a few seconds before Giorgia added:

"In this town, you have to decide whose side you're on, I'm sorry to say. And that is not always easy…"

Both the adults felt Marco's hand squeezing theirs.

"Let's walk, round the town, please," Marco said, looking forward to the thrill of being seen by as many of his school mates as possible without being recognised.

A disconcerting thing happened as they passed the Bar San Nicola where Stefano was serving visitors from outside the town who had arrived thirsty and who had headed straight for the seats on the *terrazzo.*

Stefano looked at the remarkably clad trio walking by – a Snow Queen, Pinocchio and one of the Three

149

Musketeers. He paused briefly, loaded tray resting on one arm, and looked in admiration. He smiled broadly and added "Nice one, Luca!"

The three of them froze for a second before Giorgia's trill laugh rang out from beneath behind her mask.

"You see, *amore,* even disguised you can't avoid being famous in this town!"

Luca was glad that his mask concealed what must have been a startled look of alarm. He had had the presence of mind not to acknowledge the compliment by any physical gesture – in the hope that Stefano may have had doubts about whom he had identified so readily. But he had been recognised – maybe because of his height alone or the way he walked. But in the end, as they walked down past the Town Hall, the spirit of the occasion took hold of him as they met a growing number of visitors from outside Collemaga coming up the hill. The little group of three received more than one look of admiration – and some of the crowd even applauded them silently as they marched triumphantly downhill, assuming they were part of the spectacle.

Luca nudged Giorgia as they passed his car. Somebody had placed a tarpaulin over the body of the car – but the wheel had not been refitted. His car was rendered anonymous by the fact that every single parking space had already been occupied by visitors from beyond Collemaga. The pavement was lined with brightly-coloured street stalls selling sweets, little dishes of cooked chick peas with pancetta – and right at the bottom of the hill, a stall selling armbands with a flashing white light in the shape of a cross inset into the material – to ward off the evil spirits, a publicity poster proclaimed. Luca was amazed to see that nearly everybody was stopping to buy at least one of the armbands per family.

Luca and his family had stopped to watch and applaud a lady-puppeteer who was skilfully manipulating an ugly little man on the end of six strings. The marionette would suddenly make a dart towards the watching children who scattered in fear as the diminutive figure appeared to be chasing them. The puppeteer was applauded and some of the children, issued with small change by the adults, took tentative and fearful steps towards the basket placed near the now motionless *omino*.*

Interspersed between the stalls, were a number of 'living statues' standing stock still in various poses – clowns and other recognisable figures who managed to hold a motionless stance until a spectator put money into the basket near their feet – a gesture that earned the donor an exaggerated bow of acknowledgement.

Marco was fascinated by one 'statue' in particular - a tall witch dressed in black with a half-mask that bore an ugly pimple on an ashen grey face. But the cruel sneer on her lips was, Luca realised with a shock, her real mouth made up with black lipstick. He shuddered inwardly despite himself.

"Look, *mamma,* that's a new one – we've never seen a witch before."

Whenever anyone dared to approach the witch to put a coin in the basket, she would bow sarcastically and wish a curse upon the donor in a croaky voice. It was one of the eeriest street performances of this kind that Luca had ever witnessed - totally dedicated to the black arts and performed with sinister conviction.

Marco asked if he could put a coin in the witch's basket.

"No, Marco," replied Giorgia curtly. "I don't want you to be cursed – even in fun."

Was it Luca's imagination? He could swear that he had seen the witch's lips moving to form silent words.

"Let's go," Luca said, ushering his family away from the spot. He glanced over his shoulder to take one more look at the witch. He frowned invisibly beneath the cover of his mask. The 'witch' appeared to be talking into a mobile phone clutched to her ear. She was stepping down from her plinth.

The little trio cut into the side streets at the bottom of the hill where there were only local people assembling outside their houses getting ready for the trek uphill later on. Here the lights were dim but the streets were lined with candles to mark out the route that the floats would follow later on in the evening on their route back down the hill.

Giorgia began singing. She had a soft, melodious voice and, like so many younger Italian women Luca knew, she could reproduce the words of any song which had become popular over the years. Luca believed there was an opera singer buried deep in the psyche of every Italian. Marco joined in the singing – humming when he did not know the words. Luca preferred not to mar the effect with his tuneless bass voice – the operatic gene was sadly missing from *his* make-up he had had to admit to himself many years ago.

He spotted a figure with a half mask covering his face. It was Aurelio Russo, the estate agent, with his family. The man was looking at Luca as if trying to place him – or was Luca being paranoid? It might simply be that the man was admiring their little family group as they walked by in their costumes. Luca performed an exaggerated bow with a twirl of his right arm in the direction of the estate agent. Aurelio and family briefly applauded – and the moment passed.

They were walking along a street that Luca recognised immediately. They were passing in front of the house which

Luca had gone through the motions of purchasing only a few days previously. It still looked magical in the light of the candles and the single street lamp which stood on the corner.

He stopped and pointed to it without an explanation to Giorgia or Marco. She understood immediately. The straight line of three closed into a tight circle as Giorgia hugged Luca and Marco simultaneously.

È proprio bellissima, Luca," she said with simple passion.

It produced a romantic song from her lips as they continued slowly uphill, with the bond between the three figures unbroken.

They passed in front of the *Bar Commercio* and Luca's hotel, *L'Ospite Inatteso* – which still managed to look seedy and run down even when the street was full of people and lighted candles.

Marco was becoming excited as they approached his school. He knew there would be a number of his classmates gathering outside the doors. There was to be a school procession that would materialise later on. He was happy because he was sure he could put on his Pinocchio act for a few glorious minutes without being recognised by anyone.

With the courage of one who imagines he is 'invisible', Marco broke away from his mother and his new *papà* and approached the group of his school mates as if he was being operated by strings – just like the ugly little man they had been watching minutes beforehand. His leg and arm movements were comically and accurately performed as he pranced woodenly towards the group of children – and his teacher.

The effect on the little gathering surpassed all his expectations as he was greeted by a chorus of *bravos* and *bravissimos* coming from nearly everyone, including his teacher. His hope of prolonged anonymity was sabotaged by a pretty, raven-haired girl who broke away from the applauding group and planted a kiss on Pinocchio's cheek. She had recognised who he was and wanted to show her affection towards her friend.

"That's his girlfriend, Monica," Giorgia explained to Luca.

There were flashes of light as someone – the teacher or some parent – took photos of the scene on a smart phone.

Luca spotted a couple of boys at the back of the group who were sniggering and pointing at Marco. The effect of Marco's comical act was about to be wrecked by a couple of insensitive young louts – very likely the same ones who had reduced Marco to tears earlier on. Without reflecting, Luca – the Musketeer – strode over towards the group of children with a Ho Ho Ho! emanating from within his mask, sounding more like a manic Santa Claus than a swashbuckling French hero. With a sweeping gesture of his right arm as if he were wielding a sword and a twiddle of his moustache with his free left hand, he succeeded in distracting the group for long enough to place an arm round Marco's shoulders and lead him back to his mother. Marco kept up his Pinocchio act until they were out of sight of his class.

"*Bravissimo,* Marco," said Giorgia hugging him. "You were brilliant!"

"*Grazie, mamma!* It was going fine until Monica recognised me, wasn't it?"

* * *

By the time the three of them had reached the main square, the spectators in the know had already staked out their territory to ensure they would have a good view of the finale. Luca, Giorgia and Marco were relegated to the fourth row back but they managed to squeeze their way on to the church steps. Luca hoisted a proud Pinocchio on to his shoulders. The seven-year-old was slim and didn't weigh as much as Luca feared; his charge was likely to be up there for at least half an hour.

After only fifteen minutes, a mass of spectators arrived from down the hill – heralding the arrival of the procession. The brass band arrived first in their brightly coloured uniforms playing a variety of patriotic sounding tunes. As expected, the church procession made its way into the *piazza* next. There were the choir boys – and girls – and the altar boys all dressed in white smocks. They were singing a hymn to San Nicola. The brass band had temporally fallen silent while the musicians regained their breath from climbing up the hill and blowing into their instruments at the same time. A handful of nuns followed the choir. Apart from one young nun barely out of her teens, most of the motley group of sisters looked about seventy years old – but they were singing the hymn to their patron saint lustily – even if out of tune. Luca looked on amazed as the elderly parish priest stumbled along under the weight of the cross he was defiantly bearing. Two young men in cassocks walked by his side, their arms at the ready to support either the crucifix or the struggling clergyman.

The priest with his improvised congregation supporting him morally from behind turned round to face the open *piazza*. At last he could rest the base of the cross on the cobble stones. He was still resisting any help from his entourage.

An expectant silence had fallen on the crowd.

Giorgia nudged Luca and whispered in his ear.

"Now you're going to see the *fattucchiera*. Be prepared for a shock, Luca."

Luca felt Marco's legs tense up on his neck and shoulders. It was the eerie effect of the discordant notes that could be heard approaching even before the float came into view that struck Luca first. Rather than any sound, he felt a vibration in his chest and stomach. He looked sideways at Giorgia who returned his glance with a knowing nod.

"It's different," she said almost reverentially. "You'll see in a minute."

The rhythm of the music was not of this world. It was like the throb of a demonic heartbeat which resonated throughout his body, but the notes being played were more like the magic of pan pipes being played in the depths of a primeval forest, redolent of the cries of wild animals. He could only describe the effect as discomforting, unnerving even. This was no amateur performance, thought Luca, impressed despite himself. The sorceress must take her role in life in deadly earnest.

Incongruously, the choir and the nuns began shakily to sing church music – plainsong from the centuries of Christianity gone by. Luca felt instinctively in the pockets of his costume for his smart phone so that he could record the atmosphere created by the conflicting music for his article. It was only then, he realised he must have left it on the kitchen table. He silently cursed his lack of preparedness.

Before the float came fully into view, Luca caught sight of two figures marching up the street. They were wearing grey costumes that made them look ugly and plumped out like a pair of giant Michelin tyre men – or some nightmare version of Tweedledum and Tweedledee, transformed from comic characters into grotesquely deformed human shapes. They seemed to be bouncing up the road on hidden springs.

Giorgia had instinctively moved closer to Luca. She looked at her son and wished for the first time that evening that she could see his face. Luca felt Marco tensing up. He too had registered the two outlandish figures coming nearer.

"They're new, Luca. They've never played a part in previous carnivals," Giorgia stated. "I don't like them."

Then the float came into sight. It was shaped like an enormous dragon with wings raised up in the air as if ready for flight. A gasp of surprise spread all around the square and the voices of the choristers faded into silence. The group accompanying Don Sandonato instinctively took a step backwards. The old priest clutching his cross stood his ground, his white alb stirring slightly in the evening breeze.

The dragon float came to a standstill twenty metres away from the priest. There were two figures on the chariot. One was all too familiar to Luca. Luigi Bonifaccio was dressed in black and his upper body was writhing with snakes, which he appeared to be handling fearlessly. The second figure was seated in a low armchair in the very front of the float. She wore black too. She was, as the mayor had hinted, a striking looking woman whose long black tresses fell over her shoulders. But she seemed diminutive.

"Is that *her,* Giorgia?" asked Luca. "She's almost a dwarf."

"Wait and see," replied Giorgia in a whisper.

The music coming from somewhere inside the chariot began a drumming sound. With a suddenness which brought a cry of fear from the crowd, the *fattucchiera* seemed to rise up from the chair as if lifted by invisible hands. She appeared to grow in stature until she towered above the crowd. She began to utter curses in some strange tongue that was not Italian, pointing an accusing outstretched finger at the priest and the crucifix. A lick of flame spurted out of the dragon's mouth seemingly aimed at the priest. His supporters recoiled instinctively, leaving the old priest standing on his own, unable to move because of the weight of his burden.

There were cries of disbelief and fear from the crowd.

"What in God's name is going on?" said Giorgia out loud.

If this was supposed to represent the forces of evil overcoming the forces of good, it certainly looked as if the evil would win, thought Luca. From the reaction which the spectacle aroused from the spectators it was obviously a departure from previous years' performances.

What happened next was so unexpected that the gasps from the crowd became cries of fear. The priest had shouldered his crucifix and was taking laborious steps forward towards the chariot.

"Leave this square! Leave this town! In the name of Jesus Christ and the Blessed Virgin Mary BE GONE!" the priest was shouting in a shaky voice filled with anger.

There was another spurt of flame from the dragon's mouth which came too close and visibly singed the base of the wooden cross.

The *fattucchiera* was cursing the priest in anger. Her voice had grown deep like a man's. A courageous few of the brass band players blew trumpet and trombone notes discordantly by way of protest – but the sorceress's voice could still be heard.

Luca was astounded and he could feel Marco trembling. He lowered him gently to the ground next to his mother.

Where had the two Michelin men gone? They seemed to have disappeared in the chaos of the last few minutes. The dragon chariot was moving. It performed a semicircle in the middle of the *piazza* and disappeared down the street which led past the school and the hotel where Luca had stayed – all that time ago. The *fattucchiera* remained standing, raining curses on the crowd in general until she was no longer visible – nor audible. People were running forward to help the priest and relieve him of the smouldering wooden cross.

Giorgia was left hugging Marco – who was trying to remove his costume. Luca stood and looked at them.

"That has NEVER happened before, Luca. The priest is supposed to retreat into the church and leave the stage to the *fattucchiera.* It's the first time he has ever defied her authority. What got into him?"

Luca had no answer but he felt something akin to respect for the old man who had made such a hopeless and defiant gesture in the name of what he believed.

The crowd had not dispersed. They were shocked at what they had witnessed and were too busily engaged in animated debate to think of moving away from the town square.

The priest was being helped up the church steps. He had finally allowed someone else to carry his cross into the church. Don Sandonato passed near where Luca was standing. He looked at the debonair figure of the French hero and paused.

"Is that you, Luca?" he said in a shaky voice. The Musketeer nodded at him. "There," said the priest. "I've finally done it! After all these years!"

He managed a tired but triumphant smile in Luca's direction before he stumbled into the candlelit church.

Giorgia, still hugging Marco after the shocking scene they had witnessed, came and stood close to Luca. She was giggling – obviously highly amused by something.

"There, you see, *amore?* You've given him the courage to fight back. You see what going to confession can do for a man?"

"Maybe it was because he won the lottery," laughed the Musketeer. "Nothing to do with me – or the Good Lord!"

"Oh, I know otherwise, Luca. It's *you* who have given some of us new hope. Now we can go and see the fireworks down the hill..."

Marco was looking uncomfortable. He whispered in his mother's ear.

"I'll just take Marco to the toilet as we're so near home. You wait for us here, *amore*. And keep your mask on... please! We'll just be five minutes."

* * *

Luca stood where he was on the bottom step of the church. The square was even more crowded than before as the various groups of men, woman and children in the official procession had arrived belatedly. They mingled with the crowd of spectators, agog to find out what had happened to the dragon chariot and the *fattucchiera.*

And where was Elpidio Pugliese while all this drama had been enacted, Luca couldn't help wondering.

While he was still puzzling over the matter of the missing mayor, Luca spotted the Michelin men. They were bouncing purposefully across the *piazza* towards the church. Luca stared at them fascinated. There was something vaguely familiar about the way one of them was walking. He could readily visualise under the obscene costume the personage of the *carabiniere* officer with whom he had crossed swords so recently. Luca realised too late that Tweedledum and Tweedledee had come to get HIM.

* * *

Giorgia had gone into the dining room-cum-kitchen. The first thing she spotted was Luca's mobile phone on the table. She looked at the screen. There had been a call from his friend Giacomo Mainardi in Rome at last! Giorgia, clutching Luca's phone, went back outside hand in hand with Marco and headed for the church. She looked around for Luca but he was not there. What she had feared most of all had come to pass in those few brief minutes of her absence.

She knew what she had to do next. Marco was looking at his mother with tears welling in his eyes.

"Luca's in trouble, isn't he, *mamma?* We've got to help him, *vero?"*

Giorgia held him close to her – and nodded.

15: With a little help from above...

"We're not talking about just *anyone, dottore!* This is Luca Fontana, the notable writer and one of the few Italians in this country who has had the courage to publish book after book exposing the inner workings of the *'ndrangheta* – regardless of the risks to himself. We cannot simply sit back and 'wait and see what transpires' – as you seem to be suggesting. The man is in danger of losing his life."

"That's a somewhat exaggerated claim, surely! He has only been out of touch for twenty-four hours, *Signor* Mainardi - if I have understood the situation correctly."

Giacomo Mainardi was seated in front of a very large desk facing the Undersecretary to the Minister of Finance – a necessary preliminary step, he had been told in response to his request to see the Minister in person. It was implied by the Undersecretary's manner that he had been very fortunate to get this far in such a short space of time.

"Take this as a sign of our respect for you as a valued team member - and the extent to which we wish to take this matter seriously," he had been told at the beginning of this interview with the imposing grey-haired official who, despite the courteous words, gave the impression that he was preoccupied by far more urgent affairs regarding Italy's shaky financial state than pursuing the matter of some journalist poking his nose into the affairs of a hilltop town in remote Abruzzo.

"This town – Collemaga – is little more than one hour's drive away from Rome, *dottore,*" Giacomo had interjected rashly, provoking a look of ill-concealed irritation on the Undersecretary's officially neutral countenance.

Giacomo drew in a deep breath and imposed a strict regime of interior patience on his habitually impulsive desire to address his superiors without the mincing of words. The tortuous verbal paths necessary to satisfy Italian officials' deep-rooted sense of hierarchy left Giacomo frustrated. On this occasion, he would have to play the game according to their rules if he was to get anywhere with this high-ranking civil servant – all too aware of his own status and, Giacomo intuited, over-sensitive to any words that might be construed as a challenge to his authority. *'Mancanza di rispetto'* – a lack of appropriate respect – was the excuse often trotted out by people of the Undersecretary's rank when they wished to terminate an unwanted audience with someone of inferior rank.

"That is absolutely true, *dottore,*" admitted Giacomo. "But, with the greatest respect for the facts, Luca Fontana first contacted me well over a week ago simply because he was concerned that he had unearthed some dark secret in Collemaga. He had already challenged the authority of certain undesirable elements at work in the town. He stated clearly during his last conversation with me that he feared reprisals against his person from these quarters."

"It would seem that *Il Dottore* Fontana has so far avoided reprisals from the Calabrian mafia. It would be unfortunate if he was to fall foul of some local cabal in a town of only two thousand inhabitants," stated the Undersecretary.

Giacomo smiled for the first time during this difficult interview.

"Funnily enough, *dottore,* you have echoed almost to a word what Luca said to me during his last conversation. Have you read any of Luca's books, by the way?"

It was the Undersecretary's turn to smile – albeit bitterly.

"*Signor* Mainardi – may I call you Giacomo? It's much less of a mouthful."

The Undersecretary did not even wait for Giacomo to nod his assent.

"Luca's books are regrettably essential reading to someone in my position. The fact that the income of the 'ndrangheta represents the equivalent of over 3% of Italy's GNP can hardly be ignored. So yes, I have read his books out of despairing necessity. They are extremely well-written and quite extraordinarily precise."

Giacomo Mainardi felt secretly pleased. He had broken the ice. If he chose his words wisely, he had a chance of convincing this man that official intervention was needed in the affairs of Collemaga.

"I am sure you recall a young man dispatched to Collemaga by our ministry some months ago, *dottore?* His brief was to ascertain whether European funds allocated to the support of rural communities – Collemaga in this case - had not been improperly spent."

"You mean...?"

The Undersecretary was struggling to remember the name.

"Mattia De Angelis – he was a young graduate of about twenty-three, straight out of *La Sapienza**" explained Giacomo.

"Yes, Mattia De Angelis, that's right. Something happened to prevent him coming back to work here, if I remember rightly," replied the Undersecretary. "A nervous breakdown, or something, wasn't it? It was a colleague of mine who set that visit up."

Giacomo paused. He could hardly tell the Undersecretary that his information was wildly off course. He began with a polite sort of cough accompanied by a regretful smile of complicity. He was hoping that the rivalry that inevitably existed between people of similar high rank within the Ministry was going to come to his aid.

"I was never entirely convinced that my colleague had made a valid judgement by sending someone as inexperienced as this De Angelis out on a solo mission..." said the Undersecretary as if to himself.

Giacomo Mainardi drew a meaningful breath and, with a look of professional chagrin on his face on finding himself in the position of having to question the judgement of a person of higher rank to himself, continued:

"I have to agree with your analysis, *dottore*. Your colleague should have thought twice before he assigned such a mission to a relative tenderfoot such as Mattia..."

"It was a lady colleague who set the visit up. De Angelis was in her section," said the Undersecretary as if he deeply regretted having to cast aspersions on anyone at all – let alone someone of the opposite sex.

Giacomo was mentally rubbing his hands with glee. He had read the situation with unerring accuracy.

"I am unsure what explanation you might have heard as to Mattia's fate, *dottore*. But the fact is that he disappeared off the face of the earth and has not been seen or heard of since. His parents are in despair. They have tried everything – even appearing on that programme on RAI 3 called *'Chi l'ha visto?** You know the one, I'm sure. But it was all to no avail."

The Undersecretary was looking hard at Giacomo.

"Are you suggesting that this boy's disappearance can be traced back to his mission to...?"

"Collemaga? Yes, *dottore*. Let me tell you what Luca told me only a few days ago."

His interlocutor nodded curtly as if to say: "Talk! What are you waiting for?" The nod was accompanied by an impatient wave of his hand.

The man was hooked, Giacomo realised – whether for the right motives or not. It was a start at least. He needed to whet the appetite of his listener – but he would have to trust his own judgement and take a risk.

"Have you come across the term *fattucchiera, dottore?* I imagine someone as widely read as you are will certainly know what the word refers to...?"

Wait for the reaction, Giacomo! Give him the chance to show off!

"Yes, Giacomo, I seem to recall it's an old dialect word for a witch or a sorceress. You are surely not going to imply that this town...Collemaga. I see! The name of the town would suggest a witch-on-the-hill. But that's all a load of superstitious nonsense, isn't it?"

"Luca's first encounter in this town was with a very dubious character called Luigi Bonifaccio. Luca's own word for this man, who trailed him round the town to spy on wherever he went or whoever he spoke to, was *Il Porco.* He picked up the rumour that this sleazy individual was the sorceress's son. Illegitimate, many said – the result of a coupling with Satan even!"

Giacomo held up his hand in a gesture which forestalled the Undersecretary's dismissive protests.

"I can guess what you are thinking, *dottore* –that it smacks of pure superstition. But Luca's conviction is that the whole town is being fed these fantasies to avert attention to what is really going on under the surface. We are talking about diverting public funds into private bank accounts on a regular basis. It is quite likely that our young colleague, Mattia, discovered, or at least suspected, that a percentage of the EU subsidy was being misappropriated. His disappearance may well have been engineered by the real powers that be in Collemaga. Mattia may still be alive, Luca believes."

Giacomo paused to give the Undersecretary time to formulate his inevitable objection to the far-fetched notion of abduction. He was amazed to hear the next words that his interlocutor spoke – not at all dismissively.

"I would be interested to know how an intelligent and perceptive man such as Luca Fontana arrived at such a conclusion. In fact, I am fascinated by your account so far."

It was almost as if this senior public servant was pleading with him not to disappoint him by ending the account unconvincingly.

Giacomo gave his interlocutor a charming smile to accompany his next words.

"I should warn you, *dottore*. Luca Fontana sometimes goes about matters in a very unconventional manner. He was told about Mattia in very unusual circumstances - not entirely of his own making."

"I'm listening to you, Giacomo. I have a very open mind you may be surprised to know."

"Just a day after his arrival, he was visited late at night by a young Moroccan woman who had been inveigled into prostitution by the man, Bonifaccio – *Il Porco.* There were two girls under this man's thrall. I don't know the details but it seems that Luca Fontana struck up an unlikely friendship with this young woman. Luca speaks fluent French and the girl was so relieved that she told him the whole sad story how she was tricked into travelling to Italy with the promise of finding employment as a baby-minder or a *badante.** Luca – in his usual spontaneous way – spirited the girl away one night and left her with a restaurant owner and his family in a neighbouring town. The restaurant owner – Bruno Vespini - is one of the two people to whom Luca had the foresight to give my phone number to – with strict instructions to call me if anything happened to him."

"So it was this Moroccan girl who told Luca about Mattia De Angelis – is that correct, Giacomo?" The question was fired at Giacomo like a bullet.

"Yes, *dottore*. She overheard a phone conversation between her pimp – Luigi Bonifaccio – and someone else with a masculine voice about 'keeping him alive' only for as long as necessary."

"So did the girl know where Mattia was being held, Giacomo?"

"Oh yes – she was in no doubt about that. He is being held prisoner in the house of the *fattucchiera.*"

"And what about your second contact? Can he shed any further light on the abduction of Mattia?"

"My second contact is a woman, *dottore*. She was distraught. I had the impression she was close to Luca. She was too upset to go into details. But I have her name and I know where to find her in Collemaga."

"But does she have any idea where Luca is?"

"Oh, *dottore* – she is in absolutely NO doubt at all. He is being held prisoner by the *fattucchiera* – in her very large house just a few hundred metres from the main square. It is more like a fortress than a house, it seems."

The Undersecretary to the Minister of Finance closed his eyes and went into deep thought until Giacomo was so embarrassed that he considered getting up and leaving the room – out of the sheer necessity to appear tactful. He had even begun to stand up.

"Sit down, please," he was ordered in peremptory fashion. Then after a pause he heard words that made him return to revolt mode.

"I have never, but never, heard such a fantastic story in all my lifetime spent sitting behind this desk, Giacomo."

Giacomo was containing his anger with the greatest of restraint. The cutting comments about officials who took it upon themselves to dismiss anything out of the ordinary that a colleague of junior rank felt the need to impart were being suppressed with great difficulty.

"It is entirely to your credit, therefore, Giacomo Mainardi, that I believe every single word you have told me."

Giacomo could hardly believe what he was hearing.

"Grazie, dottore," he answered with all the dignity he could muster. He wondered if the Undersecretary had gauged his words with deliberate dramatic effect. If so, his superior had just displayed an aspect of his character which Giacomo had never appreciated.

"Leave this with me. I shall convey the urgency of this matter to the Minister immediately. However, it might take a lot more skill and diplomacy than you can possibly imagine, to convince *him* about what you have told me. Leave the matter in my hands – and trust me, even if you do not hear from me for a day or so. The Minister has a lot on his plate at present, as you can imagine, thinking of ways to reduce our national deficit."

"Will you need me to be present, *dottore,* when the Minister...?" Giacomo asked.

"I'm not sure how to approach him. You don't know the Minister like I do. He needs to be handled with great diplomacy. If you think *I* can be obstructive, you haven't seen anything yet," concluded the Undersecretary standing up to indicate that the exchange was over. But he gave Giacomo a wry smile as he shook his hand warmly.

"Don't be too concerned, Giacomo. We'll find a way to convince him."

Giacomo left the upstairs studio and felt a wave of relief as he took the stairs down to the next level.

"Pazienza, Luca," he said to himself. "We're on our way."

* * *

Another person back in Collemaga was feeling impotent and was desperately wondering how she could bring matters to a head. She had lain awake for hours at night time over the past two days, crying softly to herself in her frustration and anger. She did not wish to wake up her son who, since Luca's disappearance, had insisted on sleeping with his mother.

Giorgia had no allies in Collemaga. A few friends of course, but none of them could be trusted not to weaken under pressure from Luigi Bonifaccio or from the mere threat of *la fattucchiera* herself. She never even considered going to see the mayor. He was in the sorceress's pocket. Luca had kept his word and said nothing about his visit to the mayor – even to the woman he loved.

She took Marco to school and kissed him goodbye before he walked reluctantly through the school's entrance door and disappeared. The glimmer of hope that he had nurtured about finding a father had been extinguished by Luca's sudden and inexplicable disappearance.

"But why does the witch want to keep Luca prisoner, *mamma?*" he had asked her repeatedly.

There was only one person who Giorgia knew she could trust. And he did not offer a great deal of hope – but she had to talk to someone about Luca's abduction. It would involve her going to confession.

Father Sandonato understood immediately what she wanted. She had cast her eye round the *piazza* to make sure nobody was watching her movements. Giorgia's shop had been 'visited' by the *carabiniere* officer only the day before. But she had been very thorough – even going to the lengths

170

of switching off Luca's mobile phone so that nobody who happened to possess his number could reveal its presence by the device ringing unexpectedly.

Giorgia knelt down on the raised prayer stool and the priest went round the other side of the partition. Giorgia noticed that he had gained a new lease of life since his act of defiance against the *fattucchiera*. There was an inner energy inside his ageing frame that had been absent for as long as Giorgia could remember.

"I take it you have not come here to confess your sins, my dear? I am quite sure that God has forgiven you long ago for any minor peccadillo you might be guilty of," he had begun in a kind voice, which echoed his renewed spiritual strength.

"Thank you, father! I have to talk to someone. I have fallen in love with Luca and I am sure he has fallen in love with me – and Marco too. But I have to tell you that he was abducted during the *festa*. I am sure he in peril of his life. *That woman* has him in her grasp. I'm sorry, but I didn't know who else to turn to."

"I was expecting you to come and see me, Giorgia. I think I knew he had disappeared and there was only one person in this town who would wish him ill. I have Luca to thank to a very large extent for giving me the strength to resist the evil in this town – and I have been giving the matter all my..."

There was a noise behind Giorgia's back. Somebody had entered the church and knelt down surreptitiously just behind her. She turned round to look and had put a warning finger to her lips for Father Sandonato's benefit.

Despite – or because of - the hood covering his face, Giorgia knew who had crept into the church and come as close as possible to the confessional so that he could eavesdrop. His intention was self-evidently to be mistaken for the priest's next penitent.

Giorgia stood up and looked down upon the kneeling figure.

"Good morning, Luigi. Have you come to confess your sins – or simply to listen to *mine?*" she said cuttingly. "I trust you will allow me to finish mine first – because YOU are likely to need the rest of the year to confess yours."

He raised his head and Giorgia saw the sneer on his face – but there was a vestige of discomfort behind the sneer that he had been so fearlessly unmasked by this woman.

Father Sandonato made the sign of the cross silently from behind the protective partition – and stood up. *"Che Dio mi aiuti!"** he muttered as he walked round into the body of the church and headed purposefully towards the two figures His heart was pounding.

The old priest's voice sounded a little strangulated by nerves, but there was no hesitation.

"Good morning, Luigi. I hope and pray that your true motive for being here is that you have come to repent your sins – both venal and mortal."

The face of the son of the sorceress was contorted in a look of disdain.

"Your hopes are in vain, *father!*"

The last word had been spat out in hatred. But Luigi remained kneeling – in the position of humility, the old priest sensed.

"Then I would beg you to leave this sacred place where only God rules, my son. I shall continue to pray for you."

Father Sandonato's voice had grown more self-assured.

"Who is going to make me leave if I don't want to? An elderly priest and a *woman?*" replied Luigi with venom. He

172

was disconcerted by the look of sheer anger on Giorgia's face – and by the response of the priest who had walked casually towards the church's entrance door. Luigi was unable to make out what the priest was doing - without straining his neck round at an impossible angle. Father Sandonato returned holding a brass urn in one hand and a silver aspergillum in the other. Luigi was looking at him with what was intended to be a look of scorn. But his discomfort was betrayed by the uneasy look in his eyes.

"Holy water, my son," stated the priest, dipping the sprinkler meaningfully into the brass urn. "If you are without sin, the water will be like a baptism. If you are truly in league with Satan, then the water will burn your flesh and leave a permanent mark..."

Both Giorgia and the priest jumped out of their skins when Luigi leapt to his feet and ran for his life out of the church.

They looked at each other and burst into uncontrollable laughter.

"And to think I'm not sure I even remembered to bless the water in the font," said the priest with glee – as tears of mirth trickled down his wrinkled face.

"Oh, father! You were magnificent! But it begs the question whether Luigi ran out of the church because he was afraid of being burnt – or because he secretly knew he *wouldn't*. That way, WE would have known his claim was all a sham."

"The latter, I suspect," chuckled the old priest. "Now, what was it you wanted to tell me about Luca? I think we can just sit out here, now don't you, Giorgia?"

"Yes, father. My knees were already getting sore."

Father Sandonato listened thoughtfully to what Giorgia was saying.

"Now I understand what I thought I saw two nights ago after the *festa*. It all makes sense now. I saw Luca walking away with those two carnival figures – you remember, Giorgia, the ones who looked like a couple of overblown motorcar tyres! They were frogmarching Luca off in the direction of the sorceress's house."

"But what can we do, father?" asked Giorgia, the note of desperation returning in her voice.

"Apart from praying, you mean, *cara* Giorgia?"

She did not reply.

"Well, I shall tell you what we are going to do," said Father Sandonato. "But I could do with your help and moral support."

A new quality in the priest's tone of voice alerted Giorgia that he was about to say something out of the ordinary. But nothing could have prepared her for what came next.

"Would you be able to give me a lift to Pontefalco this afternoon? I have to take the overnight bus to Rome. I have an appointment to see His Holiness tomorrow morning at noon. I have never been to the Vatican or met a pope in the flesh before in my life. I am so happy that it will be *Papa Benedetto.* I feel blessed beyond all expectations."

"But how ever did you...?" began Giorgia.

Don Sandonato merely pointed skywards and smiled mysteriously.

"So, it *wasn't* because he won the lottery at all!" thought Giorgia with a secret smile on her face.

16: Unlooked-for interventions...

Giorgia's car was well worn– and yellow! It spent most of its life hidden in a *box auto** in the little back street behind the shop. It only emerged from hiding once a week when she and Marco went shopping – at a supermarket in Pontefalco. Giorgia was aware of looking conspicuous as she, Marco, Father Sandonato and an outsized battered brown suitcase all squeezed into her Panda and drove downhill out of Collemaga. But what did it matter at this stage if Luigi or one of his spies spotted the mismatched little group furtively leaving the town? She told herself it was too late to care. She must already be a marked woman in the eyes of the sorceress and her son.

Neither Giorgia nor Don Sandonato was inclined to indulge in conversation – both preoccupied with their own thoughts. Marco, in his child seat in the back of the Panda, was the one to break the meditative silence with an innocent question.

"Where are you going, father?"

"To Rome, Marco."

"Why are you going there? What are you going to do there? Is it a holiday?" he asked.

"No, figlio mio – vado a vedere il Papa."*

"You mean Luca? He's not in Rome, father. He's locked up in the witch's house."

The priest sighed. Marco's revelation, delivered out of the blue, did not come as a huge surprise.

Giorgia explained to her son the subtle difference between *papÀ and Il pApa.** The first one is 'your dad' and the second one is the Pope – confusing, isn't it?"

Marco remained silent for all of five seconds before he said with a giggle:

"So you are going to see Il Papa about *my* papà, father."

175

The priest turned round to look at Marco.

"Yes, I shall tell him about Luca and then we shall pray together for his safety, Marco."

"But, father…" began Marco, wishing to seek clarification.

"*Basta,** Marco," intervened his mother. "Leave Father Sandonato in peace now."

The short journey to Pontefalcone was soon over. Giorgia drove to the coach terminus and got out of the car to embrace the priest.

"*In bocca al lupo,** father. We'll be praying for you. And ring me when you get back so we can pick you up."

"*Grazie mille,* Giorgia. *Dio sia con voi.*"*

The elderly priest walked away purposefully, handling his suitcase with ease.

"I bet he's only got a pair of pyjamas and a tooth brush in that case," she thought. "Plus his rosary, of course!"

On the way home, Giorgia was obliged to take a different route because of the one way road system in Pontefalco. She passed in front of a *trattoria*. She read the name of the restaurant – *La Buona Forchetta*. It rang a bell. Of course – it was where Luca had taken Marianne.

Without premeditation, Giorgia pulled over and parked her car half on the pavement a few metres down the road.

"Let's go and have something to eat, Marco. Are you hungry?"

It was a rhetorical question. Marco was *always* hungry. But as they walked through the door into the deserted restaurant – it was barely 7 o'clock – Marco instinctively put his hand over his face. Giorgia knew from sad experience that her son always made this gesture without thinking whenever they entered an unfamiliar place. She put an arm round his shoulder and whispered the words:

176

"Corraggio, amore!"

The owner was standing behind the bar, cleaning glasses. He was almost as tall as Luca – and almost as good-looking, Giorgia registered in amusement. It must be him! Bruno looked up suspiciously at the unexpected arrival of the woman and child. He frowned, obviously wary of newcomers – for very good reasons.

"You must be Bruno Vespini, I suppose," said Giorgia.

"I might well be," was the curt reply. "And you are...?"

"My name is Giorgia Calvera. I'm Luca's..." she did not complete the sentence immediately because she was unsure how to express their status. The owner of *La Buona Forchetta* just stared at her, with a discouraging look.

"Luca's our friend, Bruno. He's gone missing, you know."

"None of the names you have mentioned mean anything to me, *signora,*" he added gruffly.

"And this is my son, Marco," she continued desperately. "Luca has taken us under his wing."

"Ciao, Marco," said Bruno Vespini with a hesitant smile in the child's direction.

Instinctively, Marco waved his hand at the man and returned the smile, thereby revealing his face. Bruno took one look at Marco. His expression was transformed into one of pleasure. Luca must have told him about Marco's affliction – and of course, about her, Giorgia realised.

"I am so sorry, Giorgia. I have to be so cautious these days. I have had two visits from people who purport to be Luca's friends from Collemaga – including that creepy individual who Luca calls..."

"Il Porco!" said Giorgia laughing.

"Elena!" shouted Bruno to his wife, who was working in the kitchen preparing the evening meal. "Come and meet Luca's friends."

A cheerfully well-fed lady stepped into the dining room wiping her hands on her cook's apron. She took in the newcomers with one glance and smiled in welcome.

"You must join us for dinner, Giorgia and Marco. We always eat early before the evening diners arrive."

"We don't want to…" began Giorgia.

"No arguments please!" insisted Elena. "Kids, downstairs with you – we've got guests this evening," she called out.

To Giorgia's surprise, three people came down the stairs from above the restaurant.

"This is Roberto and this is Stella…" she said as the children shook hands with Giorgia. Instinctively, Marco's right hand had covered his face again. With a gesture that brought tears to Giorgia's eyes, Stella took Marco's hand gently in hers, obliging him to grasp her hand. Roberto, only slightly more cautious than his sister, held Marco's hand in his and managed a smile. They must have discussed Marco *in famiglia,* thought Giorgia. Marco was very soon at his ease – since he made no move to cover his face again.

"And this young lady is…" began Bruno,

"*You* must be Marianne!" said Giorgia, taking her hand in turn. "But Luca told me you had gone away to stay in Sulmona with…"

"I got bored and I missed my family in Pontefalco," said Marianne. "I came back again the next day."

"I'm sure you will be safe here," said Giorgia. "Besides which, certain people in Collemaga have got much more on their plate right now than wondering where you are, *mia cara.** There has been a change in atmosphere in Collemaga since the *festa* – thanks to one very old priest."

The two children ate quickly and, after the dessert of fruit, they disappeared upstairs again after shaking hands and saying *buona notte** all round. Marianne stayed downstairs.

"I am so glad that you came, Giorgia – even if I didn't know you existed," said Marianne. Dinner over, the conversation inevitably turned to the subject of the *festa* and the extraordinary incident of the burning of the crucifix. Giorgia left out no details of the events which had led up to the moment when she had taken Marco back home to use the toilet – followed by the total shock of discovering that Luca had been abducted by the two Rubber Tyre men during her brief absence.

Marianne had become increasingly preoccupied as the narrative unfolded. The parents had got up from the dinner table and gone back into the kitchen to prepare for the arrival of the fifteen or so diners who had begun to trickle in. Giorgia, Marianne and Marco remained at the table.

"I'm coming back to Collemaga with you two," she stated. "Could I stay with you for a time?"

"No, Marianne! It would be crazy for you to return to that town! You would be in great danger if you were seen..."

"I would not be in as much danger as Luca is at the moment," she replied. "That man gave me hope for a better future. I know exactly where he is being held captive, you see. I can help him..."

"I don't know what to say, Marianne. I would love your company and so would Marco - *vero* Marco?"

Marco nodded seriously. He had been staring in fascination at Marianne throughout the meal.

"But, can't wait for a day or so until you are sure...?

"I AM sure, Giorgia. You and Luca are lovely people. You are together, aren't you?"

"Yes, we are – yes, we were. So briefly that I did not even have time to appreciate just how fortunate I was. And

Marco already calls him *papà*. But I don't want to be the cause of you falling foul of that evil crew again…"

"I truly believe their days are numbered, Giorgia. And I can help. I owe it to Luca. I can really put the cat among the pigeons, you see. If you don't take me with you, I shall walk there!" stated Marianne in all seriousness.

Giorgia smiled at this remarkable young woman's determination and courage.

"I do believe you want to take your revenge on them, don't you Marianne!"

"That too if I get the chance – but mainly I want to save Luca."

"I can see why he wanted to rescue you, Marianne. You are a remarkable person. *Va bene. D'accordo!** I'll take you back with us."

"Let me talk to Bruno and Elena. It's only fair I help them serve tonight's customers first. It'll only take me a few minutes to pack."

Left on their own, Giorgia looked at a sleepy Marco and asked him:

"Are you happy about this, *amore?*"

"*Sì mamma,*" he smiled and fell asleep at the table.

Marianne returned and nodded.

"*Tutto a posto,*"* she said and took Marco in her arms, carried him upstairs and laid his sleeping form on her bed.

It was past eleven o'clock before the little group walked out of the restaurant. Bruno and Elena stood on the pavement and solemnly waved them good-bye.

"Come back and see us soon," said Elena.

"*Salutatemi I ragazzi,*"* whispered Marianne.

"They're going to miss you, Marianne."

* * *

Giacomo Mainardi had got to the stage of tearing his hair out after five days had elapsed since he had spoken to the Undersecretary to the Minister of Finance. Luca must have been in captivity for just over a week by now. But Giacomo knew that if he made any attempt to contact his superior, it would be construed as *'una mancanza di fiducia'** which would risk jeopardising his mission completely. He had sent a text message to his two 'contacts' in Collemaga and Pontefalco to warn them that he was up against an 'administrative delay' from 'up above'. He adjured them to be patient and never to give up hope.

Giacomo's tried and tested theory - that relief magically comes only when one has been distracted by more trivial matters - proved to be the case on this occasion.

He had sent his young and very pregnant secretary on an errand to the 'upper reaches' of the ministry. She had assured him that it would not overtax her at all, that she preferred to be moving about rather than sitting 'doubled up' at a desk. When she had not returned after thirty minutes, Luca began to be concerned. She had taken the lift up to the top floor – he had seen her getting into the ancient apparatus. He decided he would go and see if she had run into difficulties with the official whom he had sent her off to liaise with. It was, as chance would have it, the self-same lady who had dispatched Mattia De Angelis off to Collemaga.

His insistent button-pushing had failed to produce the lift. He had an awful thought that the lift must have got stuck between floors. He ran up the stairs. The lift cage travelled through a non-enclosed shaft. He had to run up to the stairway which led to the top floor before he saw the lower half of the cage and a pair of female legs. He could hear her crying for help.

"Gloria!" he shouted. "It's me – Giacomo."

She tearfully explained she had been pushing the emergency button but no-one had answered. He could hear the panic in her voice.

He did not waste time getting the reception staff at ground level to call out the lift company, but called out the fire brigade directly. A young and pregnant woman stuck in a lift was enough to put the *Vigili del Fuoco* on full alert. They were outside the Ministry within ten minutes. The arrival of the fire engine, sirens blazing, and the sight of firemen running upstairs set off a state of panic which spread faster than a fire could ever have done.

"Why hasn't there been a fire warning bell?" people were calling out. Most of the staff didn't wait and simply headed *en masse* to the stairwell and assembled outside the building. The firemen took only fifteen minutes to free Gloria – who shot off to the toilet as soon as she had been freed. She subconsciously noticed that the whole building seemed to be deserted – except for Giacomo standing shaking the firemen's hands in gratitude for their prompt action.

As word spread to the crowd of people out in the street, normality was gradually restored. One of Giacomo's staff – a witty individual noted for his acute sense of the absurd - provoked much laughter when he pointed out that the only people who had not escaped the fire were the Minister and his Under Secretaries on the top two floors. They had remained blissfully unaware of the chaos below them.

"If ever we wanted a change of government," he announced to those standing about in Giacomo's vicinity, "all we need to do is vacate the lower floors and set fire to all the filing cabinets without telling them upstairs."

Giacomo laughed heartily along with the others. That was the moment when his desk phone rang. The Undersecretary was summoning him upstairs.

"You and I have an appointment in twenty minutes time with the Minister, Signor Mainardi. I want you upstairs immediately so I can brief you as to your role."

* * *

"The only thing you have to remember, *Signor* Mainardi, is not to react angrily to anything I say. You must trust me to know what I am doing. If the Minister asks *you* a question, answer it simply – and stick to the simple, unembellished truth."

The Undersecretary knocked on the door and waited to hear the word *'avanti'* before he pushed open the door. As the pair of them covered what seemed like a kilometre's walk between the door and the huge mahogany desk, Giacomo was struck anew by the apparent youth of the Minister. He knew the man must be at least twenty-five since one could not become a representative of the people until that age. But really... he looked barely that age with his sharp patrician features and his black, short-cropped hair brushed back from his high forehead. Young and ambitious were the words that went through Giacomo's mind as he sat down nervously.

The Minister looked at his watch as he smiled a quickly stifled parting of the lips to reveal pearly white teeth for the space of no more than two seconds before the official – patrician – face was firmly back in place.

"Gentlemen, convince me in five minutes that we are not wasting state money and time on a mission that involves some sorceress and an imprisoned writer," said the Minister curtly. "Cosimo…?" he said, looking at his Undersecretary.

"I have listened to my colleague most carefully and given the matter much thought over the past few days, *Signor Ministro.* I am entirely convinced that he has grasped the facts of this unusual situation with accuracy. But a rescue attempt would be costly and time-consuming. I am not entirely convinced that the effort or expense are justified in light of the low level of risk involved to this admittedly notable and important author. I am, of course entirely ready to be persuaded otherwise if *Il Signor Ministro* is disposed to consider this situation warrants State intervention."

Giacomo was seething inside at this high-ranking official's devastating words. How could the man be such a treacherous turncoat?

"A bit of a negative assessment of the case," said the Minister turning his attention to Giacomo, who was having to stifle his interior wrath at this apparent betrayal. "What do you have to say on this issue, *Signor* Mainardi?"

Giacomo began talking quietly, calmly covering all the points of the case one by one. He emphasised the importance of Luca Fontana as a writer and supporter of a decent mafia-free society. He laid particular emphasis on the unexplained disappearance of one of their own staff – Mattia De Angelis. Giacomo was about to threaten the minister's authority by inferring that, if Mattia's disappearance became widely reported by the media, then ministerial inaction over the case could create a scandal. He thought – or hoped – that he had begun to understand the Undersecretary's approach. Thus he contented himself by underlining how it appeared that a whole town – little under one hundred or so kilometres from where they were sitting – had ended up under the sway of some undesirable dynasty, apparently led by a *fattucchiera.*

"The two people with whom I am in contact on site, so to speak, seem convinced that Luca Fontana is likely to suffer the same fate as our young colleague, Mattia De Angelis."

The Minister turned back to his Undersecretary.

"That account seems to contradict your rather over-cautious assessment of the seriousness of this situation, wouldn't you say, Cosimo?"

"It is my duty, *Signor Ministro,* to caution you against rash political decisions. I stand by what I say."

The minister had become pensive. He was obviously weighing up the political risk to himself of making a wrong decision – in either direction.

"Leave this with me for a day or so longer," he said.

The Undersecretary glanced briefly and despairingly at his watch. Giacomo caught sight of an anxious face. His 'ally' had seriously misjudged his own tactics and his cleverness, thought Giacomo angrily.

Just as they were about to leave, the Minister's desk telephone rang. He wrenched the receiver irritably from its cradle.

"I thought I said I didn't want to be disturbed, Tamara…. What on Earth can be so important that…? WHO did you say?" he asked incredulously. Well of course, you must put him through. Are you sure you…? Yes, you are sure" After a pause: "What can I do for Your Holiness?"

Cosimo, the Undersecretary, was looking more relaxed, even smug, thought Giacomo.

There followed a lengthy monologue from the caller, during which the Minister did a lot of nodding. The gentle voice which could be heard on the other end of the line sounded just like that of the Pontiff - but surely, that would be impossible, wouldn't it?

After what seemed like an age, the voice from the Vatican finished on an interrogative note. The Minister finally spoke:

"Yes, Your Holiness. Of course we are taking the matter seriously. We shall act upon this matter without delay. Rest assured..."

He replaced the receiver and looked at his Undersecretary, who was careful to resume his previous deferential demeanour.

"Whilst I respect your sound and invaluable advice, Cosimo, it would seem your junior colleague was right all along. We cannot delay dealing with the matter of this small town called..."

"Collemaga, *Signor Ministro.*"

"Collemaga... yes of course."

* * *

"There, Giacomo. I think we managed to get our own way in the end, don't you?" said the Undersecretary to his junior colleague as they walked side by side down the marble stairs.

"I cannot thank you enough, *dottore.* I am sorry I ever doubted your integrity and diplomatic skills. But, did you *know* the Pope was intending to call at that minute in time? If so, how could you possibly...?

The Undersecretary, Cosimo De Cesaris, tapped the side of his nose.

"Me l'ha detto l'uccellino, Signor Mainardi!"*

"Some little bird! More like some wily OLD bird!" muttered Giacomo after Cosimo De Cesaris had left him to return to his office down below.

186

He was brought back down to Earth as he walked into his office by a grateful Gloria, who propelled herself and future child into his arms in wordless gratitude for his prompt action in rescuing her.

Just before going home, Giacomo sent the same message to two people who lived some hundred kilometres away – telling them that help should be on its way.

Had his boss, Cosimo De Cesaris, not taken so great a delight in being secretive, Giacomo might well have added a third person to his short list of recipients in Abruzzo.

17: A special kind of evil...

When Luca became aware that he was still alive, he did not know where he was. Some confined space which smelt of mould. The only light was from a bare bulb dangling from a wire in the ceiling, which looked as if it formed part of a cave. It was too gloomy to make out the dimensions of the space he was occupying. The feeble light bulb cast more shadows than it did light. It was the sort of bulb that he had fitted up in his kids' bedroom when they were little - because they had both been afraid of the dark. His body, he worked out after a few seconds, appeared to be stretched out on a bed. His head did not seem right. It felt very much as he remembered feeling after a minor operation he had had as a teenager – groggy. He must have been given some drug to be in this state, he realised. He wondered what time it was. He felt for his wrist watch. It had been removed.

He felt anger. That was good. It would keep him from feeling any negative emotions – such as fear. Memories of his moment of capture were coming back to his conscious mind. He even smiled at the recollection of the two rubber tyre men who had tried to frogmarch him down the narrow side street.

He recalled shaking himself free of their grip without too much difficulty.

"Get your hands off me you couple of goons," he had shouted out – motivated by a desire to attract as much public attention as possible to his abduction. "I *want* to meet the good lady who claims to be the witch of this town. Without you two, I might never have got an invitation."

The two men were obviously taken aback by his reaction to being kidnapped. Luca had made matters worse for his captors by turning to the shorter, stockier version of the Michelin brothers with the words:

"And as for YOU, *Tenente-whatever-your-name-is,* you should be ashamed of yourself. Yes, I recognised who you are immediately. No amount of rubber coating can conceal *your* identity. If this performance of yours is the best the *Carabinieri* can come up with, little wonder there is no real law and order in this town."

Luca remembered the comical, wordless reaction from his captors. The one who was not the junior *carabiniere* officer had half turned towards his companion on the other side of Luca. If their faces had not been concealed by their outlandish disguises, Luca was certain that he would have intercepted an accusatory glare from Tweedledum directed at Tweedledee.

Luca had laughed out loud, he seemed to recall. The only trouble now, was that Luca had no means of telling how long ago his capture had taken place. Stoke up the anger, his subconscious mind told him. It would clear his head. He stood up and began to explore the cell in which he had been imprisoned. It couldn't be more than twenty square metres – if that. His eyes grew more accustomed to the gloom. Yes, the roof consisted of roughly hewn stone, so he must be in a cellar carved out of the cliff face. He found the door – which of course was locked. Although solid enough, it was only made of wood. He would have kicked the door to vent his anger but realised just in time that he had no shoes on. So he banged the door with his fist instead. The noise made a suitably resounding echo in what he assumed must be a corridor on the other side of the door.

Further groping in the gloom soon revealed a metal table and chair against the stone wall on the opposite side to the bed. There was a small plastic bottle of water on the table. As he moved on round the confined space his foot kicked something metallic. He identified it as a makeshift toilet – of the portable variety. How delightful! That seemed to be it. Fighting off an encroaching attack of panic, he kept on walking up and down the cell – venting his feelings on the door whenever he felt like it. He did some press-ups and lifted the metal chair up and down above his head to keep his arms moving. The woolly sensation in his head had cleared, but he felt thirsty. He reached for the bottle of water. Twisting the plastic top did not break the seal however. That could indicate that the water inside had been contaminated in some way. He took a few sips just to see if he had any reaction.

He lay down on the hard bed again and drew a deep breath, summoning up his reserves of courage and patience. They obviously wanted him alive – for whatever reason. Otherwise, he reasoned, they would have bumped him off immediately. He wondered what on earth the *fattucchiera* had in store for him.

Despite the hardness of the bed and the temperature in his cell, he felt himself dozing off. But, in a trice, his mind was alert again. He thought at first someone was unlocking his door. But he realised he had heard the sound of a door slamming in the corridor and a key turning in the lock to secure it – not to open it. The next sound was so totally unexpected that he stood up in shock. Someone was sobbing and – so it seemed – reciting the Hail Mary.

Luca struck his forehead – if he could hear this voice so easily, there must be another room next to his. But the important thing was – since he could hear another person speaking and crying -the wall must be very insubstantial. In a trice, Luca put two and two together.

He tapped firmly on the wall, which sounded hollow – just plaster board maybe.

"Mattia? Is that you?"

There was total silence from the other side of the petition wall. The sobbing had ceased and the prayer to the Virgin Mary was left suspended between Earth and Paradise. Luca tapped on the wall again.

"Mattia, can you hear me? You *are* Mattia De Angelis, aren't you?"

A feeble voice, little more than a whisper could be heard.

"Yes, I think so. Sometimes I'm no longer sure... Are you the Mother of Jesus?" asked the voice in disbelief.

"I trust Mary didn't have a baritone voice like mine, Mattia," replied Luca. Mattia's voice sounded younger and softer than it should have been – more like a twelve year old whose voice had not quite broken. He sounded traumatised.

"Who are you?" asked the voice. "Have you been sent by that awful woman to torment me even more?"

"No, Mattia. I am a prisoner like you. My name is Luca."

"Luca?" repeated the voice of Mattia.

"Yes. I'm a friend of Giacomo Mainardi – in the Finance Ministry. He remembers you well."

"Giacomo?" echoed Mattia – as if he was testing to see if his brain and his powers of speech were still in working order.

"Are you alright, Mattia? Don't worry. We shall soon be out of here. It's only a matter of days."

The sobbing had begun again and the young man's plaintive voice had relapsed into childlike tones again.

"You're just telling me that to give me hope, aren't you Luca? Then I shall find out that it's just another trick to cast me down onto the ground so SHE can trample on me all over again."

"No, Mattia. I'm telling you the simple truth; I'm her prisoner. But I shan't allow that woman to get the better of us, I promise."

"Just you wait...Luca. You'll find out when it's your turn. She can make you do, say and think things that you've never even dreamt of..."

Mattia seemed to be reliving some horrendous experience. His voice was shaking with emotion.

"Be careful, Luca. When the time comes and it's your turn..."

There was somebody in the corridor jangling a set of keys. This time it *was* Luca's door being unlocked. His 'turn' had apparently already come.

"Coraggio, Mattia," he whispered fiercely before the cell door was pushed open and a brighter light flooded his cell.

Luca had lain down again on the rudimentary bed. He wished to appear totally nonchalant in the face of his captors.

A familiar voice said:

"Get up *Signor* Fontana. *Mamma* wishes to talk to you...now!"

Without moving from his bed, Luca called out cheerfully:

"Why, Luigi! What a pleasure to run into you again! I want to talk to your mother too. But I can't, you see."

"Why not, *Signor* Fontana?" asked Luigi petulantly in his barely comprehensible dialect.

"No shoes, Luigi. Somebody has taken them away. And I would like my watch back too. It was a gift from my wife...several years ago," Luca added as if for his own benefit.

"Go on, Fortunato," the voice of Luigi said, obviously speaking to someone with him.

"Ah, you've come with the heavy mob, have you Luigi? That won't help you at all. I want my shoes – and my watch back before I go anywhere."

Luca was banking on the fact that the *fattucchiera* would want her 'guest' to be in one piece at this stage. Indeed, a gruff voice which was not Luigi Bonifaccio's was muttering in even heavier dialect than his companion:

"We'd better go and ask first. I don't want no trouble, Luigi."

The cell door was relocked and the two men could be heard muttering – none too civilly – as they tramped off to another part of the house.

A different sound came from the cell next door which Luca could not quite make out. Then he realised that Mattia was clapping his hands together in applause.

"There, I told you I was a prisoner just like you, Mattia."

"But you must still be wary Luca. Those two are just vassals – they wouldn't dare do *anything* without her permission. SHE is different, believe me! *PERICOLOSISSIMA!*"* insisted Mattia, the hint of terror back in his voice.

"So am I, Mattia! Very dangerous indeed when roused," he reassured his new companion. It felt like a whole hour had elapsed before the sound of keys rattling in the corridor alerted Luca to the return of his prison warders. Once again, the light from the corridor flooded into his cell thereby restoring something resembling normal visibility.

Fortunato was short and stocky – more like a local farmer. He placed what Luca assumed was his watch on the metal table and handed Luca a pair of shoes – *his* shoes, but not the ones he had been wearing when he had been captured. Of course, he had been wearing those ornamental shoes with pointed toes from his carnival outfit.

193

They must have been round to Giorgia's house, thought Luca in alarm. They would have seized his suitcase. He hoped to God that she had thought to rescue his computer before *they* had arrived. And, even worse, what about his mobile phone? A stab of fear was undermining his pretence at bravado. But he must not let any sign of vulnerability be perceived by his captors.

Luca was being 'accompanied' by Luigi on his left and Fortunato on his right flank. Neither of them attempted to hustle him along in any way. I guess they know there is no escape route, thought Luca. At one point, Luca looked up a steep flight of steps at the top of which a battered door allowed fractured beams of sunlight to penetrate through the cracks.

"If you ever get the chance, *Signor* Fontana, you can always escape through that doorway," Luigi sneered.

The sheer callousness of the 'invitation' to self-destruction made Luca's heart rate increase. Luigi Bonifaccio obviously felt entirely self-assured living beneath the mantle of his mother's protection. Luca must maintain his cool exterior at all costs.

"Luigi, you really must stop attempting to use these childish tactics on me. I am not impressed at all. That doorway can only lead to empty space with, I imagine, a thirty metre drop to the river below."

"Knock it off, Luigi," muttered Fortunato in such strong dialect that Luca could only guess what he had said by the tone of his voice. *"This* guy's too intelligent."

Luigi retorted in equally pure dialect. It sounded to Luca as if he was trying to reassert his authority over his minion.

The trio went up a flight of stairs out of the basement. The air was warmer and did not smell of mould. There was a subtle hint of incense and autumn leaves pervading the air – but it was a perfume he had not come across before. The only word that sprang to Luca's mind to identify the effect of the scent was 'pagan'. Strange how smells can influence the way we interpret our surroundings, thought Luca – not feeling particularly reassured by the memory of the scent of rain-soaked autumn leaves which he always associated with his own mother's funeral. Was that the smell which he could detect here in the sorceress's house? Almost, but with a hint of some obscure oriental spice added to it.

Luigi knocked on an old panelled door.

"Mamma, your guest is here."

No answer. He knocked again – and again after that. But he gave the impression that this was a regular 'ritual'.

"Avanti!" said a softly modulated female voice which contained just a hint of matriarchal impatience.

The deadly game of charades was about to begin, thought Luca, unable to prevent his heartbeat increasing despite his mental efforts to quell his nerves. The opening of the door brought with it a waft of the heady perfume he had detected in the corridor. It was disquieting – as if the occupant already knew how to reach his inner soul.

The room was heavily curtained, making it impossible to tell whether it was daylight or night time. If Luca had not spotted sunlight through the cracks in the 'suicide' door a few minutes beforehand, he would have assumed it was night time. Perhaps the sorceress worked better in this artificial twilight zone.

And there she was, standing tall wearing a reassuring smile on her unobtrusively rouged lips.

"Benvenuto, Signor Fontana – Luca!"

The voice was soft - holding no hint of menace. Her raven hair fell over a face which was darkly beautiful and beguiling.

Luca decided on the spot not to respond in predictable manner.

"Ah, I can see now, Margherita – it really WAS you driving that dragon chariot through the streets yesterday evening, wasn't it? And I fancy the *fattucchiera* statue issuing curses to whoever put coins in the basket was also you. A masterful performance, if I may say so!"

Luca was assuming it *was* only yesterday evening when he had been abducted. He had instinctively taken the chance of using her first name – simply to match her use of *his* first name. He wished to establish a kind of moral balance from the outset.

He detected the most fleeting hint of surprise on the *fattucchiera's* face – so swift as to be almost undetectable. Her reply, however, almost whispered, was delivered with quiet and unnerving grace.

"You are a most perceptive man, Luca, as I was sure would be the case. But you have been with us now for three whole days."

Inwardly, Luca felt an initial jolt of physical shock. Was it possible that so much time had elapsed? The notion was disconcerting. No, he considered. Three days was logically impossible – he would have been suffering from hunger and thirst to a far greater extent. She was toying with him in a deliberate attempt to confuse him. Mattia's warning words came back to him.

"Three days!" he replied in easily feigned surprise. "It must have been quite some drug you administered to me to have lasted that long!"

The lips parted in a smile revealing a perfect set of white teeth, in sharp contrast to so many of the citizens of Collemaga, who looked as if a visit to the dentist was long overdue.

"I apologise, Luca. It was necessary to calm you down. You were quite energetic in your resistance to being captured."

It was a lie, he was sure. But he must make her believe he had been taken in.

"No wonder, then, I feel ravenously hungry and thirsty – Margherita!"

She winced again at the use of her first name.

"Today, you will eat with me, Luca. The table is laid."

She led him – hips swaying – into an anti-chamber. Her tight-fitting, full-length black dress did more than hint at her shapely contours - another disconcerting aspect of this creature.

She invited Luca to sit halfway down the longer side of the table and took up her position opposite him. Luca had never in his life seen a black tablecloth before. A young woman in her twenties brought in two dishes of pasta and placed one dish in front of the lady of the house and the second dish a few seconds later in front of Luca. No notion of the guest being served first. He was being reminded of his status.

"This is Marta," said the *fattucchiera* in the same manner as she would have pointed out a piece of valued furniture. "She is from this town and acts as my cook."

"Grazie, Marta," said Luca kindly. Was there the tiniest hint of appeal in the eyes of this young woman – quickly cancelled from her dark features?

Luca was very hungry. He picked up his fork and was about to break an obvious house rule – and not wait for the *fattucchiera* to take the first mouthful. He looked in astonishment at his sorceress – she was about to go through the ritual of saying grace. But she made the sign of the cross in reverse – her forefinger touching her forehead last of all. She muttered a few words which had nothing in common with the Italian language.

When she opened her eyes again, Luca had quite deliberately ladled a mouthful of pasta into his mouth.

"Buon appetito," he said boldly. "Your Marta is a very good cook."

The frown of suppressed anger on the face of his hostess was plain to see.

"In this house..." began the *fattucchiera.*

A shocking moment for Luca - the former sweetly modulated female voice had issued from her lips as a broken male voice which crackled with anger.

She rapidly recovered, smiled at Luca, saying the words 'Enjoy your meal, Luca' in her woman's voice, but with an edge to it that implied it might be his last. But the eyes glared at him with dark anger. She had allowed the mask to slip, thought Luca, overwhelmed by a sense of the alien nature of his adversary. Luca was allowed a few mouthfuls more of his pasta before the *fattucchiera* addressed him again – her gentle voice belying the venom behind her words.

"So you're a writer," she stated with total assurance. "Not an architect as you initially told the mayor."

Luca took a sip of the red wine and drank a tumbler full of water. He must have been well on the road to dehydration by this time – even after only one day. He nodded as amiably as he could. Marta arrived with the second course, which turned out to be a tasty horse meat stew. The sorceress was looking at him appraisingly – as if she was working out how the new 'guest' was faring emotionally and mentally.

"Delicious!" stated Luca, tasting the stew. *"Complimenti al cuoco!"* he added smiling at Marta, who did not dare return the smile.

"We'll let you know when we need coffee," said the hostess dismissively.

"And I suppose you thought you were going to write about my town, didn't you *Signor* Fontana. You seem to have been spending your life writing a number of very biased books against the *'ndrangheta* – yes, I know this to be true. I employ a team of researchers who are devoted to me. They have obtained one of your books..."

"*Buona lettura,** Margherita!" was all Luca deigned to say. To all intents and purposes, he was totally engaged in enjoying his meal.

"The Calabrian mafia are merely providing an alternative economy to the State and they keep more people happy and in employment than the government can ever hope to achieve."

Luca looked at the *fattucchiera* in mild disbelief. Still he refused to react. He wanted to see where his refusal to be drawn into the conversation would lead. By his silence, he wanted to provoke his adversary.

"In Collemaga, I have established the rule of law – there is no crime in this town," she stated.

"Except you allow your son to exploit foreign girls against their will. Living off immoral earnings *is* a serious crime, madam!" Luca had spoken in a low clear voice, looking straight into the woman's eyes. Once again the almost beautiful face was distorted in anger. She was not used to being contradicted. But yet again, she was back in control of the situation within seconds.

"Come now, Luca," she said smoothly. "You are a man of the world! The girls are only providing a service which helps to keep destabilising male libidos in check. No harm is being done – until you saw fit to interfere."

"I don't suppose that argument will stand up in a court of law, Margherita," he said smiling sweetly.

"A court of law, Luca? We are never going to have to answer to such ineffectual institutions here in Collemaga, I assure you, *Signor* Luca. She scoffed the words scornfully in his face.

They had both reverted to first names again, but it had become a deadly game and the use of first names had become a form of insult.

"You will never publish your book. We have taken your computer."

"Oh good – I hope you will find it enlightening," replied Luca. The words of the *fattucchiera* had left him reeling. If what she said was true, she would find out that she had been betrayed by Elpidio Pugliese. Why, oh why had he not had the foresight to conceal his computer properly?

"I should point out to you that I have already decided not to publish what I have written so far," said Luca evenly. "Events in my life here have overtaken my desire to write about Collemaga. I have decided to come and live here. As I am sure you are aware, I have officially purchased a house…"

The *fattucchiera* rose from her chair. She had scarcely touched the plate of food whereas Luca had even cleaned his plate with a piece of bread. She seemed to have grown in stature – how did she manage to achieve this diabolic effect? Drugs, thought Luca. Had he fallen for the oldest trick in the book – meat with some hallucinogen injected into it – or the sauce that had accompanied the meat? He drank another tumbler full of water to quench his thirst. Or even in the water, heaven help him! The *fattucchiera* seemed to be towering above him. She had a sneering grin on a face whose beautiful features were distorted with sadistic pleasure.

"And as for your new bed-mate, Giorgia… She is one of MINE, Luca. She will do anything for me. She even succeeded in seducing YOU with the greatest of ease. How do you think we picked you out of the crowd so readily?"

A couple of minutes later, Luca was being escorted roughly back to his cell, inwardly cursing his own naivety. The only thing he had achieved was to pocket the serrated knife he had been eating with. He had had an idea whilst at the table. Now, his scheme seemed laughably puerile...

18: Rappresaglie... *(Reprisals : Fighting back)*

Luca lay down on his apology for a bed and began to consider what had transpired upstairs. Above all, he was feeling a deep and heart-rending sadness that he had been so wrong about Giorgia. Of course he should have known that Giorgia's financial survival must depend on this woman's grace and favour. How gullible he had been in allowing himself to indulge in such naive romanticism!

La fattucchiera had unerringly succeeded in striking at the heart of his most cherished desire – that of finding his true *anima gemella** in his complex life. He had instinctively singled out Giorgia as the one who had appeared to have all the qualities he had ever looked for in a partner. Surely he could not have been so mistaken in his feelings for Giorgia – or rather hers for him? He fell into a deep depression which risked casting him into the abyss of despair. How impotent he felt when the natural reaction to his sense of loss was to seek out the woman he had been so attracted to and simply ask for the reassurance only she could provide. Now he truly understood what it meant to be a prisoner. He felt the tears welling up inside him. He was going to cry dammit!

He was shaken out of his immediate desire to surrender to his feelings by a discrete knocking on the wall. Mattia! Luca had not given the young man a second thought since he had been dumped back in his cell.

"Are you alright, Luca?" asked an anxious voice through the wall.

"No, not really, Mattia. I should have taken what you told me more seriously. I underestimated the maliciousness of which she is capable."

Mattia, bless him, did not say 'I told you so'. Instead, Luca could just make out the words:

"It's quite understandable, Luca. You had never met her before."

"I want to tell you what happened, Mattia, but I'm tired of communicating through this wall. Let's try something to see if we can get back at this ungodly set-up. Is your bed up against this wall on your side of things?"

"I guess so, Luca. But what can we…?

With an energy that had to be summonsed up from the brink of defeat, Luca stood up and pulled his bed frame away from the wall. A good job he now had shoes on his feet. He would need their protection in the next hour or so.

"I'm going to try and make a hole in this wall, Mattia. Low down at floor level."

The 'hour or so' which he had predicted took nearer six hours hard labour and a lot of swearing – inevitably directed against his main adversary upstairs. Mattia kept silent throughout. He dared hardly hope that this futile gesture on the part of his 'saviour' would yield any advantage to either of them.

The knife which he had purloined was hardly up to the job and was half blunt by the time he had succeeded in making a deep enough score in the plaster board to ensure that it would only be a small section of the wall that would cave in when it came to kicking it. But there was still a risk that the whole wall would split if he wasn't careful. In the end, he managed to cut a tiny hole right through the plaster board by twisting the knife round in circles while putting a lot of pressure on the knife.

Mattia looked at the tip of the blade as it edged its way through the wall. For the first time in months, he felt a glimmer of hope. This unseen person was going to change things after all!

Finally, Luca succeeded in pushing the whole knife through the hole.

"Now it's your turn, Mattia! I'm going to tap on the wall and I want you to make a mark with the tip of the blade as precisely as you can where you hear me tapping."

The process took another twenty minutes off their lives.

"Now you have to join up the dots, Mattia. Make a cut as deep as you can – I'm sure that knife will give up the ghost very soon.

A weakened Mattia, who had suffered from malnutrition and sleep-deprivation, had to take agonisingly frequent breaks between his efforts. It took him hours to complete – Luca was glad he had his watch back, otherwise the Herculean task might have seemed like an eternal one.

"OK Mattia, stand back," commanded Luca through the little hole gauged out of the wall. Luca aimed one mighty kick at the plaster board wall. To his amazement the section came away cleanly.

"I hope you're not very fat, Mattia," he said in jest. "Otherwise I shall have to steal another knife."

"For the first time in my life, I am glad to be skinny, Luca."

"OK Mattia – hero number one – can you push all the debris through this way before you come through? I would hate for them to discover our trick just because we were untidy workmen."

Luca collected the bits and stuck them in his toilet. There *was* nowhere else to put it, he reasoned.

"Alright, Mattia. It's time we met," said Luca.

Mattia was taller than Luca had imagined – like a lanky teenage schoolboy. But the smile on his face and the tears running down his cheeks as they both shook hands like lost travellers in a foreign land endeared the lad to him immediately.

"We shouldn't linger around, Luca. *THEY* will be down soon, I reckon. They bring some kind of food and a bottle of water down – and we slop out and have a cold shower once every day."

"Well done, Mattia. We'll catch up after they've gone. Whatever happens, make sure you act exactly as you always have done," warned Luca.

Mattia hugged Luca and crawled back into his cell. They both shifted their beds back into place to cover the hole in the wall - which to Mattia's sensitive soul seemed like a portal to a new dimension.

* * *

Mattia was right in his assumption that the pair of them would be subjected to the humiliating ritual of being taken to a sordid bathroom along the corridor. Mattia was standing outside Luca's cell in the company of Luigi and the man named Fortunato – who looked anything but 'fortunate'. Mattia was carrying a chamber pot covered with a filthy rag.

"Muoviti, Fontana!" said Luigi Bonifaccio rudely to Luca. "Bring that toilet with you to empty it."

"There's nothing in it yet," replied Luca, lying smoothly. "I haven't even been here a full day yet! Besides which, I insist on being taken to a proper toilet – every time!"

It was interesting that Luigi Bonifaccio did not contradict Luca's statement about the length of time he had been held prisoner. One lie from the *fattucchiera*, thought Luca, might well indicate that she had deliberately lied about everything else too. A glimmer of hope, maybe!

Mattia was standing looking at Luca with wild fear in his eyes. It occurred to Luca that Mattia was acting – if so, it was a truly professional performance.

"And who is *this* poor sod?" asked Luca gruffly, jabbing a finger in Mattia's direction. He took one threatening pace towards Luigi, who instinctively backed away from the taller man – the one who had not even been scared by his snakes. "Some other poor soul you are torturing? You're going to pay for this one day, Luigi Bonifaccio!"

Luigi managed a sneer and indicated that the pair of them should head down the darkened corridor. There *was* a filthy toilet cubicle which flushed reluctantly after pumping the handle up and down several times. And the shower cubicle did not even have a curtain to ensure a minimum of privacy. A miniscule stream of tepid water emerged from the shower head.

After the 'ablutions' had been carried out, they returned to their cells. Fortunato was left to guard them while Luigi went to pick up two bowls of food and two bottles of mineral water from a small table just a few metres up the corridor.

Before his cell door was locked, Luca took his bottle of water and twisted the cap to ensure the seal was unbroken – whilst glaring at Luigi ferociously.

"No more of your drugs in my water bottle from now on, Luigi. Is that understood?"

He was gratified to see a look of something resembling guilt briefly cross the man's face. It was one of his 'special talents' to add the most effective drug in the appropriate quantity to his victims' food or drink. He had never been faced with anyone who challenged him in this way - on every conceivable occasion.

"You can tell that to your mother from me!" was Luca's parting shot.

His cell door was slammed shut and locked. Neither the door nor the lock seemed particularly resistant, noted Luca for future reference.

As soon as they were left alone, Luca called out to Mattia.

"Come on into my place. Let's dine together, this evening."

The food, although almost cold, was surprisingly good. Mattia commented on the fact.

"This is the first time I've been given anything edible, Luca. How did you manage to...?

Luca remembered Marta's fleeting expression of complicity when she had served him upstairs.

"Maybe we have an ally in the camp," he explained to Mattia.

"Now tell me everything that has happened to you since your arrival here, Mattia," invited Luca. "By the way, congratulations on your performance in the corridor! It was entirely convincing."

"In Rome, I belong to a drama group in my spare time, Luca. I think it is going to prove essential over the next few days."

Mattia began by describing his discovery of the fraudulent financial transactions involving European funds. Luca quickly abandoned his earlier assessment of Mattia - a boy sent to do a man's job. It rapidly became evident that he must be highly competent. Luca then listened in horrified silence to the catalogue of abuses to which the 'sorceress' had subjected him over the weeks he had been held prisoner.

"So as well as destroying any hope of seeing your family again, she has been exploiting you sexually since your arrival?" asked Luca incredulously.

Mattia nodded in shame.

"If I refused, she threatened to kidnap my little sister and bring her here too. She seemed to know exactly where my family live in Rome. She is completely ruthless and totally sadistic, Luca," said Mattia, who could not keep back the tears from his eyes. The look of terror had returned.

Luca took one look at this abused and dejected young man and hugged him tightly as a father would.

"There's one more thing I should tell you about *her*, Luca. But I can't say it out aloud. It's too embarrassing."

He leant over to Luca and whispered in his ear.

"Ahhh – that explains a great deal! Now I understand what was puzzling me," said Luca enigmatically. To Mattia's astonishment, Luca was chortling to himself and couldn't bring himself to stop. Mattia looked at his companion with a disconcerted look which brought Luca back to earth. He looked at his young cell mate with deep concern.

"I am so sorry, Mattia. I'm not sure how you will ever put behind you the abuse you must have suffered. For now, we must both be strong – and fight as best we can. We will make sure you are not subjected to any more degradation."

"The really scary thing is that I have almost grown to accept it as normal," stuttered Mattia, his eyes cast down to the floor.

Luca had to change the atmosphere of horror created by Mattia's words. Instead, he told Mattia in great detail what had happened to him since his arrival, including his relationship with Giorgia and Marco. The only thing he omitted was his meeting with Elpidio Pugliese. Mattia actually showed signs of unrestrained amusement as Luca told him about Luigi's snakes – and admiration when he related his rescue of Marianne.

"She was really good to me," whispered Mattia.

"The worst aspect of my meeting upstairs," continued Luca ,"was her revelation that Giorgia had seduced me under her orders. I was on the brink of despair by the time I was put back in this hole…"

"That's what she does, Luca. She is entirely convincing. That is the nature of her evil…her witchcraft. You must believe me. She was almost certainly lying about everything – yes, including the length of time you have been here. Be reassured, Luca!"

It was *he* who was being consoled by his young cell mate, thought Luca struck by the irony of the role reversal.

It was midnight – thank heaven for his watch – before Mattia crawled back with difficulty into his own cell. They resolved to keep a careful check on the amount of time that elapsed between each 'visit' from the floor above over the next few days. Luca was already devising a scheme to avoid Mattia being subjected to the reign of sexual tyranny he had had to endure. He could do nothing about what was happening in the real world. He had to maintain his faith in the fact that Giacomo Mainardi would realise he was in trouble. He sighed a deep sigh and lay down on his bed, exhausted by the day's events.

One thought kept returning as he mulled over what Mattia had told him.

The *fattucchiera* must be Luigi's father – not his mother. There had been some subtle element that had seemed out of place when he was with 'Margherita' – an anomaly he had not been able to put his finger on at the time.

* * *

Apart from their nightly scheduled visit to the shower and bathroom, Luca and Mattia calculated they had been left alone for three whole days. An unusually long time commented Mattia. The only event that cheered Luca up was when he had banged loudly on his door whilst shouting that he needed to go to the *bagno**. The man called Fortunato arrived after about ten minutes and ushered Luca to the toilet. When Luca re-emerged, Fortunato spoke to him.

"I'm sorry it took so long for me to reach you, *Signor* Fontana. I'll be listening out for you in future."

The words were spoken by a man who looked genuinely contrite.

Luca took a risk – any ally in the camp, however wary, needed to be encouraged.

"Thank you for your kindness, Fortunato. When we are free again, I shall put in a good word for you. That is a promise."

Luca placed a reassuring hand on the man's shoulder.

"You shouldn't be put through this ordeal," the man whispered – in more or less good Italian.

Luca and Mattia thought it would be best to err on the side of caution. They agreed that Mattia should only crawl into Luca's cell after their nightly 'official' visit to the bathroom. Luca had jokingly suggested he should enlarge the hole in the wall so he could reciprocate. He also pondered how he could get rid of the broken plaster in his portable toilet. Pouring it all into the almost defunct lavatory bowl might simply block it completely – and set alarm bells ringing.

Between lengthy periods of silence, they told and retold each other their life stories – embellishing the narratives each time. At Mattia's suggestion, they played mental chess. The games never extended beyond ten moves because Luca lost track each time round about the eleventh move. Mattia seemed to be able to visualise the layout of the chess board with no effort. In the end, Luca admitted defeat and bowed to his companion's superior mental aptitude. They played word games instead - at which they were more equally matched.

It must have been on the fourth day when the routine they had been obliged to follow was finally interrupted, just as the feeling of renewed despair was beginning to take hold of them. It was Luca whom Luigi and a subtly altered Fortunato came to escort upstairs. Even Luigi seemed less down-trodden. Luca could never have prepared himself for what was about to transpire during his second meeting with 'Margherita'.

That alien smell again! The ritual of Luigi Bonifaccio knocking three times on the door to his 'mother's' vast apartment – as if it was the traditional prelude to some dramatic French stage performance.* An apt analogy, thought Luca. Once again, the matriarchal voice calling out the word *"Avanti".*

Despite his best efforts to remain detached, Luca's face must have revealed his astonishment. Margherita's raven black hair had been tied tightly back and up on the top of her head. Her olive skin and dark eyes positively glowed. She had a beautifully shaped face. She was wearing a different, even tighter-fitting black outfit which emphasised the ample curves of a younger woman's body. Luca had to make a supreme effort to remain impervious to the alluring figure before him, which needed no help in creating its seductive appeal.

"Buongiorno, Signor Luca," said the female voice with a sexually appealing catch to it coming from deep within her throat.

Margherita was smiling at him, challenging him to continue staring. Luca's brain was, despite the temptation to stare, working overtime. She must have known somehow with an acute grasp of human foibles that Mattia might have revealed her secret to Luca. This magnificent show

211

was her means of reasserting her persona. Luca could only admire the effect – not entirely dispassionately. This was the true nature of her witchcraft, he admitted silently.

"*Lei sembra bellissima,* * *Margherita,*" said Luca as coolly as he could.

The smile vanished from the face of this modern day *fattucchiera,* to be replaced by something softer and sadder. Luca had chosen his words with consummate skill: "You *seem* truly beautiful, Margherita."

Luca had to suppress the treacherous thought which had come to mind that young Mattia might not have been so unfortunate after all. He cleared his mind of this destructive falsehood. Margherita was a dangerous woman who could transform into a harsher, malevolent being within the space of half a second.

The *fattucchiera* had regained her poise with devilish speed. Luca was sure she had grown in stature since his entering the room. Somehow, she could create this illusion – as if by magic.

"Sit down, Luca," she said patting the four seater sofa invitingly. It would be churlish to refuse, he considered, taking his place but leaving a gap between them. He instinctively sensed that the true purpose of the invitation was about to be revealed. He steeled his mind in readiness.

"Today we are celebrating, Luca," she said softly.

Luca remained silent, waiting for the inevitable change of tone and the words which would be designed to crush his spirit again.

"You will be glad to know that we have recaptured your little friend Marianne. She is safely back in Collemaga now – so she can continue to do what she does best."

The jolt that went through Luca's body at these entirely unexpected words must have been visible to the observant eyes of 'Margherita'. She was leering at him in a

212

way which distorted her whole face. Then seeing Luca's shocked features, she began to laugh – a laugh that turned into an ugly cackle. It gave Luca the will power necessary to react.

It was *la fattucchiera's* turn to be shocked. Luca had dared to stand up and was towering over her.

"I do not believe you, Margherita."

She relaxed and looked at Luca insolently.

"We discovered her very easily in that trattoria called *La Buona Forchetta,* Luca. She took the kids to school and on the way back we forced her into the car kicking and screaming. Luigi had to quieten her down with one of his injections. What a pity all your puerile heroics have been a total waste of time!"

Luca had his emotions under control in a trice. He was looking at her in sorrow.

"I pity you, Margherita, truly I do!"

At the mention of the word 'pity', she bridled and made as if to stand up.

"Sit down, please," said Luca quietly, almost kindly. "I haven't quite finished. I pity you that you can take so much pleasure in causing pain to others. Look at you – you could be walking along the catwalk in any fashion parade in the world..."

Luca's voice was hypnotic.

"And yet you take pleasure in satisfying your lust on an innocent boy, time after time. Yes, Mattia has told me what happens each time you summon him upstairs and taunt him with false promises about seeing his little sister again. Have you no fear of divine retribution at some point in the future?"

She laughed in his face.

"You mean from that parish priest? From your god?" she mocked him for the triteness of his words.

"Your god has deserted this world! I obey a much more powerful lord than you can ever conjure up in your puny mind, *Signor* Luca."

"You mean... Satan, I presume?"

"Call it what you like, little man. It has no earthly name!"

Time to plunge the knife in, thought Luca. There was no point in playing out this war of attrition any longer.

"*Margherita,* do you claim that Luigi is Satan's son? Or is it not more accurate to say that *you* are Luigi's biological father?"

La Fattucchiera rose up from the chair. She had done it again, Luca registered in his mind. How did she manage to give the impression of 'floating' up? It defied logic – and gravity!

Her face – almost level with his – was horribly contorted. Her body was undergoing a series of convulsions beneath the tight-fitting black dress. Luca had the overwhelming sensation that something - or someone - was trying to escape from within. There was that odour of rotting leaves again – stronger than before. But it was the metamorphosis of the voice which terrified him most. A raucous male voice issued from her throat issuing curses in another tongue altogether.

He looked at the writhing form before him and uttered the words:

"I am sorry, Margherita," as he turned away and headed for the door. The words had almost stuck in his throat out of uncontrollable emotion – one of pity, however misplaced it might be.

* * *

Of his escorts, there had been no sign. So Luca trod the now familiar descent back to his cell. With something resembling a sense of freedom, he decided to walk up the steep stone staircase which seemed to lead towards daylight. He gingerly pushed open one slat of the door at the top. He had been correct in his assumption that the escape route led 'nowhere' – save to certain extinction on the rocks below where the river flowed lazily by.

His cell door was not locked – evidently Luigi had not considered it necessary. He must have assumed that the audience with his 'mother' would have taken much longer. Luca wondered whether Luigi was aware of his mother's true sexuality. Probably not, he reckoned. Luca went into his cell and lay down on the bed. He felt drained of energy. He must have unconsciously let out a deep sigh.

"Luca? Why are you back so soon?" asked Mattia in concern. "Has something gone wrong?"

"In a sense, yes, I suppose it has. If my interpretation of events is accurate, I fear *she* will seek to take out her wrath on you – very soon. I think you should come through into my room pretty soon."

Luca's assessment of *la fattucchiera's* reaction was proved to be correct in every respect. He did not even have time to relate the details of his latest encounter to Mattia. In fact, the voice of Margherita could be heard shrieking out orders to Luigi to fetch that 'puny little wimp' up from his cell immediately.

Mattia had turned as white as a sheet.

"Under the bed, Mattia! And make sure you don't sneeze!"

This injunction to his new *protégé* was not an idle one – Mattia, allergic to something in this dark place, had frequent sneezing fits in the night.

Luca lay down on his bed – determined to appear nonchalant when, inevitably, Luigi would open *his* cell door after he had discovered that Mattia was missing.

He heard Luigi's sniggering, coaxing voice saying: "Time to go upstairs again, Mattia. *Mamma* is so anxious for your company this evening."

Mattia was shivering – even from the relative protection given by Luca and his bed.

They heard Luigi unlocking the door to Mattia's cell.

"Cazzo! Che diavolo sta succedendo…?* Cazzo, cazzo, cazzo," swore *Il Porco* at this unforeseen crisis. His voice was trembling with shock. Just as Luca had predicted, Luigi came out and tried to unlock Luca's cell door. He could not at first work out why nothing appeared to be happening. As soon as he realised that the door was not locked, he began swearing all over again – absolute panic in his voice.

"No, Luigi, you fool! You left it unlocked when you took Luca upstairs earlier on…" Luca could hear Luigi comically reasoning with himself. "But *mamma* got shot of Luca only a few minutes ago…"

Luigi swung open the cell door violently so that it crashed into the rocky wall of the cave. In the light coming from the corridor, he could see the prone figure of his second prisoner on the bed.

"Where's Mattia?" he snarled at Luca.

"You mean he has vanished, Luigi? Sounds like a bit of black magic to me," chuckled Luca. "Maybe he didn't want to see your *mamma* again. Maybe he heard her ravings upstairs. Did you look under his bed by any chance?"

It was a bit of a risk suggesting this to Luigi – but Luca and Mattia had tested to see if the bedding, which partly overlapped their hole in the wall, was enough to hide the result of their labours in the dim light available.

Luigi had obviously not considered this possibility and hurried back in a panic to look under the bed, leaving Luca's door open.

A kind of strangulated cry emerged from Luigi. A brief probe with one hand passing to-and-fro under the bed told him his prisoner was not there. But he had not locked the cell door before going into Luca's cell. It was obvious! Mattia had escaped and was roaming about the house. Luca got up and stood in the corridor, with every hope of rubbing more salt in the wound. He found Luigi standing at the foot of the suicide stair-well, staring up with horror at the half open door. Now he was too shocked even to swear.

"Oh dear!" taunted Luca. "You really are in trouble! Your *mamma* is going to be really mad at you now!"

Luca had the overwhelming sense of satisfaction of hearing Luigi run around on the floor above calling out *'mamma'* in a terrified voice. Luca wondered what kind of punishment would be exacted. He returned to his cell. Mattia was still cowering under the bed.

"You're safe to come out now, Mattia. Luigi thinks you jumped out into the void and killed yourself in desperation. It'll keep them busy for ages."

Luca realised he must have left the door open by mistake when he took a look up the 'suicide' staircase. What a fortuitous oversight on his part!

The two of them listened enthralled to the hysterics and the angry voice of the frustrated sorceress berating her 'stupid and incompetent' son – accompanied by the pitiful pleading on Luigi's part. He even tried to shift the blame on to his mother for letting Luca go without telling him. That silenced her for all of five seconds as she remembered her total humiliation as Luca had dismissed himself from her presence of his own accord.

Hours passed without anything happening. Things had settled down upstairs. It was well past their 'ablutions' time, but it dawned belatedly on them both that they were free to see to themselves since their cell doors had been left unlocked in the confusion. Luca took the opportunity of emptying his portable toilet of its content of plaster at the far end of the bathroom, which was shrouded in darkness.

"My guess is, Mattia, that Luigi and someone else have been sent down to the river to retrieve your body! They'll be looking for a long time – it must be dark by now," he said looking at his watch.

"We should behave like model prisoners, I suppose," said Mattia thoughtfully. "When they come back down again, they'll be amazed to find us both in our own cells, as good as gold."

Luca looked admiringly at his fellow prisoner.

"Well done, Mattia. You're right! But do you mind going back to your cell? Aren't you scared of…?

"I don't know – yes, a bit scared. But I feel that something has changed. It's hard to explain. I don't feel frightened of *her* any longer."

"*Bravo,* Mattia! *Bravissimo!*" said Luca hugging his companion warmly. "We're winning, aren't we!"

If the sentiment expressed by Luca was a statement of his most optimistic hopes, it soon turned into something far more concrete.

There was a discreet knock on his door and the gentler voice of Fortunato whispered:

"There's somebody here who wants to see you Luca. Are you decent?"

Mattia dived under the bed again – despite his claim to have lost his fear of the inhabitants of this weird dwelling.

"Door's not locked, Fortunato," he said amiably.

He looked up to smile at the man whom he was expecting to see framed in the doorway.

Before Luca could register his astonishment, he found Marianne rushing into his arms with a joyous smile on her face.

"Oh Luca! I'm so glad you're safe. I haven't stopped thinking about you since you left me with that lovely family."

Luca was repressing tears of pure joy.

"But you're their prisoner again, Marianne. I was told they found out where you were hiding and dragged you back here again..."

The look on Marianne's face showed total incredulity.

"Luca, who told you that? No, you don't have to tell me... I can guess who told you. *Écoute, mon cher Luca.* I came back of my own free will to help rescue you. Giorgia brought me back with her from Pontefalco in her car."

The lump in Luca's throat prevented him from asking Marianne what he was so anxious to know. Before he found his voice, Marianne was speaking, with a hint of curiosity in her voice. She had just spotted a pair of feet jutting out from beneath Luca's bed.

"Oh, that's Mattia – he's hiding under my bed. We thought you were someone else, Marianne."

Luca heard the magic sound of rippling laughter for the first time in days. Mattia emerged from his hiding place, looking sheepish. He smiled at Marianne – and shook her hand formally.

"Go on, Mattia!" said Luca. "Give her a proper *abbraccio** for heaven's sake!"

"I had better go now, Luca," said Marianne. "Fortunato let me into the house and brought me down here. I need to get out of the house before anyone finds me here. *Il Porco* knows I'm back in Collemaga and he'll try to get me back

219

working for him. I told him I came back because I missed him so much," she said laughing. "I told him I suddenly had to go to the hospital in Pontefalco because I had some 'woman's problem' which needed medical attention."

Marianne stood on tiptoe and kissed Luca for one warm, wet, electric second on his mouth before heading for the door.

She turned round at the last minute and said:

"By the way, Luca, the police are arriving in force at dawn tomorrow morning -with your friend Giacomo too. The pope with one of his cardinals is already here staying with Don Sandonato at the presbytery..."

"The pope...?" began Luca in total mystification. But Marianne had vanished down the corridor, accompanied by a grinning Fortunato.

19: There's no such thing as witchcraft...

"And before you ask, Mattia, I have absolutely no idea why the pope should be here in Collemaga. But I guess his presence can only be a positive force."

"I was only going to say, Luca, that I would bet you €100 that the cardinal who is accompanying him is Monsignor Romani."

Luca was mindful that the one bet which he had lost to Mattia was over their first game of mental chess.

"I shan't make the mistake of making bets with *you* again, Mattia – without being very sure of my ground. Why do you think the pope would select this cardinal…?"

"He specialises in exorcism. He's famous for it."

"Mattia – you are a very interesting young man. You will go far, I am sure. Now – more immediately, how are we going to celebrate our rescue tonight?"

"Do you believe that Marianne is in a position to know what she was talking about, Luca?"

Mattia was desperately wanting to believe their salvation was imminent but he had received so many blows to his hopes of freedom that he did not dare to put too much faith in Marianne's words.

"Yes, I am sure, Mattia. I just about managed to contact the outside world before I was abducted – mainly my friend Giacomo who works in your building at the Ministry. I am now almost certain that our *fattucchiera* has fed me lies since I have been here…"

"Well, I told you that all along, Luca. But can we really believe…?"

"A prostitute, do you mean, Mattia?" asked Luca sternly.

Mattia was silent. In the end he just said: "Sorry Luca. I didn't mean…"

"Come on. I know what we can do to celebrate," Luca interrupted his young friend.

Luca pulled the bed from the wall and aimed two or three massive kicks at the plaster wall. Most of it collapsed under the violent attack.

"There, Mattia. Now we have a suite of rooms for our last evening here," he declared. They were both covered with white dust from the plaster.

"I'm hungry," said Mattia.

Luca glanced at his watch. It was well after the time when Luigi and Fortunato usually descended to the basement.

"Maybe they are still down near the river looking for your body."

Mattia was silent. He was thinking of the time when Luigi had taunted him to climb the stairs to 'freedom'. He remembered all too vividly how it was only his cowardice which had prevented him from launching himself into that dizzying void. He had not told Luca about that incident.

Luca was very sensitive to other people's reactions. He half guessed that a painful memory had been evoked by his words from the way that Mattia's body had appeared to freeze momentarily.

"Well, Mattia, do you know where the kitchens are?"

Mattia nodded.

"Why don't you go up and see if Marta can give us something to eat? There's just one more little precaution I want to take while the coast seems to be clear."

"What? On my own, Luca?" stammered a not so brave Mattia.

"*Dai, Mattia!** You might run into Fortunato. He's not a threat. Remember you told me you were no longer afraid of anyone in this house."

222

Mattia was regretting his rash declaration of courage, but he could think of no convincing argument not to carry out his mission. He smiled guiltily at his saviour – and walked along the corridor towards the stairs under his own steam.

"He really must be hungry!" thought Luca to himself as he headed off to the bathroom. He picked up some bits of plaster and stuck them into a plastic mug that must have been intended for the use of the 'guests'. He mixed the broken bits of plaster into a thick paste and headed back towards his cell. It took him only a minute to plug the key hole full of plaster and pray that it would solidify quickly enough.

Mattia stepped unopposed into the kitchen where he found Marta spooning pasta into a single bowl. He stood rooted to the spot. His pallid, plaster covered countenance produced a look of abject horror on the girl's face as she slopped the next spoonful on to the floor with a scream of terror.

"You're supposed to be dead! If this is your ghost, please believe me, Mattia, I never wanted to cook that awful food for you..." she squealed in alarm.

It must have been the first time in weeks that Mattia had smiled, his gaunt features lighting up for a few life-restoring seconds.

"So they really do think I'm dead, do they? How wonderful!" he said to Marta. "But we are *both* alive – and starving!"

"I'm sorry I panicked just now – I thought you must have passed through your cell door in spirit form. *O Dio mio – come sono stupida!**" she declared.

"Well, ghosts don't need food, Marta – not as far as I know!"

Mattia took the bowl of food and two forks downstairs where they shared the contents between them.

"I'm still hungry, Luca," said Mattia.

* * *

The 'search party' eventually returned from the valley below in ugly mood, judging by the acerbic comments that the sorceress was hurling at her son and her entourage; several obsequious voices were heard offering their abject apologies for the failure of their mission, mixed in with feeble protests from the bolder members of the household trying to assert that Mattia's demise had been totally beyond *their* control. The voices which dared to object seemed to be coming from much younger people. Luca shot a questioning glance at Mattia.

"It's her staff, Luca. She employs – or rather subjugates - two or three young post-graduates to do internet research for her. They usually dig up information on anyone, including you and me, Luca... That's what I have gathered over the months I've been here."

The arguments were still raging up above. Silence fell abruptly as a chorus of two male voices, one baritone and one tenor could be heard from the floor below singing in tune to *Fratelli d'Italia*: "WE WANT OUR FOOD! WE WANT A SHOWER! Plus a few other ingenious lines, until the final melody had resolved itself back into the home key - when the two singers managed to finish almost in harmony.

When the singing had stopped, Luca and Mattia heard a few titters from what he supposed was the admin staff, followed by the broken male voice of *la fattucchiera* – this change in voice seemed to be triggered whenever her *persona* was challenged, Luca had worked out.

"Go down and see what's going on, Luigi. And after that, go and fetch me that girl, Marianne. I'll have *her* tonight instead."

"But *mamma* – she won't come. She's being protected by..."

"Get her, you little worm, or I'll have *you* cast on to the rocks below. *Sono chiara...chiaro...chiara...chiaro?*"* Margherita's voice seemed to have become stuck in a groove.

Mattia looked quizzically at Luca.

"She seems to be having some kind of sexual identity crisis, Luca."

"I think this conflict is at the heart of her dilemma, Mattia. Come on! Let's put on a final show for Luigi.

Luigi Bonifaccio found Mattia lying on his bed, looking at him scornfully. His new self-confidence was alarming but *Il Porco* would soon change all that! But he could not prevent himself from asking Mattia the obvious question.

"Just a bit of black magic, Luigi. It's not just your mother who can play tricks like that, you know."

Il Porco snarled at him, went out into the corridor and locked his cell door. Mattia felt an involuntary stab of fear returning at the sound of the key in the lock, which signified that he was back in captivity. He was unaware that Luca had taken precautions against such an eventuality. He did not have time to dwell on his dilemma before Luca was in his cell.

"Go and lie down on my bed, Mattia. That will faze him out completely."

The exchange of places was affected within ten seconds while Luigi was attempting to fathom out why he could not insert the key in the lock to Luca's cell. It took him a confused sixty seconds to work out that the lock had been sabotaged.

"Cazzo!" shouted Luigi, reverting to the vernacular, which was always present just below the surface. His reaction on seeing Mattia on the bed inside Luca's cell reduced him to a state of quivering fear. He knelt down on the hard stone floor and wailed a fearful lament. Mattia could not resist taking his revenge for weeks of subjugation at the hands of this individual.

"Now *that* is real magic, isn't it, Luigi. I can pass through walls."

But the ever sensitive Luca, was feeling pity towards the Sleazeball. His humanity prevailed – after all, Luca reasoned, his freedom would be over in a few hours and his version of events would form part of the case against his mother.

Luca helped Luigi gently to his feet and showed him the hole in the wall.

"We needed each other's company, Luigi. There's no magic involved."

Luigi staggered to his feet and walked unsteadily towards the door which he could not lock.

There were no audible recriminations from the floor above. Margherita must have retired to some inner sanctum. But after a few minutes, Fortunato appeared at their door.

"I've been told to keep an eye on you both to make sure you don't escape. Don't worry - I'll let in the cavalry tomorrow morning. You two can get some sleep."

"You are our *angelo custode,** Fortunato," said Luca hugging the man who had had the courage to defy *la fattucchiera.* Luca left him sitting on a wooden chair which he had brought down with him and lay down on his bed. His final waking thoughts before his exhausted body took over was a silent prayer that Marianne was out of reach of Margherita – just this one last time, please, said Luca

226

directing the prayer to his own version of the unseen powers which encompass human life.

* * *

The sound of the rescue party arriving at dawn was impossible to sleep through. A banging of something solid against the outer door of the house was accompanied by the sound of a male voice calling out in stentorian tones:

POLIZIA – APRITE LA PORTA!

Luca and Mattia were alert in an instant. But the first sound they heard after the barked order to open the door was a cry of agony from above.

Luca looked at Mattia.

"Fortunato!" stated Luca fearfully.

The men ran upstairs and reached the hallway above to see Fortunato doubled up in pain with his hand over his heart. *La fattucchiera* was standing in the hall with an accusatory finger jabbing in Fortunato's direction. It looked for all the worlds as if she had just uttered a curse directed at the man gasping for breath on the floor at her feet. Luca ignored Margherita and crouched down next to Fortunato.

"Fortunato... what has she done to you?"

He was shaking his head while grimacing with pain.

"Door...electrified. My heart...weak..."

Luca leapt to his feet and glared at Margherita, who was still dressed in her daytime clothes despite the hour. She was staring at Luca with a look of unadulterated hatred in her eyes.

Luca ignored her and banged on the door, careful not to touch the metal door handle.

"The door's electrified. Man down! We need an ambulance!"

He could just make out male voices talking in muted tones on the other side of the massive wooden door. Then Luca heard a voice which changed everything.

"Luca, is that you?" said a voice which he instantly recognised.

"Giacomo! Thank God!"

"There's an ambulance outside. We feared someone might be in need of help..."

Luca could hear more voices. Someone in authority said:

"This is no time for discussion. Just do it!

"Make sure everyone is standing well clear of the door, Luca," said the voice of Giacomo.

Luca and Mattia gently moved Fortunato, still clutching his heart and looking petrified at the proximity of death.

And then their world was transformed as the double doors flew open, crashing into the wall.

The first people through the door were two ambulance crew carrying medical apparatus. They wasted no time before giving life support to the man on the ground, gently asking Fortunato for his name and speaking reassuring words to him as they treated him.

Next to enter were three burly *carabinieri* officers who quickly pursued the vanishing figure of Margherita – who seemed to be floating down the corridor away from them.

"It must be hypnotism – or something. She really is a remarkable woman," he was thinking. Any further conjecture was cut short by the sight of Giacomo stepping over the threshold. Luca simply hugged his friend in wordless gratitude. Giacomo then turned to Mattia, who was still staring at what was happening, unable to come to terms with the reality that his months' long ordeal was over.

"Welcome back to the normal world Mattia," said Giacomo. "Here's my phone. You should call your parents immediately. They know nothing about this rescue mission – we didn't dare raise false hopes beforehand.

"I...I... can't remember our phone number," stuttered Mattia.

Giacomo had added Mattia's home number to his phone. He selected the number for him and passed the phone to him as soon as the ring tone sounded.

The hysterical and disbelieving sound of a woman's voice was clear for all to hear. Mattia took his phone outside – his first steps towards freedom into the still dark streets of Collemaga. He was brought to a halt in shock - whilst his mother's voice continued unabated - simply because he appeared to be walking towards the instantly recognisable figure of *Papa Benedetto*, accompanied by his cardinal. They were both dressed in ordinary cassocks.

Pope Benedict smiled that warm and reassuring smile at Mattia, touched his arm gently and stepped inside the house of *la fattucchiera,* making the sign of the cross.

Luca was recovering his composure as the two ambulance crew accompanied Fortunato gently outside supporting him either side as they walked him towards the waiting vehicle.

"We'll take him to the hospital in Pontefalcone and then we'll be back, *signore."* The words were addressed to Luca.

"Giacomo, I don't know how to thank you enough..." began Luca.

His friend merely shook his head to indicate he did not need thanks.

"All my other friends call me Mino,* Luca. I think you should do the same from now on."

"Mino," began Luca, "there's just one question I need to ask you," said Luca – who was looking guilty for reasons which Giacomo failed to grasp.

"Who was it who first contacted you to tell you I had been abducted?"

Giacomo was taken aback – quite unaware of the underlying fear behind his friend's question.

"Your lady friend Giorgia, of course! Who else would it have been? She has been beside herself with grief. She's been phoning me at least three times a day badgering me for news about your rescue. Why do ask, Luca?"

Luca couldn't answer, because he had begun to shed tears of relief and joy. When he had recovered sufficiently, he smiled apologetically.

"Just never tell Giorgia that I asked you that question, Mino," Luca pleaded.

Giacomo shrugged his shoulders.

"Why should I tell her, Luca? I don't know what you're talking about."

Mattia came back in to the house, gratefully returning Giacomo's mobile phone. Three more policemen appeared from outside somewhere. But they belonged to the *Guardia di Finanza** to Luca and Mattia's surprise. They really were taking things seriously. Introductions were made all round.

"We will interview you first, Mattia – just to get a preliminary statement from you. You have become a very important person for us," smiled the senior officer. "Later on, we shall be taking you home to Rome with us – if you can wait just another few hours."

Mattia nodded. Now that he was free and his baby sister knew he was safe, he wanted to stay and be part of the action. He wanted to absorb some more of the beginnings of self-confidence he had begun to acquire because of his contact with Luca.

"What about Giorgia, Mino? Is she at home?"

"Yes, on the edge of her seat. Marianne is with her. The police wouldn't let them come here before you had been rescued. It might have been dangerous – especially as that amazing little kid Marco would have insisted on coming too. He kept going on about how you would want to see Pinocchio again."

Mio Dio! The tears again that had to be kept under control! Business first! The tumultuous day ahead had one more major shock awaiting them all – before Luca would see Giorgia again.

* * *

The morning proceeded in a state of organised confusion. Occasionally, the police officers from Rome would consult with Luca, sometimes with Mattia. Giacomo seemed to be hovering about equally at a loss as to what to do. By eight o'clock, three police officers from L'Aquila arrived. The local police had been summonsed out of 'courtesy' following the correct procedure, which stipulated that any crime committed on their patch entitled them to be present.

"Expect some local cops to arrive," the *Guardia di Finanza* officers from Rome had informed the *carabiniere* officer who had been put on guard duty by the now wide open – and electrically disabled - front door. "We could do with some more feet on the ground."

The local police arrived – a team of three young officers, who had introduced themselves to the three men hanging around in the hallway as Officers Oriana Salvati, Giovanni Palena and Simona Gambino – of whom the latter was constantly being told by casual observers that she reminded them of some famous Italian actress.*

The new arrivals were introduced to the *carabiniere* colonel in charge of the operation.

"I would be grateful if you two ladies would look after our main suspect – but be wary! She is a very artful woman who has already used her feminine charms on my men to try and slip away out of our grasp. Accompany her wherever she goes. She's very manipulative. She claims to be the local sorceress. And I'm inclined to believe that is not so far from the truth."

"Where is she now, *colonnello?*" enquired the officer called Oriana Salvati.

"Talking to Pope Benedetto – and no, Officer Salvati," stated the colonel, seeing the expression of fury on the young police woman's face which was plainly intended to convey that she had not travelled all this way merely to put up with vacuous jests from some fancy senior male officer from Rome.

"I am not being facetious, but it's too long to explain," said the colonel from Rome with an amicable grin directed at Oriana Salvati. "So far, His Holiness – who is trying to make our sorceress understand she is on the path to eternal damnation – is the only one present whom our suspect seems to be in the least bit in awe of."

"The *colonnello* is right, Officer Salvati," Luca joined in. "She can mesmerise the unwary. She's as slippery as a serpent. I've had dealings with her over the last few days."

Luca had taken an immediate liking to the three officers from L'Aquila who had arrived out of the blue – and addressed him as if *he* had been in charge of proceedings, despite the fact he must have looked like a neglected scarecrow.

Luca was becoming increasingly aware that he was in need of a change of clothing – and he suspected that Mattia was feeling the same. Mattia still had nothing on his feet except a pair of worn socks. Luca knew that the officers who had arrived from Rome – and even his friend Giacomo – ran the risk of underestimating *la fattucchiera*. He needed to be on site in case of an emergency. Luca had the instinctive feeling that *Margherita* would attempt to evade capture and prison, by magic or by trickery, before the day was out. Only Giacomo was free to go back to Giorgia's house and rescue some spare clothes.

"Of course I'll go, Luca! What message should I give Giorgia from you?" asked Giacomo pointedly.

"Tell her I can't wait till I'm in her arms again, Mino. But that I shall need a shower beforehand."

"That will have to do, I suppose," said Giacomo good-humouredly.

* * *

Some forty minutes later, Luca and Mattia were more or less showered and presentable again. They had reluctantly used their sordid shower and bathroom one last time. Luca had paused at the foot of that steep staircase which led to open space. Something was different. Luca had to work out what it was for a second. No doors – or they had been pushed open wide. Rays of sunlight were streaming in through the aperture. Luca frowned deeply. Mattia was looking at him, puzzled, but did not say what, if anything, he thought it might signify.

When they rejoined Giacomo upstairs – still standing around waiting to be told if they were needed or not – Luca was feeling alert and presentable enough to ask a question which had been nagging him all morning.

"Can you explain how on earth the pope ended up here, Mino?"

Giacomo replied that he was almost as completely in the dark as Luca.

"My boss received the call from the Vatican while we were locked in discussion as to whether the State could spare the human resources needed to effect your rescue. The intervention of the Pope – in person – was a turning point which finally mobilised the mission to rescue you two. That's all I know, I'm afraid."

Luca was looking very thoughtful. He had an image of a very old priest who had stood his ground when faced with the 'chariot of dragon fire' on the *piazza* that evening so many days ago.

"Is it possible...?" Luca thought to himself.

Now he had recovered his dignity and a few clothes which did not smell, Luca remarked on the fact that there had been no sight or sound of one Luigi Bonifaccio throughout the morning. It was already nearly noon.

The obvious person to ask was the *carabiniere* officer on guard by the main door. He shook his head and phoned his senior officer, who instantly emerged from *la fattucchiera's* suite, which had out of necessity become the interrogation room.

"There is one room upstairs which was securely locked. The officers assumed it was a store room after they had banged on the door to no effect," explained the senior officer.

Luca's description of *Il Porco* rang no bells.

"We certainly haven't met anyone fitting that description," added the officer.

"He's the sorceress's son – or so we understand, *colonnello.*"

Luigi was finally unearthed lurking in the room in question. The police officers could not believe what they saw when the door was finally opened by Luigi himself. It was seething with snakes of different species in glass tanks. The whole set-up looked just like a laboratory. But the reason why the officers could not immediately apprehend Luigi Bonifaccio was because he was crawling with vipers. No one of the officers was willing to approach him.

Luca sighed. Reluctantly, he offered to go upstairs – to a part of the house he had never realised existed. On seeing Luca, Luigi's face underwent a transformation. He looked almost contrite. Here was *that* man who had no fear of him or his snakes. He knew he had met his match.

"Come on Luigi, let's put your pets back in their tank, shall we? You are needed downstairs to be with your mother."

Luca had gritted his teeth and picked up one of the docile reptiles from Luigi's shoulder. After all, he had been reliably informed that the snakes' venom had been extracted.

Luigi went downstairs with Luca like a lamb to the slaughter. All he said on the way downstairs were a few words in dialect.

"You *are* brave, Luca. I hadn't milked those snakes yet."

* * *

The two officers from the *Guardia di Finanza* had summoned Luca and Mattia into Margherita's suite. The whole household had been accommodated there, including some young people whom Luca had never seen before. *La fattucchiera* was sitting at the head of her huge dining table, looking the picture of contrition and obedience. She even smiled sweetly in Luca's direction.

"*Signor* Fontana...Luca – how many of these people do you consider we can safely let go? On the understanding, of

235

course, that they must remain available for questioning at a later date."

The three young people, two men and a girl, had been discovered in an ultra-modern computer studio. They looked relieved and petrified in equal measure. They must have been Margherita's 'research' team.

"Are you all local people?" asked Luca of the three nervous individuals.

Two nodded and the girl shook her head.

"We'll answer all your questions whenever you want, *generale,*" the girl said. "But it might take a very long time. We have been held here as virtual prisoners. We cannot tell you how relieved we feel to be freed at last. We will gladly cooperate."

Their contact details were rapidly communicated and the three young people were told to go home.

"And this is Martha, our cook," explained Luca. "She is completely blameless in all this fiasco. I might suggest you free her immediately so she can prepare lunch for everyone."

Marta glowed with pleasure and nodded in agreement.

There was one rather plump looking girl left – she was obviously of North African descent. Of course – it must be Fatima, Marianne's 'companion'. Luca had never seen her close up and face to face.

"I think it quite safe to let Fatima go for now," said Luca. "She has been more sinned against than sinning. But I think she will need to be cared for until she decides what she wants to do with her life."

Luca looked at Luigi Bonifaccio and said:

"She has been rather dependent on this individual - and I am quite sure it is not safe to let *him* loose just yet. He will have a great deal to tell you."

Margherita was still sitting at the head of the table, looking serene and repentant.

"L'apparenza inganna!" thought Luca. Appearances were indeed deceptive whenever *she* was involved.

* * *

By four o'clock that afternoon, the number of people being detained in the house had been reduced to one single individual – Margherita. She had disturbingly remained perfectly amenable towards her captors. She had adopted a kind of surprised innocence that she should have so unexpectedly found herself in her present predicament.

The two *Guardia di Finanza* officials had saved up their formal interrogation of the 'sorceress' until last. The senior of the two officers had explained to Mattia that they would be obliged to take Margherita back to Rome that night.

"We shall have to come back to Collemaga and pick up all the physical evidence of her financial misdeeds in a day or so's time, Mattia. You may not feel like sharing a car with the lady concerned. I gather you have been...eh...severely maltreated since your incarceration."

"Yes, officer," replied Mattia, "you are right. And my parents have already offered to come and fetch me tomorrow. But, I thank you all the same for your kind offer."

Now, for Luca, the grand finale was about to take place. Present round the big table, where Luca had sat and shared her food several days earlier, were the two lady police officers from L'Aquila – the third officer was taking his turn to rest for the next hour – Luca and *La Fattucchiera* herself. She was still dressed in her tight-fitting black outfit, which the two *Guardia* officials were studiously ignoring as best they could.

Since midday, events had proved to be both rewarding and revealing for Luca, who had been growing impatient as the prospect of an early reunion with Giorgia and Marco receded.

At lunchtime, which had of necessity been carried out in three separate sittings, Luca found himself in the presence of Pope Benedetto. His initial embarrassment evaporated within the first few seconds. The pope seemed to be enjoying Marta's cooking and smiled appreciatively at her as soon as he had taken the first mouthful of the pasta cooked with a cheese, cauliflower and tomato sauce. He had not even bothered to say grace. There was just nothing formal about him. Luca felt a wave of tranquillity pass through his body. Good – as opposed to evil – gave off a totally different 'scent', thought Luca – more like the smell of the ocean and sandy beaches on a warm summer's day – with a hint of the interior of old churches thrown in.

"I'm so pleased to meet you finally, Luca," began the pontiff. "I've heard so much about you from Father Sandonato. He thinks the world of you."

"Kind of him, Your Holiness, but..." began Luca.

"If you must call me anything, Luca, please just call me 'father'. My official title is just so out-of-keeping with the realities of life on Earth, don't you think?"

"Thank you, father."

"You are aware, I suppose, that Father Sandonato came to see me in Rome, aren't you?" continued the pope.

"Ah! So that's how it all happened!" exclaimed Luca, finally enlightened. They chatted about Don Sandonato for a time.

"Yes, I believe your own mayor here in Collemaga had a great deal to do with my presence here too, Luca."

So Elpidio Pugliese had played his part in the rescue too!

The pope went on to tell Luca about the ritual exorcism of the house which had been carried out in every room during the course of the morning – including a satanic chapel tucked away in one corner of the vast house.

"I hope you believe in the power of evil as well as the power of good, Luca. I would imagine you do, judging by those amazing books you have written," the pope was saying.

Luca contented himself with a look of astonishment while Pope Benedetto smiled, pleased that he had been able to catch Luca off guard.

"I will just tell you one thing which happened this morning, Luca. Your sorceress happened to be near my cardinal while he was sprinkling holy water around each room. A tiny drop of water fell on her bare arm. She jumped out of her skin at the shock. I noticed a tiny burn mark where the water had touched her. My cardinal was not surprised. It's happened before during this ceremony, he told me. It really makes one wonder, doesn't it, Luca? But I fear there is little I can do for that unfortunate woman apart from praying for her soul."

What a truly remarkable man, thought Luca as the Pope touched him on the arm and took his leave.

"We are holding a special mass of thanksgiving on Friday, Luca. I hope you will be present."

"Father, of course I will be there," promised Luca. "Actually, I forgot to ask anybody what day it is today. I have lost all sense of time."

"Just like God!" added the pope with a chuckle, as he walked with dignity out of the kitchen.

Luca was requested to go to the 'interrogation' room, where the *colonnello* was debating with himself and his colleague what to do with Luigi Bonifaccio. Luca suggested he might be accommodated in one of the two cells in the police station in Collemaga. He warned the *carabiniere colonnello* that the two local officers' allegiance to the sorceress had been stronger than their allegiance to a strict upholding of the laws of the land.

"And one of them disabled my hire car by removing a front wheel – which is probably still sitting behind the counter," explained Luca. He mentioned that the older of the two officers was closer to retirement and had 'merely gone along with the situation' in Collemaga, while he saw out his remaining time.

Luigi Bonifaccio looked alarmed at the notion of imprisonment and, in an obsequious, whiny voice, protested that he hadn't done anything wrong.

The *colonnello* listed all the offences which he had been told about by Luca – plus a few more of his own.

"How about living off immoral earnings, illegally importing poisonous snakes from foreign countries, intimidation of innocent citizens...? Shall I continue, *Signor* Bonifaccio?"

"But who will look after my snakes?" pleaded Luigi. "Can't I just continue to live in this house – like what I've always done?"

The colonnello let out a sigh as the catalogue of unforeseen obstacles mounted at every turn.

"No, Luigi, you cannot continue to live here. This property is sequestered and will probably be sold by the state to compensate for the funds illegally misappropriated by your mother."

The two local *carabinieri* arrived, looking uncomfortable – especially the one who had abducted Luca in his rubber tyre costume. With a degree of sympathy towards Luigi, the *colonnello* escorted his prisoner outside into the corridor – without handcuffing him.

"*Ciao, mamma,*" Luigi said pitifully. His 'mother' completely ignored him and went on looking detached and serene.

Outside the room, the *colonnello* addressed the two policemen sternly.

"I shall want to interview you two at a later date for the part you have played in the corruption in this town. Meanwhile you can redeem yourselves by behaving in a manner that befits our great force. Remember, *tenente,* from now on you are serving only one mistress!"

The porn-ogling *tenente,* not cerebrally gifted, stood to attention and said in dialect:

"I have only ever served one mistress, SIR!"

The *colonnello* looked at the man disdainfully.

"Yes, *tenente,* I am aware of that. The 'mistress' I am referring to is the Democratic State of Italy! Oh, and by the way, you will also replace the wheel on this gentleman's car – before nightfall."

Luigi was led off with his head hanging low.

"Grazie, colonnello – for the wheel."

"Ho fatto solo il mio dovere,* Luca."

"Well, I thank you for considering rescuing my car part of your duty. I feel sorry for Luigi," added Luca watching the sad individual being escorted away.

The *colonnello* let out another sigh - for the fragility of mankind.

* * *

Before going back into the house, Luca had a word with the two ambulance crew.

"Any news of Fortunato?" he asked them.

"Don't worry, *signore,* he will survive. We left him in good hands."

The pair were getting ready to return to Pontefalco, having been told by the *Guardia di Finanza* that there was no need for them to hang around.

That left only *la fattucchiera* – still looking dignified and submissive. She had not uttered a word or shown any sign of agitation for hours.

"What supreme and unnatural self-control," thought Luca. "She's got some scheme up her sleeve - I'm sure of it!"

He would need to summon up his last reserves of mental alertness at the end of this tumultuous day. He did not share his suspicions with the others - although Giacomo was eyeing him keenly. He had known his friend for too long not to detect the tell-tale signs.

20: A magnificent downfall...

Margherita, *la fattucchiera* was still seated nobly at the head of her table. Officers Simona Gambino and Oriana Salvati flanked their prisoner, looking ready to pounce if she made an unexpected move. Officer Giovanni Palena had returned and taken an unobtrusive seat in the corner of the room. Giacomo, Luca and the two senior financial police officers lined each side of the ceremonial dinner table. The *carabiniere* colonel was sitting further down the table, unabashedly eyeing their prisoner up and down.

A strained silence had fallen over the proceedings, which did not seem to ruffle Margherita's calm self-assuredness. Indeed, Luca detected the hint of a superior smile on the lips of their 'sorceress'.

"We will be taking you to Rome with us this evening...*signora.*" The senior *Guardia* officer seemed to be searching for an appropriate title with which to address the striking-looking woman sitting regally at the head of table.

"We will be returning here with a team of investigators to ascertain to what extent you have misappropriated public funds – and held the town of Collemaga to ransom under a regime of suspicion and suppression over the past few decades. The gravity of your crimes will guarantee that you will remain a guest of the *Guardia di Finanza* for some time to come – before your trial."

After hours of silence, Margherita spoke her first words. Luca had listened to her speaking, or cursing, in a whole gamut of voices. Right now she was addressing the *Guardia* officer in a timbre of voice which Luca had never heard before. Soft, persuasive and soothing – it was like rich dark honey dripping from a silver spoon.

"May I say, officers, that you have treated me with the greatest respect today – far more than I deserve. Would it

make your task easier if I told you I will cooperate fully with you and help you in every way I can? I shall hide nothing and be totally open with you about everything I have done. I can only say to you all that I admit that I have allowed ambition and the practice of my arts to take me far into unchartered lands. I was aiming for the stars but I have descended into the trough. Too many innocent people have suffered at my hands. Now, I only wish to repent and make amends..."

Even Giacomo had been staring at *la fattucchiera* spellbound by the mellifluous sound of her voice. He glanced over at Luca as soon as Margherita had finished speaking, only to find that Luca was looking at him meaningfully in a way that was clearly intended as a reproach for his gullibility.

Nearly all of the police officers still looked as if they were in a trance.

Luca had been studying the face of the young police woman from L'Aquila, called Oriana Salvati. Throughout the sorceress's speech, her eyes had been darting around in amusement at all these men apparently bewitched by the mesmerising voice.

"Good! That's settled then!"

Everybody was startled. It was Margherita speaking again in a business-like manner. The spell was broken.

"If you will allow these two delightful police officers from L'Aquila to accompany me to my private quarters, I would like to change into something more comfortable and pack a suitcase. Then I shall be ready to accompany you to Rome."

It was quite unthinkable that any of the officers in charge would refuse her request. It had been brilliantly done, thought Luca. She had succeeded in putting nearly everyone off their guard.

The two police women from L'Aquila stood up, ready to escort *la fattucchiera* to her own private suite of rooms. Luca intercepted a fleeting exchange between Oriana Salvati and the male officer, Giovanni Palena. Officer Salvati was declining his offer to accompany the three women with the briefest shake of her head.

Luca excused himself from the company and walked rapidly down the stairs which led to the cellar where they had been held prisoner. He made a similar gesture to Mattia as Oriana had done to her male colleague when he noticed Mattia wanted to accompany him. Luca went and stood at the foot of the stairwell which led 'nowhere'. If his instinct had been wrong, he could always make the excuse he had had a call of nature. Nobody would be any the wiser.

The two women accompanying the sorceress followed her up a short spiral staircase. Margherita's 'dressing room' was spacious, dark – and circular. They must be in the tower. Heavy curtains were drawn keeping out all of the afternoon sunlight apart from one stray beam which lit up the section of wall opposite the windows. The wall itself seemed to be covered with dark images. Margherita knew exactly where everything she needed was to be found. Oriana and Simona were trying to get used to the unaccustomed darkness and the disconcerting sensation of the room having no corners. They looked at each other questioningly, wondering how closely they should supervise her. Officer Oriana Salvati shrugged her shoulders as if to say *'vada come vada'** There was little they could do to interfere with the simple process of their charge getting undressed. Margherita was trundling a hold-sized black suitcase retrieved from a walk-in wardrobe over towards a folding screen on the far side of the room. The screen unfolded into five sections – smoothly and silently as if it had been on runners – revealing panels ornately decorated with diabolical images from an underworld that even the worldly-wise officer Simona Gambino felt disturbed by. *La fattucchiera* emerged from behind the screen and walked rapidly towards her wardrobe and disappeared inside it. Officer Oriana Salvati followed her in – fearful that there might be an exit or another stairway leading out of the tower. But their prisoner was merely selecting underwear, trousers, dresses and a cloak covered by a plastic sleeve on a coat hanger and depositing everything behind the screen. *La Fattucchiera* made three separate journeys. But she seemed to be speeding up. Not simply in a hurry but via a steady acceleration of pace which seemed to defy normal time. The final walk from wardrobe to screen was akin to watching a speeded up film. It was mesmerising.

Oriana looked at her colleague to see if she had experienced the same sensation. Simona was frowning but totally absorbed by Margherita's movements.

A friendly voice from behind the screen invited them to open the curtains a bit more if they found the darkness disturbing. Oriana walked over to the nearest window and pulled one of the heavy curtains to one side.

The officers watched fascinated as the elaborate costume which Margherita had been wearing since they arrived six or so hours ago began to be slung over the panels of the screen one item at a time - the black dress, blouse, bra, stockings until the length of the open panels were covered by more gear than they could have imagined possible. Margherita had begun humming a monotonous song, the likes of which they had never heard before. It was more like a Buddhist chant than a recognisable tune.

And then the two officers were abruptly aware that silence had fallen. They waited motionless for all of twenty seconds to see if 'she' would emerge from behind the screen – as they felt she was bound to do. Then they ran across the room and tugged at the screen. The clothes which *La Fattucchiera* had selected were strewn on top of the unopened suitcase and over the floor surrounding it. But the lady herself was nowhere to be seen. Simona Gambino had the presence of mind to run back into the room and open more curtains so that light flooded into the room. But it made no difference. Margherita had vanished into thin air. Instinctively, the two police officers ran downstairs to raise the alarm. Their cries galvanised the seated *Guardia* and *carabinieri* officers into confused action. Mattia had turned pallid. He, out of all those present, was aware they were dealing with a being endowed with powers seemingly beyond the reach of ordinary mortals. Giacomo made the simple deduction that the front door of the house was wide open with only one man to block the path to freedom. He looked at the 'junior' *carabiniere* officer on dozy guard duty and shouted at him:

"Has anybody come through this door, officer?"

The man had leapt to his feet, shaking his head.

"Nossignore – nobody visible at least!"

* * *

Luca was waiting downstairs in the cellar. He heard the commotion above him and knew that he had read *la fattucchiera's* mind correctly. His wisdom of foresight gave Luca little consolation as he perceived her tall figure gliding down the stairs in his direction, enveloped in a black cloak which reached down to her feet.

He stood blocking the way to the staircase that lead to the outside world.

She came to a halt one metre in front of Luca. She seemed to her adversary to have grown centimetres taller. On her face was a wild smile of wicked jubilation.

"Come on, dear Luca! Try and stop me. I know you want my body for yourself. *Dai!* Only you can save me now!"

Her voice was seductive and challenging – almost disembodied. Luca closed the gap between them. Then his whole body went into shock. He felt an enormous pressure on his chest, as if a pair of massive hands was preventing him from moving forward. Next moment his nostrils were assailed by that repellent stench of rotting autumn leaves which caused him to step back in horror – images of his mother's coffin being lowered into the ground haunting his imagination.

Luca had been helpless to prevent *la fattucchiera* mounting the steps and speeding up towards the sky above. For the time it takes to blink an eyelid, Luca swore he had seen some other figure preceding Margherita up the stairway. It looked like the shadow of something with arms and legs bounding energetically upwards – something nameless which appeared to be causing a 'vibration' in physical space. His last image was that of Margherita launching herself into the void with a cry of triumph - before he passed out unconscious on the stone floor.

Luca opened his eyes to find himself being supported by Marianne and Giacomo raising him up into a sitting position. The whole household was gathered round him looking on with alarmed concern.

"*Grâce à Dieu, Luca,*" said Marianne, with a look of relief on her smiling face as it became obvious that he had not suffered any permanent damage. He was led to the kitchen and sat round the huge table where the food was prepared. A glass of something which he hoped was *grappa* was set before him.

He emptied the glass too quickly and began choking on the fiery liquid. Giacomo patted him hard on the back and Marianne fetched a glass of water.

When he had obviously begun to recover, the senior *Guardia di Finanza* officer spoke with reassuring authority:

"I guess it is you, Luca, who may be able to throw some light on the disappearance of our missing sorceress?"

Luca nodded, still in a state of semi-shock.

"I think she might well have saved you the trouble of conducting a major enquiry into her past antics, *comandante.*"* stated Luca solemnly.

The *Guardia* officer instinctively touched his insignia, pleased yet self-conscious that this famous author was able to identify his high rank without hesitation.

"Now, Luca Fontana, I order you and Mattia to get out of this house. We shall meet again soon, I am sure," he said, looking at Luca. "I assume you will be around to help us for another few days yet?"

Luca nodded once again and felt it was safe to smile briefly before the shocking images of the last few disturbing minutes came flooding back.

The *comandante* could see that Luca was disturbed by what he had witnessed but needed a minimum of information from him before he headed home.

"I gather she jumped out of this doorway into empty space?" probed the *Guardia* officer as gently as he could. "Should we send someone down to see if we can find her?"

Luca remained thoughtful for a second or two, trying to assess what he had witnessed.

"I would say she flew out of that doorway. But I am acutely aware that I may be talking nonsense," replied Luca. "Yes, *comandante,* if I were in your shoes, I would send someone down to the river valley to look for her. But I have an intuitive feeling that the search may find nothing down there..."

Luca's voice trailed off. He looked and felt drained of all his former vigorous energy.

"Go home, Luca," repeated the *comandante.* "I cannot thank you enough for all you have done to help us."

Luca shook hands with all the police in turn. He reserved a special farewell for the three young officers from L'Aquila.

"Come and visit us in L'Aquila when you have recovered, *Signor* Luca," said Giovanni Palena.

Then Luca finally dragged himself away from the house of the sorceress – in the company of Giacomo, Marianne and Mattia. Outside they found an abandoned Fatima, her tear-stained face making her look like a forlorn orphan on the streets of Rabat.

"Come along with us, Fatima. You can't stay there all night."

It was Luca who had spoken the words, prompted by the last vestige of emotional energy he could muster. The little group walked silently back to the main square and led their hero back to the door of Giorgia's tobacconist's shop.

It was Marianne who took charge of Mattia and Fatima.

"We're staying at *L'ospite Inatteso* tonight, *ragazzi,*" she informed them in motherly tones. "Giacomo, you too if you can stand the thought of spending the night in Collemaga? *Signor* Frassica is expecting us."

Luca was finding it difficult to realise he was a free man, that Giorgia was only ten metres away from him. He hugged Giacomo and promised to see him the following day before he drove back to Rome. He hugged everybody else too - Mattia and even Fatima, who burst into uncontrollable tears at the first sign of real affection she had known since childhood. The warmest embrace was reserved for Marianne. Luca could not find any words for her – but knew they were not necessary.

"*A domani,* everybody! See you all tomorrow – but not before midday!" suggested Luca wearily. He was about to turn round and go into the shop when he spotted another figure walking swiftly across the *piazza* in their direction. It was Stefano, the lad from the bar opposite.

Stefano simply came up to him and shook his hand in both of his.

"*Bravo,* Luca! You are the hero of Collemaga!"

How could he possibly have learnt what had happened so soon, wondered Luca?

Stefano turned round and walked back the way he had come without another word.

The little group laughed at the almost comical effect of this brief encounter. Stefano waved a cheery hand without turning round as he strode back across the *piazza.*

"Loads of gossipy customers waiting!" he called out over his shoulder.

And a few seconds later, Luca pushed open the door of Giorgia's shop. The sound of the shop bell brought Giorgia into view. She simply ran into his arms without a word and rocked him from side to side for several eternal minutes.

"Marco!" she called out.

Luca was too far gone to be surprised at seeing Marco run towards him fully clad in his Pinocchio outfit. Luca bent down and hugged the seven-year-old until Marco broke away.

"What made you wear your Pinocchio costume, Marco?" Luca managed to ask.

Marco shrugged.

"I just wanted to," he replied.

"He's been expecting you since he woke up this morning. He didn't want you to see his tears, Luca, so he put the costume on," explained Giorgia. "He's been wearing the costume ever since he got back from school."

Luca looked at Pinocchio and said quietly:

"Marco, please take your costume off now – and let me hug the real Marco, tears and all. We're together again now. So we don't need to put on an act anymore."

Pinocchio nodded and ran upstairs.

"What day is it today, Giorgia?" asked Luca irrelevantly – his loss of any sense of normal time seemed to be troubling him.

"Absolutely and without a doubt the happiest day in all my life, Luca," was the only answer he received. "But Giacomo was right – you do need a shower and intimate contact with the contents of a bottle of hair shampoo!"

21: Aftermath...

When Luca came out of the shower room, dressed in a lounger suit retrieved from his suitcase, he found his mobile phone and computer sitting waiting for him on the kitchen table. Giorgia was looking at him expectantly.

"But *she* told me..." began Luca in disbelief.

"SHE would tell you *anything* to destroy your faith in yourself and your nearest and dearest, *amore mio.* I can see she has really worked her evil spells on you. She is a viciously destructive woman."

Luca was disinclined to substitute the 'is' for a 'was'. He still could not be sure exactly what he had witnessed so recently. Besides, he was still too emotionally disturbed by Margherita's violent disappearance to put it into words.

"But didn't Luigi or someone come and raid this house, Giorgia? Those shoes...?" he asked instead.

"Oh yes, Luigi came with one of his stooges and had a quick snoop around – but a pair of shoes was the only thing they left with."

"But how come they didn't find my phone...? The computer...?"

Giorgia was looking smug.

"It was the first thing I did as soon as I realised you'd been taken away from me. I switched the phone off so it wouldn't ring unexpectedly and give its position away. I taped it to a rafter up in our attic. As for the computer, I hung it in a waterproof beach bag out of a back window. It never occurred to Luigi to look outside. I'm not daft you know, Luca!" Giorgia said with that sharp, playful tone of voice that Luca only then realised he had missed so profoundly.

"It's me that's daft," he muttered as if to himself.

"You are a hero, Luca, and I love you. I cannot begin to imagine what you have been through. But the little I found out from Marianne after her visit to your cell yesterday evening was enough to give us a clear idea about your bravery. Marianne was tickled pink while she was telling me about the wall you had knocked down and Mattia's feet sticking out from under the bed. Now all that matters is you're safely home again. It doesn't matter how much time you need to recover, *amore.* I'm here for you."

Finally, the barrier of his pent up emotions was breached and he shed tears of relief. Marco came back downstairs at that moment, took one look at Luca – and began laughing.

"Oh no, Luca!" he exclaimed. "Would you like to borrow my Pinocchio disguise?"

Then the three of them hugged in a tight circle before sitting down round the table for a simple bowl of pasta. After which, Luca was sent off to bed to sleep.

"I'll join you as soon as I've put Marco to bed, *amore.*" said Giorgia, quietly in charge of their embryonic family.

Outside, the street lights were coming on in the *Piazza San Nicola.* There was an unusually large number of townsfolk of all ages gathering in the square. Rumours as to what had happened had begun to circulate around Collemaga. And the more people gossiped, the wilder the fantastic tales became.

Luca switched his phone on but was assailed by an endless stream of missed call signals – including three from his wife – and at least fifty text messages. He switched the phone off again and went to bed.

He remained fast asleep until dawn. When he opened his eyes, the woman who seemed to have selected him to be her lifetime partner was there. She drew her body close to his and whispered intimately into his ear the words:

254

"It's Thursday today, *amore,* in answer to your question."

* * *

Luca had forced himself to get out of bed when he had finally had his fill of slumber – full of strange and disturbing dreams about plunging off the ridge of a canyon into a swiftly flowing torrent below. He apologised to Giorgia for his lack of physical response to her presence.

"This is merely day one of our life together, *amore,*" she had replied. "What's the hurry?"

She had taken Marco to school on her own despite her son's disappointment that his new father was not coming too.

"I'll come with you tomorrow," he had promised faithfully.

"No you won't, Luca," said Giorgia with a smile. "The mayor has declared tomorrow a holiday for everybody. The pope is going to hold a mass of thanksgiving tomorrow morning. Nobody would have gone to school or work – so the mayor decided to make it official."

"Then we three will go to church together tomorrow, Marco," Luca had told Marco.

"Can I wear my Pinocchio costume?" Marco asked with a grin on his face.

"We shall have to ask *Papa Benedetto's* permission first," was Giorgia's prompt reply to pre-empt any further discussion.

"How about if we get out of Collemaga tonight, Luca? We could go to Pontefalco together and have dinner at *La Buona Forchetta...*"

Marco was thrilled at the prospect.

"*Dai,* Luca! It's a brilliant idea!" he said.

"It's a date," said Luca.

He held Giorgia in a warm embrace, cupping the back of her head in one hand as he did so – feeling the first hint of a return to normal emotions.

"Can I wear my...?" began Marco and ran out into the square laughing at his own joke.

"*A dopo,* amore,*" said Giorgia as they both smiled at Marco's secret, seven-year-old way of coping with his own dilemma.

* * *

When Giorgia returned from her school run, there was already a queue of customers waiting for the shop to open. Apparently, the demand for stamps, scratch cards and cigarettes had tripled overnight. Giorgia singled out Giacomo and Mattia amongst the queuing customers.

"I guess you two would like to see Luca. I'll get him to come out and talk to you if he's up. He had a couple of nightmares last night, but he seems more normal today than he did yesterday," she gaily informed them.

Luca came out almost immediately still looking a bit dazed. Instead of going into the shop straightaway, the customers formed up in a straight line and began clapping and calling out "*Bravo Signor Luca!*" – each and every one insisting on shaking him personally by the hand. Only one of the customers, a sour looking seventy-year-old, pushed rudely past his fellow citizens and went into the shop with a scowl on his face. Luca was to discover very quickly that this preliminary reaction was in direct proportion to that of the rest of Collemaga – roughly one in every ten inhabitants of the town was unhappy about the sudden collapse of the power of *la fattucchiera.* With few exceptions, his detractors would be old men in their seventies, discontented with the destruction of the status quo, for reasons which Luca could only speculate upon.

"Is it true, *Signor* Luca, that she flew out of a window and escaped?" asked one of the hand-shakers.

Luca was tempted to say: "Yes, she did – on a broomstick!" but limited himself to laughing at the notion and telling the man concerned that he had been watching too many Harry Potter films – much to the amusement of the others.

Just over half of the queue actually went into the shop to make purchases. The other three followed Luca as he, Mattia and Giacomo headed for the *Bar San Nicola.* Luca realised they had no ulterior motive in following him. He had merely become the centre of attraction in this shaken township. More than a handful of the passers-by looked dazed, as if they were uncertain how their daily lives would be affected.

Luca and his companions sat outside in the warm sunshine. Mattia was waiting for his parents and little sister to arrive – in about twenty minutes, his mobile device informed him.

"Please, Luca, would you come and meet them? They would be mortified if they had to drive back to Rome without thanking you."

"Of course, Mattia! *Ci mancherebbe altro!*"* Luca assured his fellow sufferer.

Giacomo had a piece of information for them which he was dying to communicate. As soon as a smiling Stefano had deposited coffees and brioches on their table, Giacomo launched into his discovery of yesterday.

"I went back to *la fattucchiera's* house after I left you yesterday afternoon, Luca. I met up with that young police woman from L'Aquila – Oriana. She had been back into Margherita's dressing room. She was convinced that her disappearance from the room had nothing to do with magic. She suggested that Margherita was nothing more than an expert illusionist."

"Officer Oriana Salvati struck me as being very smart," Giacomo continued. "She and the other officer, Giovanni Palena, are married – and she's expecting a child. I bet you didn't find that out yesterday, Luca."

Luca shook his head.

"Well, to get to the point, she went back to the dressing room, as I was saying, and she noticed something different as soon as she looked behind that screen.

"Margherita's suitcase was open and the clothes were no longer lying on top of it," she told me. "Yesterday, the suitcase was closed when we first looked behind the screen. What if she was a bit of a contortionist, Giacomo? She could have been hiding inside the case and just waited until we had run out of the room in panic before she simply stepped out of it?"

"She had even gone to the lengths of persuading her colleague, Simona, to try and squeeze into the case. She's a bit shorter than Margherita was – but she managed to curl up inside the case without too much trouble – amongst a lot of girly giggles at the absurdity of their antics."

Luca remained thoughtful for a long time.

It was in the end Mattia who broke the silence.

"Did you notice, Luca, that SHE often appeared to grow shorter and then suddenly taller? If that was an illusion, it was a pretty mysterious one."

Luca nodded in agreement.

"Yes, she had many talents that would challenge the notion she was an ordinary woman. But I agree with Oriana that her disappearance must have been staged somehow. But when I met her before she jumped out of that doorway, she seemed to be wearing something quite bulky under her cloak. I would guess that the suitcase contained whatever it was she was wearing when she jumped. So, she must have found some way of tricking them into believing she had vanished."

"Maybe we shall never know," said Mattia.

"Did anyone go down to the valley to see if...?" asked Luca.

"I'm told there was an unofficial search party out at dawn this morning, Luca," replied Giacomo. "But I haven't heard anything yet."

Their conjectures were interrupted by the arrival in the square of Mattia's parents and his sister.

Luca gave them ten minutes to embrace and rejoice in their reunion before walking over to introduce himself to the tearful parents and a smiling sister who would not let go of her brother's hand.

After an emotional display of gratitude and the extraction of a promise from Luca that he would come and visit them in Rome as soon as possible, Mattia and family took their leave. Mattia gave Luca a hug and became very emotional.

"We mustn't lose touch, Luca," were Mattia's parting words, his eyes moist with tears.

"Of course we won't, Mattia."

Giacomo had remained at the table, giving Mattia a cheery wave as he got into his parents' car.

"I don't think he recognised me, Luca," said Giacomo. "But I do remember seeing *him* once or twice in the Ministry building."

"Are you going back to Rome, today?" asked Luca of his friend.

"No, I feel like hanging round another day. I want to have a look at that dressing- room myself – and wait and see if they found her down in the valley."

"I must go and see the mayor now," said Luca. "Then I'm going to spend the day with Giorgia. We're going out to celebrate this evening – not in Collemaga, however. You must come too, Giacomo – and bring Marianne with you. And Fatima as well if she wants to join us," added Luca.

"You really *are* a pretty decent chap after all, aren't you, Luca!" said Giacomo, as if he had only just discovered this facet of his friend's character.

* * *

Just one more visit, thought Luca. He was almost looking forward to meeting Elpidio Pugliese in the knowledge that there was no longer anything to hide on either side. It was akin to the pleasure of meeting someone who had become a potential friend.

After a brief visit to see Elpidio, he wanted to scuttle back home to be with Giorgia and bathe in the warmth of her affection. He was disturbed by the inner perception that he wanted her for his own protection. So far, sexual feelings towards her had been almost totally absent. It was as if he had been engulfed entirely by the overwhelming emotional flood of his confrontation with Margherita. Common sense told him that his libido would return once he was out of shock, but its unaccustomed absence was a disturbing sensation – it was almost as if he could not recall his own name. Was it all brought about by *la fattucchiera's* malevolent power? If so, it was the worst kind of magic spell she could ever have inflicted on him at the beginning of such a new and beautiful relationship.

He was shaken out of the onset of depression when, on stepping through the town hall doors, he found the reception area teeming with a crowd of Collemagasi all jostling for a ticket machine that was about to give up the ghost. The two town hall staff were trying manfully to deal with the handful of clients who had successfully made it to their *sportello.**

At the sight of Luca walking up the stairs, a sudden eerie silence descended on the gathering. All eyes were upon him – most of them registering a kind of expectancy. Luca counted five people who half-heartedly shook a fist in his direction – including a blond woman with a sour face whom Luca was convinced he had come across somewhere before. But who or where he could not recall. If his experience of the queue outside Giorgia's shop was anything to go by, it would mean there must be about fifty people present in the town hall foyer, he inwardly calculated in ironic amusement. When he reached the top step, he turned and leant on the wrought iron bannister rail as if he was about to make a speech.

All bar the fist-shakers, burst into rapturous applause, shouting *Bravo Signor Luca! Bravissimo! Grazie mille!* He could only tentatively assume that their enthusiastic response must have something to do with a perceived change for the better in their circumstances – at least for the ninety percent who were cheering. Maybe Elipidio would throw some light on what was going on.

Since they were still applauding him, he was forced to raise his hands in the air to quell the tide of enthusiasm. It worked all too well. A sudden silence fell, leaving Luca with no choice but to address his expectant audience.

I feel flattered and embarrassed by your appreciation. I certainly do not feel like a hero. I was captured and held prisoner by your fattucchiera against my will in a cell with no windows and without any toilet facilities. So please do not think for a moment that...Margherita (There was gasp of horror at the mention of her real name) *was in any way a good woman. I was imprisoned in a room next to a young man who had been sent by the Ministry in Rome to investigate financial irregularities here in Collemaga. He has been held prisoner by your sorceress – and repeatedly abused by her in a most horrific manner.* (Another gasp of horror from his captive audience) *But to those who disapprove of me, I wish to say that I did my utmost to prevent Margherita jumping to certain death. But it was her choice! Now, I beg of you all to be patient with your mayor and begin to rebuild your beautiful town now the threat of being 'the most cursed town in Italy' has been lifted.*

The applause which followed Luca's words was led by someone standing behind him. The mayor's secretary, Mariangela Di Pietro, had come out of her office to see why the appalling noise from downstairs had suddenly ceased. She wrapped her arm round his waist and led him into her office. He could feel the pressure of her thighs against his.

"You are the hero of this town, *caro* Luca! You will go down in the town's history as our saviour. Who knows? The pope may even have you canonised – you have just worked a miracle!"

"Saintly status, I simply couldn't bear!" he replied laughing at the image of himself with a halo floating above his head and his hands glued permanently together in devotion.

"Yes, it might cramp your style a bit," admitted Mariangela smiling.

Luca had an inexplicable urge to kiss the mayor's secretary – realising just in time that his mind and body had responded to the sexual stimulus of being in close physical contact with this woman, who emanated sexual energy in abundance. Had he been freed from *la fattucchiera's* spell in a distracted moment of good humour? His conversation

262

with the mayor would have to be very brief on this occasion, he decided. Giorgia could not wait.

Elpidio stood up, a beaming smile lighting up his face as he walked round his desk to greet Luca with a hug.

"You did it, *carissimo* Luca! I knew you would!"

"I understand you have played your part too, Elpidio."

"I might have pushed things along a bit, Luca, but I am still a coward. I waited until I thought it was safe for me to do so."

"Nobody, least of all me, is going to hold that against you," Luca reassured him.

"We must meet up again soon, Luca. At the moment, I have a crisis going on downstairs."

"So I see. What on earth is it all about?" asked Luca.

"Most of the people down below are tenants of...you know who. But the little bank at the bottom of the hill was owned by Margherita and her cronies. The *Guardia di Finanza* have frozen her assets. They are all downstairs demanding that they should be let off paying their rent – for all eternity, they reckon! I am trying to set up an alternative legal banking system in Collemaga. It's a nightmare, Luca. But it's the price of freedom, I suppose."

"I wish you all the best, then Elpidio. I need to come back soon with Giorgia Calvera and sort out my house down the road..."

"You mean you really intend to live here after all you've been through?" asked the mayor.

Luca nodded.

"Yes, I guess so. Giorgia Calvera and I are...together. Did you know that?"

It was the mayor's turn to nod.

"A lovely woman, Luca! She's been waiting for someone like you in her life for years! Come and see me in a few days' time. I shall get you the best builders, plumbers

263

and electricians in the area. It's going to be a beautiful house - fit for... a hero! Or a future mayor," concluded Elpidio with a sly smile.

Luca shook his hand and thanked him profusely, pretending he had not heard the mayor's last few words.

"A prestissimo,* Elpidio," said Luca as he walked towards the door.

Just as Luca was about to vanish out of sight, Elpidio Pugliese spoke to him in a quiet voice:

"By the way, Luca, they didn't find any sign of a body in the valley..."

22: Other dimensions...

It was only eleven o'clock in the morning, but the tobacconist's shop on the *Piazza San Nicola* displayed a hand written notice on its door which stated:

CHIUSO PER MOTIVI DI FAMIGLIA

'Closed for family reasons' covered a multitude of sins from baptism to bereavement – and could never be gainsaid by even the most ardent of smokers or scratch-card addicts.

Giorgia had taken one look at Luca's face as he walked into the shop and immediately locked the door to the outside world.

She smiled broadly at him, her eyes alight with passion.

"Welcome back, Luca! That didn't take too long, did it?"

Giorgia led him by the hand to the bedroom where she shed her clothes in an untidy heap on the floor. Impatiently, she began undressing him – casting his garments far and wide in the room before pulling him down on top of her with a cry of ecstasy.

Naked, they travelled together to a faraway place and plunged into the warm blue waters of the ocean, each one abandoning a part of themselves inside the other's body and soul.

Then they lay together breathless as earthly time began to reassert its rhythm once again.

"Ti amo," whispered Luca as if it had been the first time in his life he had uttered those all too often empty words. He kissed her body all over and fondled every curve with a hand that never wanted to stop exploring her.

*"Anch'io, Luca. Per sempre."** said Giorgia with a deeply satisfied sigh.

Then Luca began talking quietly as they lay side by side. He told her everything that had happened since he had been abducted and taken to the house of *la fattucchiera*. She turned towards Luca and began stroking his body with the tip of her index finger as he talked, asking questions, occasionally giggling, or gasping in horror as the narrative progressed.

Only the fact that Marco needed picking up from school finally broke the spell – and they had to get dressed again hurriedly and descend the hill at a run, laughing at their undignified haste.

Marco emerged from the school with Monica, who was holding him by the hand. They were chatting together as if they were already soul mates. Marco was pointing at his own face.

"He's telling her he's going to get a new nose," whispered Giorgia. "He talked about nothing else while you were…away."

"But he hasn't mentioned it at all since I've been back," said Luca.

"He's a very sensible and sensitive little person in many ways, Luca. He wouldn't want to seem to be pestering you. But he is secretly thinking about your promise to him – and too tactful to talk about it."

"We'll go back up to Milan tomorrow – or the day after, Giorgia. I hadn't forgotten."

Giorgia put an arm round Luca's body and held him tight.

"*Grazie, Luca,*" she said, at peace with herself and their little world.

Monica kissed Marco's cheek and ran towards her own mother. Giorgia called out Marco's name. He ran over to them with a beaming smile on his face. In his own childlike way, he had understood that his mother and new *papà* had grown together that day.

* * *

Giorgia had settled the argument with Marco about wearing his Pinocchio costume by telling him he could wear it once only – either in the *Trattoria Buona Forchetta* that evening or at mass the following morning.

"You choose which, Marco," she had told him firmly.

She knew instinctively he would select the place where he was more publicly exposed – the church – to wear the costume. She was absolutely convinced that the pope would not see this departure from normal custom as an insult to God.

The trip to the *trattoria* turned into a celebration of many things – ostensibly Luca's escape from captivity and the town of Collemaga's release from its decades' long curse. But the union between Luca, Giorgia and Marco formed the bedrock of everybody's happiness– in addition to the excellent cuisine – and was the subject of many a *brindisi.** Bruno Vespini had closed the restaurant to the public that evening. The festivities included Bruno's entire family too. His two children had already taken Marco under their wing. He was emboldened enough to tell the company that he was going to have a new nose – at least as long as Pinocchio's.

"So you want everybody to know what a lovely little liar you are, do you Marco?" Marianne had said pulling his leg.

"Well, OK then – maybe more his nose before he had started telling lies!" Marco had conceded.

Luca had been reunited with his car, which apart from having all four wheels had also been meticulously cleaned and polished. All six of them travelled in the estate car together – Fatima at her own insistence being accommodated for the short ride in the spacious boot.

After they had devoted themselves to the main courses, Giacomo told them that he had discovered a secret cubby hole behind a panel in the wall of Margherita's dressing room in which she must have hidden.

"I even found a pair of panties there – which she must have dropped accidentally. At least her vanishing act has a normal explanation," Giacomo concluded.

Luca exchanged glances with Giorgia. He was not about to reveal in public what he had confided to Giorgia earlier on that day in the intimacy of their post love-making conversation, about what he had experienced before Margherita's leap into space.

"There are all sorts of fantastic rumours flying about Pontefalco at the moment, *ragazzi,*"* said Bruno Vespini. "Somebody even suggested that a couple of fishermen on the river bank saw her flying over their heads towards the forest."

"Probably a large crow," suggested Bruno's wife.

The laughter following her explanation was more a sign of relief that such an everyday explanation had been put forward.

Warm and noisy embraces and temporary farewells all round before the Collemaga contingent set off for the return journey. Giorgia, in the back seat, was next to Marianne. She whispered something in Marianne's ear. A broad smile spread across Marianne's face as she nodded enthusiastically.

"*Grazie mille,* Giorgia," she replied quietly, containing her joy.

Back in Collemaga, it was time to say goodbye to Giacomo, who announced he had to return to Rome early the following morning. Luca gave his friend a prolonged, wordless embrace before they parted company.

The joy of the evening's celebration was marred as Luca, Marco and Giorgia approached the shop together. Someone had daubed a message all over the glass door in black paint.

Luca the lady killer! the message announced.

Giorgia shrugged – maybe concealing her shock so as not to make her lover feel guilty. Marco looked scared.

"I'm so glad we're going to Milano soon," he said in a little voice.

Luca led them into the house. His first act was to put to the test the strength of Collemaga's return to normality. He phoned the *Carabinieri*. Luca kissed Marco good night and hugged him.

"It's nothing, Marco. Just some cowardly idiot!"

Giorgia looked gratefully at Luca for his calmness. She mouthed the words *grazie amore* in his direction and led Marco upstairs to bed.

To Luca's immense surprise, the town's two upholders of the law came trotting across the *piazza* within five minutes.

Tenente-what's-his-name was a changed man. His older companion, whom Luca had not met before, shook Luca's hand warmly.

"*Capitano* Di Gregorio," he said simply.

Tenente Malfatto* – who had finally supplied his real name – was, comically, standing rigidly to attention, his right arm in a fixed salute position.

"Sincere apologies for this abhorrent manifestation, *Signor* Luca!"

Such long words, thought Luca, amused by this not too bright officer's metamorphosis.

"Know who the perpetrator is! Cleaned up by tomorrow morning, *Signor* Luca! Condolences on behalf of Collemaga!"

"And thank you, *tenente,* for having my car cleaned," Luca added in the new spirit of things, suppressing his desire to giggle at the policeman's inappropriate choice of words.

"*Mio dovere, Signor Luca,*" said Tenente Malfatto, still saluting. His older companion raised a despairing eyebrow and took his dignified leave.

"*Buona notte, Signor* Luca. Don't let this incident upset you. We'll sort it out."

* * *

Luca, Giorgia and Marco had woken up late and had had to hurry to get to the church on time. Even by half past nine there were no seats left inside the little church. A crowd of *Collemagasi* had congregated outside on the steps.

But the old parish priest was on the lookout for Luca and ushered them in – with only two minutes to spare. Any chance of anonymity for Luca and company was immediately quashed – they were led to the front row where Elpidio Pugliese was already seated in splendid isolation, looking anxiously at his watch.

An organist had been dug out of retirement and began to play a rather wheezy bit of Bach as His Holiness Pope Benedetto appeared with Father Sandonato, who was looking frail but triumphant by his side. The congregation rose to their feet in muted wonderment that this scene was being played out in *their* own little town.

Before beginning the mass, the pope had smiled warmly at the occupants of the front row and said: "It is good to meet you all – Elpidio, Luca, Giorgia and…Pinocchio."

"Marco, father," said a muffled voice from behind the mask.

The pope obviously found the scene enormously amusing. But he was looking quizzically at Luca for an explanation. Luca pointed to his own nose and mimed a snipping pair of scissors. The pope understood instantly and smiled sadly with a quick nod of his head.

"In the name of the Father, the Son and the Holy Spirit," began the pope, in the voice that the congregation had heard a hundred times on their television sets every Sunday morning. It was scary, thought some of the congregation, how his voice had grown older so quickly in the few years he had been in office. But the warmth and kindness on his face had remained unchanged.

In his homily, the pope had spoken for ten brief moments about the courage of their parish priest, the honesty of their mayor and the bravery and determination of the man who had done more than anyone else to save Collemaga from the yoke of evil to which it had been subjected over the decades.

I would ask you to remember two more names in your prayers today, continued the gentle voice. *Firstly, a member of your own community called Fortunato who is currently recovering in the hospital in Pontefalco. He was electrocuted whilst trying to open the main door of the house in Collemaga that you all know so well to allow the rescue party in. Secondly, please pray for the soul of Margherita, your sorceress – wherever she might be at present. She should be forgiven in your hearts for all the evil she has done. May God have mercy on her soul.*

There was a massive outburst of applause within the church as soon as the pope had finished speaking. Nobody but the front row witnessed the only other significant event of the morning when it came to communion time. Luca and Giorgio went up to the altar steps with Marco between them. The pope whispered something in Marco's ear.

'Pinocchio' removed his face mark with one easy gesture. The pope touched his face as he gave the boy his blessing. Marco had physically started with surprise at the gesture. He did not recoil from the touch but looked puzzled – and then he smiled happily. Giorgia and Luca looked at each other, trying to guess what had happened.

The church ran out of consecrated hosts – so the crowd outside were about to be denied their act of Sunday fulfilment. The pope whispered in the old priest's ear with a quite unholy grin on his face. More hosts were rescued from the sacristy and the service continued.

"But your holiness, those hosts weren't consecrated," said the old priest after the mass was over - quite shocked by the pope's behaviour.

"How do we know that, father?" the pope asked him. "We're not God, you know!"

Father Sandonato smiled a beatific smile. He had just learnt something important about the authority of true holiness in that brief departure from ecclesiastical correctness.

The pope finished mass quickly. He stood on the church steps and said the words he always finished up with from high up in the Vatican every Sunday on television.

"Have a good lunch – and remember to say a prayer for me."

Then he was whisked off in the papal car with the cardinal already seated inside.

* * *

Marco had not put his Pinocchio face mask on again. As soon as they got home, he ran to the nearest mirror. His mother and Luca watched him, fascinated. He was touching his face where is nose should be – and smiling at his reflexion.

"Marco," asked his mother gently. "Why did you jump when the pope touched you?"

"I was just surprised *mamma.* The pope's fingers smelt nice."

Giorgia turned to Luca and explained.

"He has no sense of smell, *amore.*"

"Time we packed our suitcases," said Luca. "We'll leave tomorrow morning early. Shall I bring the car up and park it behind the house so we can leave at dawn? The rental on that car runs out tomorrow. Time we went to Milan. We need a break!"

Luca had been shocked by Marco's words – so soon after his inexplicable experience with Margherita and the rancid smell of autumn leaves which shouldn't have been there. He needed to cling on to terrestrial reality while he digested all that had occurred over the last few days.

"Our first holiday together, Luca," said Giorgia with a broad smile. She had seen through Luca's uncharacteristically brusque reaction at once.

Luca walked down towards the police station. He went inside and found the two officers in the back of the station. *Tenente* Malfatto shot to attention and saluted him again. The captain waved a friendly hand in Luca's direction.

"We're leaving tomorrow to go back to Milan, officers. I think we might be away for some time. If you could keep an eye on the shop for Giorgia…? And thank you so much for getting that message removed. You have been super-efficient!"

"Are you really intending to return to Collemaga, *Signor* Luca?" asked *Capitano* Di Gregorio incredulously.

"Of course, *mio capitano.* We are just going to Milano to get a new nose for Marco."

Hearing these words, *Tenente* Malfatto let out a guffaw of laughter, which startled Luca.

"Sorry, *signore,*" said the *tenente,* turning a bright red in embarrassment at his outburst. "You've got a wonderful sense of humour, sir! Much appreciated!"

Capitano Di Gregorio merely shrugged a shoulder in despair in Luca's direction – as if to say: "He can't help it!"

"How is Luigi doing?" asked Luca.

"Well enough, Luca," replied the captain. "We think it safe to put him under house arrest. We can't really keep him in that cell indefinitely. He'll be looked after by the lady who claims to be his aunt. She's with him now, in fact."

As Luca was leaving, he saw the said blond lady coming up the stairs from the cellar. She was the one who had half-heartedly shaken a fist at him in the town hall. She stood still and looked hostilely at him, keeping Luigi out of sight protectively behind her.

Suddenly, Luca remembered where he had first seen her face. She was the one who had trailed him when he had abducted Marianne that night. In a flash, Luca understood something else too - she must be Luigi's natural mother.

He smiled at the scowling woman.

"*Buongiorno, signora.* I'm pleased you will be taking care of Luigi from now on. He'll be needing a maternal hand over the next few months."

It had been a shot in the dark. But the hostile expression on the woman's face had softened for a fleeting second. He had hit the nail on the head. At the sound of Luca's voice, the outline of Luigi Bonifaccio's figure had frozen.

Luca wondered if there could be any other offspring that 'Margherita' had been responsible for in the town of Collemaga – or was poor old Luigi the only unfortunate victim of some chance encounter? Did he even know how

274

he had come into this world? The chances were that he didn't.

Giorgia's description of their trip to Milan as their 'first holiday together' had to be down-graded to 'a welcome break from Collemaga'. But she embraced the change of scenery wholeheartedly – even joyfully. If she ever doubted the motive behind their pilgrimage to Italy's second largest city, she had only to look at the expression of wide-eyed anticipation on her son's face at a voyage which was destined to transform his life. A similar look of renewed hope about her future was equally apparent on Marianne's face – for whom the departure from Collemaga was in itself a gift from heaven.

"I have never been further north than Rome before this," Giorgia exclaimed during their ten-hour-long escape to that 'other Italy' which awaited them. Her comment produced a spontaneous laugh from Luca, who took his eyes momentarily off the road to glance at the engaging profile of his new partner.

"Rome is further south than Collemaga„ I think you'll find, *tesoro.*"*

Giorgia giggled at her own mistake.

"Geography was always my worst subject at school, Luca."

Over the ensuing kilometres, Luca was thinking how little he knew about Giorgia's past. So much still to discover! It was exactly as if Giorgia had read his mind.

"It's my future with *you* that counts from now on, *amore mio,*" she stated simply.

Luca sighed silently to himself. He could not help thinking that telepathy fell into the same secret category as all the other unexplained events that he had encountered in recent days. He was having to revise his former pragmatic interpretation of life quite radically. He turned his head slightly to the right and said *"Ti amo, Giorgia."*

She replied by placing her left hand on his thigh – and left it there until she felt her arm becoming stiff.

* * *

The apartment in Milan was spacious. The three 'guests' had never lived in anything so vast in their lives. Luca had contacted his wife and spoken to his son and daughter. His wife told him without beating about the bush that she had decided to bring up their children in France and that, reluctantly, she had initiated divorce proceedings. His son and daughter told Luca they missed him and promised they would come and visit him – or *vice versa* – in the near future. Luca was sad yet relieved all in one go that his son and daughter sounded cheerful. It made him feel marginally less guilty.

"As long as your father pays for your air fares," he heard Marie-Louise intoning in French in the background.

Luca had informed his wife that he intended to move to the south of Italy and that he would cease to rent the flat in Milan – after a brief but necessary stay 'to sort out some important issues'. Marie-Louise did not even trouble herself to enquire what those issues might be. A curt *'Adieu, Luca'** was the last thing she said before ringing off.

The proof that Marie-Louise meant business had quickly become apparent – she had left virtually nothing in the apartment. Luca and Giorgia had been obliged to go out to buy rudimentary bedding for their stay, leaving Marco with Marianne. She had dragged him away from the cinema-sized television set – the likes of which he had never witnessed before – and began to give him lessons in

277

French, maths and geography – plus whatever else occurred to her imagination.

Luca had been frantically busy writing up the rest of his Collemaga story, contacting his publisher and the local Rai Uno station – who had shown interest in making a documentary about 'the most cursed town in Italy', which they had only vaguely heard about.

"We all too often neglect anything that happens further south than Bologna, Luca," the chief editor had confessed.

Luca had been actively getting in touch with various entities where he felt his influence would carry some weight, with a mind to acquiring a suitable job for Marianne.

"I don't mind being a waitress as long as I'm earning some money," she had told Luca.

But Luca had more ambitious plans for her. He managed to bully, cajole and finally persuade the editor of a regional newspaper to consider taking on Marianne in a junior role on their editorial staff.

"Just meet her once, Cosimo, and you'll understand why I am recommending her to you. Her Italian is good and improving daily – and she speaks fluent French and Arabic."

The editor caved in under his favourite writer's insistence and agreed to interview Marianne with an apprenticeship in mind. He decided that Luca was right about his *protégée*- to the extent of undertaking to find her suitable accommodation near the newspaper's head offices. He contacted Luca with his decision the following day.

Marianne looked at Luca when he announced the news – and did not attempt to hide her elation.

"It won't be easy at first, Marianne," he had warned her, "but you'll make friends and feel at home there very quickly as soon as you've found your feet.

Luca and Giorgia grew daily more convinced that their partnership would last a lifetime – wherever they lived. It was only after the third week that they began to feel nostalgic about Collemaga. Even Luca, who knew Milan like the back of his hand, started to miss the quality of life and the stillness of the mountains and lakes in Abruzzo – even the quirkiness of some of its inhabitants.

But all the frantic peripheral activity came second to the main purpose of their coming to Milan – Marco's new nose.

Luca had managed to procure a preliminary meeting with the surgeons who specialised in 'nasal enhancement' at the *San Raimondo** hospital – after the family had been in Milan for a mere ten days. Luca had used his 'notoriety' as an author to great effect and, he was informed, had 'jumped one or two queues'. As soon as they clapped eyes on Marco, the hospital staff realised that they were being asked to save the life of a marvellous little boy – instead of pandering to the desires of the rich Milanese – or Muscovite - élite willing to pay out thousands of euros for surgical changes that would never succeed in making them any happier as human beings. The 'Marco' cause made the staff feel they were performing a very special operation.

Luca and Giorgia were impressed by the youth and cheerfulness of the hospital surgeon and the nurse who carried out the preliminary examination on Marco. He had felt so little, scared and insignificant as the three of them had entered the grand hospital – after his first thrilling ride on the metro. He was put at ease within five minutes by the friendly, smiling manner of the two medics who greeted him by his first name – as if they had known him for ages.

"My name is Davide Martelli, and this is my assistant, Angela," said the surgeon.

"And what shape would you like your nose to be, Marco?" the nurse had asked him cheerfully.

Giorgia had jokingly said to Luca in bed the previous night that she suspected Marco would try out his 'Pinocchio routine', just to see what the reaction would be. But to their astonishment, Marco had pulled out a crumpled piece of drawing paper from a coat pocket and showed it to the nurse.

"Well, that gives us a pretty good idea, Marco. What do you two think?" she said showing Luca and Giorgia the childlike drawing of a nose – very slightly *retroussé* – as soon as she realised that the two grown-ups were in the dark.

Giorgia was looking solemnly and very curiously at her son.

"Marco...?" she asked.

"Monica drew it for me before we left, *mamma*. It's better than my Pinocchio nose, isn't it?"

Once again, in this new and emotional life, Luca found himself stifling the warm tears that threatened to erupt. Giorgia felt no such need to suppress her feelings. She kissed Marco and hugged him, the tears pouring unbidden down her cheeks and mingling with the smile on her lips.

"Can you really work on that?" she asked the doctor.

"Just give me thirty minutes or so, *signori,*" said the nurse getting up and leaving the room.

During the nurse's absence, the doctor filled them in on the processes involved.

"People always imagine it's a long and uncomfortable operation, but that just isn't the case. Marco's will be bit longer than ninety minutes because he's having a whole new nose, but it's mainly exterior work. It's not painful at all – even with just a local anaesthetic."

280

"But what's the nose made of?" asked Giorgia. "Plastic, I suppose!"

Marco's face was a picture of muted horror. He told them afterwards that he had immediately thought of his pink lunchbox that he took to school – and suddenly feared his new nose was going to make him look worse than before.

The doctor was smiling in sympathy at the expression on his young patient's face.

"Your real skin is not far from being made of plastic – it's mainly a carbon compound. But any likeness to the plastic you're thinking of, Marco, is light years away from what your nose will be like. Don't worry!"

Davide Martelli turned back to Luca and Giorgia.

"You can have no idea what leaps and bounds science has made in recent times. The new materials we will be using today were not available even one year ago. We have to thank our brilliant scientists in universities like Lecce and Pavia for the new skin we shall be using to create Marco's nose. It's all to do with nanotechnology. It's 'intelligent' skin that can adopt the characteristics of Marco's real skin. After a few weeks, his new nose will quite literally be part of his real skin. The bridge will be created using our 3D printer – another wonder of modern science."

"It sounds more like a miracle to me," said Giorgia.

"The miracles of science are getting closer and closer to the miracles of creation, Giorgia – just because we are managing to unlock the secrets of life."

The subject of conversation became more general. Davide Martelli asked Marco a lot of questions about his life in Collemaga. He enlightened the doctor on recent events in his town which seemed to have been cursed with a wicked witch.

"He's not making this up, doctor," Luca assured him.

It had become obvious that Davide Martelli had imagined he was simply listening to the words of a very imaginative seven year old.

"You'll be able to read about the story of Collemaga in the *Corriere di Milano* next week. I'm a journalist, you see…"

"Of course! You're Luca Fontana! I apologise for not recognising the name, *dottore!*"

The nurse, Angela, returned holding a photo of the image of a young boy's face. His nose was an enhanced version of the crude drawing Marco had given the doctors. Marco's face was beaming with delight.

The doctor excused himself, saying he had to sort something out. He shook Marco's hand and briefly stroked the back of his head. Marco, thought Luca, always managed to evoke the affection of those he met.

"See you in about two weeks' time, Marco. Now I shall leave you in Angela's hands to do a few more tests – and she will need to take a little bit of your skin off you. Don't worry, it won't hurt! And the skin sample will become part of your new nose."

The 'few more tests' in a little laboratory turned out to be fun. Nurse Angela had held various pads up to Marco's nose and asked him to sniff hard.

Marco was unable to distinguish a cheese smell from a vinegar smell, but he could tell Angela if it was a nice smell or a nasty one. He recoiled visibly at a smell which, he was told, was that of cigarette smoke.

"*Che schifo!*"* he exclaimed with the force of one who has just had an unpleasant olfactory experience for the first time.

"He has some vestige of a sense of smell, Luca, Giorgia," said Angela. "That's odd – because he really shouldn't have any!"

Giorgia looked at Luca quizzically – wondering whether they should tell her. Luca nodded.

"Go on, Giorgia, tell Angela here about Pope Benedetto's finger tips!"

"They smelt nice," Marco told the nurse.

"You mean…?" began Nurse Angela.

"We are tempted to believe that it was something to do with God's miracles – rather than science's," ventured Giorgia, offering a potted version of events in the church of *San Nicola,* back home in Collemaga.

Nurse Angela was looking thoughtful.

"I am lucky to be the one who is dealing with you and your son. You are a remarkable and heart-warming family. Now will you come with me to the surgery? You can hold Marco's hand while I take a skin sample. We usually take it from the soft skin of the stomach."

Marco had turned pale.

"Don't worry, Marco, you won't feel anything. There will just be a little soreness for a time. But it's worth it, for the sake of your new nose, isn't it!"

* * *

An hour later, they had reached the final stage of their visit – in the bursar's office.

"The moment of truth," thought Luca, expecting to be effecting a credit transfer for anything upwards of €40 000.

The bursar was a smart-looking woman in her thirties. She wore glasses and looked suitably severe for one who was employed to extract large sums of money from the hospital's private clients.

"For some reason or other, *Signori,* the management of this hospital seems to have taken a liking to your son. I have to inform you that we appear to be waiving the treatment fee for Marco and would ask you only to pay €10 000 for the materials – which are *very* expensive, by the way."

She managed a smile as she imparted this totally unexpected piece of news to the little group of three sitting on the other side of her desk.

"However," the lady continued, "we would be grateful for a bit of publicity for the work of this hospital. I understand you are a famous journalist, *signore.* I am sure you would be able to arrange for our act of generosity towards your lovely son to be compensated for by a full report in the media?"

Her statement had been inflected into a pointed question.

Luca looked at Giorgia. Giorgia looked at Luca.

"MARIANNE" they both said together.

Marco fell asleep out of sheer exhaustion almost as soon as they arrived back in the apartment – clutching the photograph of his new nose. His only complaint had been that two weeks would seem to him like a lifetime – or words to that effect.

* * *

Without Marianne present, Marco had become more intensely glued to Luca's television set until forcibly stopped by his mother. Luca observed ironically that it was the only thing in the apartment that he wished Marie-Louise *had* taken with her.

One afternoon, a cry from Marco, looking diminutive on the one sofa which remained in the living-dining room, brought Luca and Giorgia running to see what the matter was.

"Look Luca! Look *mamma!*" he cried pointing at the TV.

A man in a sort of webbed suit was spread-eagled in mid-air, hurtling on a perilous downward trajectory towards a net being held in place by a frame. Two people were standing either side of the net – as if waiting to catch the descending figure before it struck the ground at high speed. Just as it looked as if the man would crash land somewhere near the net, a hump of material on his back unfurled into a compact cone-shaped parachute which opened up behind him before he crashed into the safety net.

'Sky-diving,' a commentator's voice informed them. *'Absolutely the most perilous sport ever conceived by mankind. Each time, it's a suicide mission thwarted only by a few square metres of material!'*

Marco was looking triumphantly at his mother and Luca. He did not have to say a word.

"Bravo, amore mio!" said his mother. "You might well have solved *one* big mystery."

"How did you know...?" began Luca, never finishing the sentence. A boy with intelligence, curiosity – and nearly a new nose! Quite a formidable combination!

* * *

Had it been *anyone* else in the world but Marianne who arrived a few days later in the company of a cameraman, Marco would probably have run and locked himself in the *en suite* bathroom until they had gone.

As it was, he looked enquiringly at his mother and Luca, as if seeking their approbation.

"It will help Marianne in her new job, Marco. Your story is probably unique in the whole of Italy right now. And I expect Monica will watch the film one day too," said Giorgia.

"But I want her to see me with my new nose on," Marco protested.

"We want to come back when you come out of hospital too, Marco," explained Marianne.

It felt a little bit too close to exploitation to Luca. But it *was* a beautiful story! Luca had taken the precaution of stipulating that they would retain the right to refuse to allow the story to go public in the event of 'any change in circumstance'. In the end, he nodded at Marco as if to encourage him to go ahead,

They need not have worried. Marianne asked the simplest questions in a quiet, respectful voice – and the cameraman was discreet and kept the camera focussed on both Marianne and Marco throughout the brief shooting. No prolonged close-ups of his face at all. And Marianne simply did not ask the usual senseless question that most reporters always asked: *'How do you feel about...?"* She simply closed the one minute interview with the words: *'You are very brave, Marco!"* He had smiled his happy seven-year-old smile and the technician had switched off his camera.

* * *

Days before the one on which Marco was due to go into hospital, Luca took his old and slightly battered cream and orange VW camper van out of the spacious garage in the basement and drove his little family up to Lake Como. He wanted to take everybody's mind off the impending ordeal.

"So this *is* our first holiday together after all, Luca!" cried Giorgia in delight. "I've always wanted to visit Italy's lakes."

286

"There will be many other holidays," replied Luca. "This is just a taster."

The old and faithful VW survived the journey, having struggled up every slope in second gear, much to the anger of motorists in their sleek Audis who could not overtake the camper van on the narrow winding roads. In the end they left the VW in Como and, to Marco's joy, took the ferryboat up the whole length of Lake Como, spending a night in Bellagio. Marco endured the covert looks of passers-by with fortitude. *He* knew that all this was about to change. One particular little girl could not help staring at Marco at the hotel where they stayed in Bellagio. But the expression of sympathy on her face was so acute that Marco went up to her and asked the girl:

*"Per caso, tu ti chiami Monica?"**

"No, Elena," said the girl laughing. She kissed Marco on the cheek and ran off, wondering who Monica was.

* * *

"Don't worry, Marco," said Nurse Angela, "your mum and dad will be with you all the time. Would you like to be half awake or completely asleep while we fix your new nose?"

It was undoubtedly the biggest decision he had ever had to make in his short life, thought Giorgia, whose hand instinctively grasped Luca's.

"Asleep, I think, Nurse Angela. Thank you for asking me. I just want to wake up and find I have a nose."

Luca and Giorgia sat together in the operating theatre with masks over their faces and wearing green coats and plastic shoe covers.

"It's like being in an episode of 'Men in Black'," she whispered fearfully. Luca squeezed her hand.

"Everything will be fine, *amore.*"

They had kept their promise to Marco of being present all the time, but not once did they stand up and watch what was being done to their child.

The operation took over two and a half hours to complete. Giorgia was looking anxiously at the medical staff.

"There are no problems at all, Luca, Giorgia," their doctor assured them calmly. "But we need to try and give Marco as much sense of smell as possible. It means linking a nerve or two to the new nose. Come and have a look, if you like."

They both declined the offer.

In the end it was done. A protective mask had been fitted over his nose.

"You will need to keep this cover on for two weeks," explained Nurse Angela. "It's partly for protection while the surrounding skin heals – but mainly to stop Marco looking at himself before the new skin has settled down. He will go through a phase when he appears to hate what's happened to him. It is, after all, a very traumatic experience for anyone to undergo - let alone a sensitive seven-year-old. We suggest to all our patients – even after a simple 'nose job' - to remove all mirrors in the house if you can. But don't worry. He will be the happiest boy alive after a couple more weeks. His new skin is 'live' just like real skin and it has traces of his own DNA because of the skin graft which is incorporated into the artificial skin. There... I think Marco is waking up."

* * *

It was three weeks since the operation. Marco had wanted to sleep with his mum and dad for the first five nights. He felt sore – and sorry for himself.

"I didn't know it would be like this," he said with tears gathering.

During the daytime, Giorgia hardly left his side. They did not stop him watching television – or they read him stories. Luca managed to finish his story of Collemaga, which was taken up by a weekly current affairs magazine of national importance, called *Oggi l'Italia.** He was paid an eye-wateringly large sum for it – simply because of his reputation.

Only one untoward event took place while they were waiting for Marco to convalesce. One day a letter arrived in the post. The address had been hand written and the post mark indicated the letter had been posted in Milan. The letter inside was also hand written in a strange script.

Ciao Luca. Just wanted you to know that I am alive and kicking. Thank you for caring about my fate. M.

Luca showed the letter to Giorgia, who looked incredulous.

"Now we know what being a witch really means, don't we Luca!"

"Maybe we'll be safer in Collemaga," replied Luca with a sense of irony altering his smile.

"Facciamo l'amore," said Giorgia, out of the blue.

Marco remained asleep while they made love for the first time since their return from Lake Como.

* * *

Marco had actually asked for Marianne to be present when the bandage and protective mask were removed. The cameraman stayed in the street waiting for a phone call from the newly arrived journalist on the *Corriere di Milano,* whom every male on the staff was attempting to seduce.

The atmosphere was so tense that it hurt to be there. Marco himself removed the mask and looked at their faces in fearful expectation. He was not sure whether to be reassured or in despair at their reaction. The spectacle of his new *papà,* his mother and his beloved Marianne all gawping at him with their mouths open was too much for him.

It was Marianne who had the presence of mind to take a picture of Marco on her smart phone well before anyone else suggested finding a mirror.

He took one look at himself and burst into tears of joy. He cried so much that a stream of mucus began to flow from his nose. With a tissue, Giorgia gently wiped his nose while Marco began to laugh. He had a runny nose to wipe!

One small part of Collemaga's curse had been cancelled for ever.

Epilogo

It was the VW camper van's last journey ever. Since he had terminated his rental agreement and left the Milan apartment for ever, Luca would have had to dispose of it in Milan so as to leave the garage free. Thus Luca, Giorgia and Marco had travelled back down to Collemaga at a dignified pace, taking only the television set and the bedding with them. Marianne had come round to see them off, waving until they were long out of sight.

"It's downhill most of the way," Luca had jokingly pointed out as they headed south. It was the steep hill leading up to the piazza in Collemaga when some internal organ of the camper van finally gave up the ghost. There were funeral candles and what looked like half the population of Collemaga lining the road. It was as if they had all turned out to salute the end of the camper van's long life. Luca had to pull the VW into the roadside where the motor died and refused to start up again.

The piazza was full of people all dressed in black.

"It's Father Sandonato," one of the crowd told him. "He died peacefully in his sleep three nights ago. The funeral service is about to be held."

"What a sad homecoming!" thought Giorgia, wishing she had had more time for the elderly priest while he was alive. She would always remember him for his defiant stand against the fattucchiera during the festa. That too had been an act of real courage!

* * *

It was Elpidio Pugliese who handed Luca the letter written by Father Sandonato before he had departed this life. It was clear and lucid. He thanked Luca for 'saving his soul'

291

just in time. 'You gave me the courage to defy the evil that reigned in this town. Now I can go in the knowledge that Collemaga is in safe hands. Grazie mille, caro Luca. Che Dio sia con voi.'*

It was a pointer which Luca could not avoid. He had, inadvertently, created circumstances in his public life – and his intimate life – which he could never turn his back on. Like it or not, Collemaga had become an inescapable part of his life on Earth.

He took one look at Giorgia when he stepped inside the house behind the tobacconist's shop and knew he could never regret what had happened.

"You know I can never leave you, don't you Giorgia?" said Luca.

"And why might that be?" Giorgia had asked pertly.

"Because of the joy I feel when I wake up in the morning and see your face near mine."

"That's cool, Luca," was all she said.

Only the intense light in her eyes told Luca how she really felt. It was in bed much later that evening when Giorgia threw her body weight on top of him and said:

"I knew from the moment you first stepped inside the shop and bought those cigars that you were the one for me. È stato un colpo di fulmine."*

"Do you know, I've still got two of those cigars left somewhere," said Luca,

"Well, don't kiss me just after you've been smoking them, Luca."

"Do you know what, amore? I don't want to smoke again…"

* * *

The rest of their long story happened as it was destined to happen. The new house down the road was, as Elpidio Pugliese had promised, renovated to a high standard within six months. Luca knew that his friend the mayor was grooming him in preparation for his own imminent retirement. Luca put up only a token resistance. After all, he reasoned, there were much worse ways of spending life than striving to complete the process of regeneration of Collemaga which he had himself unintentionally initiated. Luca and Giorgia had a son and a daughter – to Marco's delight. They grew up in the three storey house, plus wine cellar, that Luca had purchased for €1 – originally as a pretext to justify his presence in the town. As elected mayor of Collemaga – with a massive majority - his first act of kindness performed in office was to employ a gentleman called Fortunato as a general handyman in the town hall. His second act of charity involved persuading the authorities to drop all charges against one Luigi Bonifaccio. It was in nobody's interest, Luca argued, to punish someone who had been so completely under the thumb of a person such as Margherita. He found a semi-derelict house in the country where Luigi could continue his 'vital' work of extracting venom from his snakes to enable a local laboratory to produce antidotes. Luigi extended his hobby to spiders too. He continued to live with the lady who claimed to be his aunt.

Eventually, Luca's son and daughter from his first marriage were able to spend their summer holidays with them all in their new, spacious home.

Before becoming mayor, Luca was instrumental in helping Elpidio Pugliese set up a proper bank, which opened up as a subsidiary branch of the Banca di Napoli. The supermarket was enlarged to sell a wider range of food stuff – under the ownership of the commune of Collemaga. The store was managed by the two local boys and the girl from

Pontefalco who had been rescued from the clutches of la fattucchiera a few weeks beforehand. Luca had been able to confirm that the youngsters had in point of fact been ordered by Margherita to discover Luca's address in Milan.

*The fattucchiera's house was not sold, but under strict supervision, became a simple hostel where the growing number of visitors to Collemaga could obtain cheap rooms and simple meals – re-employing Marta as cook. Collemaga had become a tourist attraction since an article about the town had been widely read by people from all over Italy – a story which had also been aired on Rai Uno.**

Luca and family frequently ate out at La Buona Forchetta. The friendship between the two families survived well beyond Bruno Vespini's eventual retirement from catering.

Most importantly, the tradition of the Festa of Collemaga continued as before –its 'black magic' past was celebrated as it always had been, to uphold the town's traditional reputation for witchcraft and sorcery. The firework display in the valley was one of the most spectacular in Abruzzo, people claimed.

* * *

But all that was in the future. Marco's school had closed for the summer break. Marco had walked round to see Monica who lived only a couple of hundred metres away from the piazza so he could show her his new nose. Giorgia had let him walk round on his own since it was still daylight. On the way home, Marco was accosted by the two boys in his class who had constantly taunted him about his lack of nose.

"Just look what we've got here!" the bigger one jeered. "Little Marco's got a new big nose. Shall we just pull it off, Tomaso?"

Marco was scared stiff. But the feeling that was foremost in his mind was anger that he should be treated in this way. Without premeditation, he bunched his fist tightly and punched the lout hard on the nose. The blood poured out. The couple were so astonished that Marco had retaliated violently that they did not react. The boy was clutching his nose and screaming out in exaggerated pain. Marco legged it before they could recover. Giorgia was horrified at the look of fear on Marco's face as he blurted out what had happened. Luca was out of the door in seconds. He found the two young louts very quickly. He grabbed them both angrily by their collars and frogmarched them back to the shop. They were made to apologise to a shaken Marco. Giorgia stuck two cotton bud sticks up the culprit's nose and warned him never to come near her son again. Her quiet fury was not feigned. At the sight of Giorgia's fury, the second boy apologised to Marco again and shook his hand.

"Your nose looks great, Marco," he said kindly. "You look stupid, Dario, with those things sticking out of your nose," he added cruelly to his mate.

Luca accompanied the boys back to their homes and delivered them to their parents - one at a time. Luca enjoyed the sight of Dario being slapped smartly in the face by his mother before she removed the cotton buds and cleaned his face up.

"Grazie papà," said Marco, on Luca's return. He was still shaking from the shock of his encounter at a time when he had been feeling so happy and grateful. But a secret part of him felt proud of what he had done.

* * *

'The three wise people' as Marco had christened his family had moved into the new house seven days previously.

It had become a pre-bedtime ritual for Marco to sit for fifteen minutes between his papà and his mother and watch just anything on the giant screen. Marco was allowed to flick through the channels until he spotted something that caught his interest – which happened only occasionally.

"Wait, Marco! Go back to the previous channel a minute."

"But, mamma, it was just a boring fashion show."

What they saw was so surprising that Luca started in his chair. Walking down the catwalk, dressed up to the nines, was the unmistakable figure of Margherita – followed by a line of three seemingly very attractive young Asian women.

The commentator was enthusiastically proclaiming that this was the first time in the history of Italian Fashion that the models had belonged to what he referred to as 'the third sex'.

The three wise people switched the television off, looked at each other's faces and burst out laughing.

"Well, we cannot claim that witches are not versatile these days!" said Giorgia.

"And they never cease to amaze us," added Luca.

"And they can fly without broomsticks," was Marco's only contribution.

His parents were assuming optimistically that he had not understood the full significance of what he had just heard.

Luca could not help feeling that the events of the last few months left more questions unanswered than had been resolved. 'What did it mean exactly to be a human being?' he wondered. There was no simple answer to that question.

They had succeeded in rationalising many aspects of Margherita's fate - but Luca was poignantly aware that he could not explain away his brush with the occult at the moment of la fattucchiera's leap to her 'death'.

That night, Luca and Giorgia took steps to reassert what they knew to be beautiful about their own lives – never mind about the outside world.

FINE

GLOSSARY AND EXPLANATIONS OF ITALIAN EXPRESSIONS USED IN THE STORY

This list of phrases is intended for anyone who is curious about the use of the Italian language throughout the story. Many of you will have got the 'gist' from the context and can ignore this part of the book. There is a note about the author on the last page.

Prologo

Il sindaco = the mayor
L'ospite inatteso ='The Unexpected Guest' (Name of the hotel where Luca stays)
Il comune = village : small town (an official definition of political status)

Chapter 1

Il Corriere della Sera = 'The Evening Mail'. A prominent national newspaper from Milan
La 'ndrangheta = The notorious Calabrian mafia.
Alla prossima = Until we meet again
Il Porco = lit: 'the pig' = a sleazebag : a creep
Un volantino = a flyer: a hand-out
Lei è molto simpatico = You are very nice / friendly
A presto   = See you soon

Chapter 2

Le faccio strada = I'll lead the way
Collemagasi = The noun for the inhabitants of Collemaga

Chapter 3

Una brava persona = a good 'reliable' person

La targa = a car number plate

La Buona Forchetta = Lit: 'The Good Fork' = name of the trattoria. Also a person who appreciates good food

Acqua pazza = Lit: 'Crazy water' = a fish stew from the islands off the Naples coast

'quel paese' ='That country' – which shall not be named

Chi l'ha visto? = 'Who has seen him?' = A programme on Rai 3 for missing persons

Chi diavola…? = 'Who the devil…?

Chapter 4

Mi dispiace = I'm sorry… Lit: It is displeasing to me

Una ragazza squillo = A call girl. 'uno squillo' is a telephone call

Chapter 5

Piazza di San Nicola (di Bari) = The main square named after Collemaga's patron saint

Abbracci   = 'Hugs' The name of a biscuit made by Molino Bianco.

Le faccio sapere = I'll let you know

Chapter 6

Alors, on part cette nuit? = So, we're leaving tonight?

Chapter 7

Dimmi = tell me

Porca miseria! = Lit: Pork poverty (?) A commonly used expletive to denote frustration

Ne t'inquiète pas! = Don't worry

È normale, Luca = It's what anybody would do (in the circumstances), Luca

Chapter 8

CHIUSO / APERTO = closed / open

Chapter 9

Morticia = The mother in the Addams family

Chapter 10

E bravo, Signor Luca = Well done
Abbacchio = A Roman lamb stew/ah back yo/
I Promessi Sposi = A very long novel which every school child
in Italy is obliged to read!

Chapter 11

'another pair of sleeves' = 'un altro paio di maniche' = another
kettle of fish. Too English for our mayor!

Chapter 12

Tenente = 'Lieutenant'. Luca is trying to prompt this low-
ranking officer to supply his name.
Buona sera, padre = Good evening, father (to the priest)
Fusilli alla Putanesca = a Roman pasta dish with anchovies,
capers, olives and tomato sauce and chillies.
Sogni d'oro = Lit: Dreams of Gold = Sweet dreams
Anima gemella = Lit: Twin soul = Soul mate

Chapter 13

Sei pazzo, amore = You're crazy, my love
Hai dormito bene? = Did you sleep well?
L'acqua in bocca = My lips are sealed. Lit: Water in mouth
Che palle! = What a pain in the neck! (palle = balls = testicles)

Pollo alla cacciatora = Poulet chasseur / Hunter's Chicken
(Italian version) Chicken casserole with mushrooms and red
wine

Chapter 14

Un omino = a little man – often a puppet
Vero? = True? Haven't we? Doesn't he? Etc

Chapter 15

La Sapienza = A prestigious university in Rome
Chi l'ha visto? = Who has seen him? A missing persons
programme on Rai 3
Una badante = a person who looks after elderly or disabled
people
Che Dio mi aiuti! = May God help me!

Chapter 16

Box-auto = a lock-up garage
No, figlio mio – vado a vedere il papa = No, my child – I'm
going to see the pope
Papà = emphasis on final 'a' = dad
Papa = emphasis on first 'a' = pope
Basta! = That's enough!
In bocca al lupo = best of luck Lit: In the mouth of the wolf (!?)
Dio sia con voi = May God be with you
Mia cara   = my dear
Buona notte = Good night
Vero Marco? = True Marco?
Va bene, d'accordo = All right, agreed
Tutto a posto = Everything's fine   Lit: All in its place
Salutami I ragazzi = Say 'hi' to the kids
Una mancanza di fiducia = a lack of trust

Me l'ha detto l'uccellino = a little bird told me uccello = bird :
uccellino = little bird

Chapter 17

Pericolosissima = -issimo/a onthe end of an adjective is
superlative. Very dangerous
Buona lettura = Have a good read

Chapter 18

Anima gemella = soul mate Lit: twin soul
Bagno = bathroom – euphemism for 'toilet'
dramatic French stage performance =The commencement of a
play in a French theatre is announced by three knocks on the
floor before the curtain rises.
Cazzo! Che diavolo sta succedendo? = says Luigi. "F..k! What
the devil is going on?
Écoute mon cher Luca = Listen, my dear Luca...
Un abbraccio = a hug

Chapter 19

Dai Mattia' = 'Dai' means 'give', but here used as a goad into
action. 'Go on'
O Dio mio – come sono stupida! = Good heavens – how stupid
I am
Fratelli d'Italia = 'Brothers and Sisters of Italy' The Italian
national anthem
Sono chiaro / chiara = Do I make myself clear? But Margherita
is unsure whether to apply the masculine or the feminine
adjective to herself.
Angelo custode = guardian angel
Mino = the familiar diminutive of 'Giacomo' = Giacomino =
Mino. That's how it works in Italian!

La Guardia di Finanza = The Financial Police

Oriana Salvati etc   = Three characters from "The Vanishing Physicist" make a cameo appearance – since they work in nearby L'Aquila.

A famous Italian actress = Simona Gambino from 'The Vanishing Physicist' bears a resemblance to a well-known actress, Sabrina Ferilli.

Ho fatto solo il mio dovere = Just doing my duty

Chapter 20

Vada come vada = Come what may

commandante = a high ranking officer = commander

Chapter 21

A dopo = See you later Lit: Until afterwards

Ci mancherebbe altro! = A much heard expression meaning "Of course I will!"

Sportello = The partition separating customer from employer - eg in a bank

A prestissimo = See you very soon

Chapter 22

Anch'io Luca, per sempre = Me too, Luca – for ever

Un brindisi = a toast – ie your good health

Ragazzi - lads (including lasses if present)

Tenente Malfatto = 'Malfatto' an Italian surname meaning literally 'badly made'

Chapter 23

Tesoro = treasure – as a term of endearment

Adieu = Farewell – when you see someone for the last time. (French)

San Raimondo = There is a real hospital which specialises in nasal surgery in Milan. I have changed its name.

Che schifo! = says Marco – How disgusting! How gross!

Omino - little man also for a seven-year-old boy like Marco

Per caso tu ti chiami Monica? = Is your name Monica by any chance?

Oggi l'Italia = Italy Today – a made-up title.

Facciamo l'amore   = Let's make love

Epilogo

Che Dio sia con voi = May God be with you

È stato un colpo di fulmine = It was love at first sight (Lit: a bolt of lightning)

Rai Uno = Italy's principle publicly owned TV station.

About the author...

Richard Walmsley spent his professional life teaching French and Italian in various schools and colleges in the UK until he took early retirement at the tender age of fifty-six.

He has two sons and four grandchildren – in England and Australia.

Armed with a qualification to teach English as a Foreign Language, he lived, loved - and taught English at the University of Salento, Lecce, in Puglia, until he was reluctantly obliged to retire properly at sixty-five. At which point, he began to write. His love of Italy, its language and its people are the inspiration for all seven novels and one travelogue about Puglia.

An ardent Remainer and a European at heart, Richard Walmsley is appalled at the political mess that is tearing our nation apart year on year. He, in common with a swelling number of his fellow citizens, feels he is being robbed of his European identity at the whim of a handful of misguided and self-interested politicians.

Che Dio ci aiuti! (May God help us!) as one of the characters in this novel says – in a very different context, however.

December 2019

Printed in Great Britain
by Amazon

69172052R00180